ST. T5-CWL-552

The COPY-CAT
& Other Stories

See page 350

HE TOOK HER BY THE ARM AND LED HER INTO THE HOUSE

44589

The COPY-CAT & Other Stories

BY
MARY E. (WILKINS) FREEMAN

ILLUSTRATED

Short Story Index Reprint Series

BOOKS FOR LIBRARIES PRESS
FREEPORT, NEW YORK

First Published 1914
Reprinted 1970

STANDARD BOOK NUMBER:
8369-3540-3

LIBRARY OF CONGRESS CATALOG CARD NUMBER:
71-122707

PRINTED IN THE UNITED STATES OF AMERICA

CONTENTS

ILLUSTRATIONS

THE COPY-CAT

THE COPY-CAT

THAT affair of Jim Simmons's cats never became known. Two little boys and a little girl can keep a secret—that is, sometimes. The two little boys had the advantage of the little girl because they could talk over the affair together, and the little girl, Lily Jennings, had no intimate girl friend to tempt her to confidence. She had only little Amelia Wheeler, commonly called by the pupils of Madame's school "The Copy-Cat."

Amelia was an odd little girl—that is, everybody called her odd. She was that rather unusual creature, a child with a definite ideal; and that ideal was Lily Jennings. However, nobody knew that. If Amelia's mother, who was a woman of strong character, had suspected, she would have taken strenuous measures to prevent such a peculiar state of affairs; the more so because she herself did not in the least approve of Lily Jennings. Mrs. Diantha Wheeler (Amelia's father had died when she was a baby) often remarked to her own mother, Mrs. Stark, and to her mother-in-law, Mrs. Samuel Wheeler, that she did not feel that Mrs. Jennings was bringing up Lily exactly as she should. "That child thinks entirely too much of her looks," said Mrs. Diantha. "When she walks past here she switches those ridiculous frilled frocks of hers as if she were entering a ball-room, and she tosses her head and looks about to see if anybody is watching her. If I were to see Amelia doing such things I should be very firm with her."

"Lily Jennings is a very pretty child," said Mother-in-law Wheeler, with an under-meaning, and Mrs. Diantha flushed. Amelia did not in the least resemble the Wheelers, who were a handsome set. She looked remarkably like her mother, who was a plain woman, only little Amelia did not have a square chin. Her chin was pretty and round, with a little dimple in it. In fact, Amelia's chin was the pretti-est feature she had. Her hair was phenomenally straight. It would not even yield to hot curling-irons, which her grandmother Wheeler had tried sur-reptitiously several times when there was a little girls' party. "I never saw such hair as that poor child has in all my life," she told the other grand-mother, Mrs. Stark. "Have the Starks always had such very straight hair?"

Mrs. Stark stiffened her chin. Her own hair was very straight. "I don't know," said she, "that the Starks have had any straighter hair than other people. If Amelia does not have anything worse to contend with than straight hair I rather think she will get along in the world as well as most people."

"It's thin, too," said Grandmother Wheeler, with a sigh, "and it hasn't a mite of color. Oh, well, Amelia is a good child, and beauty isn't everything." Grandmother Wheeler said that as if beauty were a great deal, and Grandmother Stark arose and shook out her black silk skirts. She had money, and loved to dress in rich black silks and laces.

"It is very little, very little indeed," said she, and she eyed Grandmother Wheeler's lovely old face, like a wrinkled old rose as to color, faultless as to feature, and swept about by the loveliest waves of shining silver hair.

Then she went out of the room, and Grandmother Wheeler, left alone, smiled. She knew the worth of beauty for those who possess it and those who do not. She had never been quite reconciled to her son's marrying such a plain girl as Diantha Stark, although she had money. She considered beauty on the whole as a more valuable asset than mere gold. She regretted always that poor little Amelia, her only grandchild, was so very plain-looking. She always knew that Amelia was very plain, and yet sometimes the child puzzled her. She seemed to see reflections of beauty, if not beauty itself, in the little colorless face, in the figure, with its too-large joints and utter absence of curves. She sometimes even wondered privately if some subtle resemblance to the handsome Wheelers might not be in the child and yet appear. But she was mistaken. What she saw was pure mimicry of a beautiful ideal.

Little Amelia tried to stand like Lily Jennings; she tried to walk like her; she tried to smile like her; she made endeavors, very often futile, to dress like her. Mrs. Wheeler did not in the least approve of furbelows for children. Poor little Amelia went clad in severe simplicity; durable woolen frocks in

5

winter, and washable, unfadable, and non-soil-show-
ing frocks in summer. She, although her mother had
perhaps more money wherewith to dress her than had
any of the other mothers, was the plainest-clad little
girl in school. Amelia, moreover, never tore a frock,
and, as she did not grow rapidly, one lasted several
seasons. Lily Jennings was destructive, although
dainty. Her pretty clothes were renewed every
year. Amelia was helpless before that problem.
For a little girl burning with aspirations to be and
look like another little girl who was beautiful and
wore beautiful clothes, to be obliged to set forth for
Madame's on a lovely spring morning, when thin
attire was in evidence, dressed in dark-blue-and-
white-checked gingham, which she had worn for
three summers, and with sleeves which, even to
childish eyes, were anachronisms, was a trial. Then
to see Lily flutter in a frock like a perfectly new white
flower was torture; not because of jealousy—Amelia
was not jealous; but she so admired the other little
girl, and so loved her, and so wanted to be like her.

As for Lily, she hardly ever noticed Amelia. She
was not aware that she herself was an object of
adoration; for she was a little girl who searched for
admiration in the eyes of little boys rather than
little girls, although very innocently. She always
glanced slyly at Johnny Trumbull when she wore a
pretty new frock, to see if he noticed. He never did,
and she was sharp enough to know it. She was also
child enough not to care a bit, but to take a queer
pleasure in the sensation of scorn which she felt in
consequence. She would eye Johnny from head to

foot, his boy's clothing somewhat spotted, his bulging pockets, his always dusty shoes, and when he twisted uneasily, not understanding why, she had a thrill of purely feminine delight. It was on one such occasion that she first noticed Amelia Wheeler particularly.

It was a lovely warm morning in May, and Lily was a darling to behold—in a big hat with a wreath of blue flowers, her hair tied with enormous blue silk bows, her short skirts frilled with eyelet embroidery, her slender silk legs, her little white sandals. Madame's maid had not yet struck the Japanese gong, and all the pupils were out on the lawn, Amelia, in her clean, ugly gingham and her serviceable brown sailor hat, hovering near Lily, as usual, like a common, very plain butterfly near a particularly resplendent blossom. Lily really noticed her. She spoke to her confidentially; she recognized her fully as another of her own sex, and presumably of similar opinions.

"Ain't boys ugly, anyway?" inquired Lily of Amelia, and a wonderful change came over Amelia. Her sallow cheeks bloomed; her eyes showed blue glitters; her little skinny figure became instinct with nervous life. She smiled charmingly, with such eagerness that it smote with pathos and bewitched.

"Oh yes, oh yes," she agreed, in a voice like a quick flute obbligato. "Boys are ugly."

"Such clothes!" said Lily.

"Yes, such clothes!" said Amelia.

"Always spotted," said Lily.

"Always covered all over with spots," said Amelia.

"And their pockets always full of horrid things," said Lily.

"Yes," said Amelia.

Amelia glanced openly at Johnny Trumbull; Lily with a sidewise effect.

Johnny had heard every word. Suddenly he arose to action and knocked down Lee Westminster, and sat on him.

"Lemme up!" said Lee.

Johnny had no quarrel whatever with Lee. He grinned, but he sat still. Lee, the sat-upon, was a sharp little boy. "Showing off before the gals!" he said, in a thin whisper.

"Hush up!" returned Johnny.

"Will you give me a writing-pad—I lost mine, and mother said I couldn't have another for a week if I did—if I don't holler?" inquired Lee.

"Yes. Hush up!"

Lee lay still, and Johnny continued to sit upon his prostrate form. Both were out of sight of Madame's windows, behind a clump of the cedars which graced her lawn.

"Always fighting," said Lily, with a fine crescendo of scorn. She lifted her chin high, and also her nose.

"Always fighting," said Amelia, and also lifted her chin and nose. Amelia was a born mimic. She actually looked like Lily, and she spoke like her.

Then Lily did a wonderful thing. She doubled her soft little arm into an inviting loop for Amelia's little claw of a hand.

"Come along, Amelia Wheeler," said she. "We don't want to stay near horrid, fighting boys. We will go by ourselves."

And they went. Madame had a headache that

8

THE COPY-CAT

morning, and the Japanese gong did not ring for fifteen minutes longer. During that time Lily and Amelia sat together on a little rustic bench under a twinkling poplar, and they talked, and a sort of miniature sun-and-satellite relation was established between them, although neither was aware of it. Lily, being on the whole a very normal little girl, and not disposed to even a full estimate of herself as compared with others of her own sex, did not dream of Amelia's adoration, and Amelia, being rarely destitute of self-consciousness, did not understand the whole scope of her own sentiments. It was quite sufficient that she was seated close to this wonderful Lily, and agreeing with her to the verge of immolation.

"Of course," said Lily, "girls are pretty, and boys are just as ugly as they can be."

"Oh yes," said Amelia, fervently.

"But," said Lily, thoughtfully, "it is queer how Johnny Trumbull always comes out ahead in a fight, and he is not so very large, either."

"Yes," said Amelia, but she realized a pang of jealousy. "Girls could fight, I suppose," said she.

"Oh yes, and get their clothes all torn and messy," said Lily.

"I shouldn't care," said Amelia. Then she added, with a little toss, "I almost know I could fight." The thought even floated through her wicked little mind that fighting might be a method of wearing out obnoxious and durable clothes.

"You!" said Lily, and the scorn in her voice wilted Amelia.

9

"Maybe I couldn't," said she.

"Of course you couldn't, and if you could, what a sight you'd be. Of course it wouldn't hurt your clothes as much as some, because your mother dresses you in strong things, but you'd be sure to get black and blue, and what would be the use, anyway? You couldn't be a boy, if you did fight."

"No. I know I couldn't."

"Then what is the use? We are a good deal prettier than boys, and cleaner, and have nicer manners, and we must be satisfied."

"You are prettier," said Amelia, with a look of worshipful admiration at Lily's sweet little face.

'You are prettier," said Lily. Then she added, equivocally, "Even the very homeliest girl is prettier than a boy."

Poor Amelia, it was a good deal for her to be called prettier than a very dusty boy in a fight. She fairly dimpled with delight, and again she smiled charmingly. Lily eyed her critically.

"You aren't so very homely, after all, Amelia," she said. "You needn't think you are."

Amelia smiled again.

"When you look like you do now you are real pretty," said Lily, not knowing or even suspecting the truth, that she was regarding in the face of this little ardent soul her own, as in a mirror.

However, it was after that episode that Amelia Wheeler was called "Copy-Cat." The two little girls entered Madame's select school arm in arm, when the musical gong sounded, and behind them came Lee Westminster and Johnny Trumbull, sur-reptitiously dusting their garments, and ever after the fact of Amelia's adoration and imitation of Lily Jennings was evident to all. Even Madame became aware of it, and held conferences with two of the under teachers.

"It is not at all healthy for one child to model herself so entirely upon the pattern of another," said Miss Parmalee.

"Most certainly it is not," agreed Miss Acton, the music-teacher.

"Why, that poor little Amelia Wheeler had the rudiments of a fairly good contralto. I had begun to wonder if the poor child might not be able at least to sing a little, and so make up for—other things; and now she tries to sing high like Lily Jennings, and I simply cannot prevent it. She has heard Lily play, too, and has lost her own touch, and now it is neither one thing nor the other."

"I might speak to her mother," said Madame, thoughtfully. Madame was American born, but she married a French gentleman, long since deceased, and his name sounded well on her circulars. She and her two under teachers were drinking tea in her library.

Miss Parmalee, who was a true lover of her pupils, gasped at Madame's proposition. "Whatever you do, please do not tell that poor child's mother," said she.

"I do not think it would be quite wise, if I may venture to express an opinion," said Miss Acton, who was a timid soul, and always inclined to shy at her own ideas.

THE COPY-CAT

"But why?" asked Madame.

"Her mother," said Miss Parmalee, "is a quite remarkable woman, with great strength of character, but she would utterly fail to grasp the situation."

"I must confess," said Madame, sipping her tea, "that I fail to understand it. Why any child not an absolute idiot should so lose her own identity in another's absolutely bewilders me. I never heard of such a case."

Miss Parmalee, who had a sense of humor, laughed a little. "It is bewildering," she admitted. "And now the other children see how it is, and call her 'Copy-Cat' to her face, but she does not mind. I doubt if she understands, and neither does Lily, for that matter. Lily Jennings is full of mischief, but she moves in straight lines; she is not conceited or self-conscious, and she really likes Amelia, without knowing why."

"I fear Lily will lead Amelia into mischief," said Madame, "and Amelia has always been such a good child."

"Lily will never *mean* to lead Amelia into mischief," said loyal Miss Parmalee.

"But she will," said Madame.

"If Lily goes, I cannot answer for Amelia's not following," admitted Miss Parmalee.

"I regret it all very much indeed," sighed Madame, "but it does seem to me still that Amelia's mother—"

"Amelia's mother would not even believe it, in the first place," said Miss Parmalee.

"Well, there is something in that," admitted Ma-

12

dame. "I myself could not even imagine such a situation. I would not know of it now, if you and Miss Acton had not told me."

"There is not the slightest use in telling Amelia not to imitate Lily, because she does not know that she is imitating her," said Miss Parmalee. "If she were to be punished for it, she could never comprehend the reason."

"That is true," said Miss Acton. "I realize that when the poor child squeaks instead of singing. All I could think of this morning was a little mouse caught in a trap which she could not see. She does actually squeak!—and some of her low notes, although, of course, she is only a child, and has never attempted much, promised to be very good."

"She will have to squeak, for all I can see," said Miss Parmalee. "It looks to me like one of those situations that no human being can change for better or worse."

"I suppose you are right," said Madame, "but it is most unfortunate, and Mrs. Wheeler is such a superior woman, and Amelia is her only child, and this is such a very subtle and regrettable affair. Well, we have to leave a great deal to Providence."

"If," said Miss Parmalee, "she could only get angry when she is called 'Copy-Cat.'" Miss Parmalee laughed, and so did Miss Acton. Then all the ladies had their cups refilled, and left Providence to look out for poor little Amelia Wheeler, in her mad pursuit of her ideal in the shape of another little girl possessed of the exterior graces which she had not.

Meantime the little "Copy-Cat" had never been so happy. She began to improve in her looks also. Her grandmother Wheeler noticed it first, and spoke of it to Grandmother Stark. "That child may not be so plain, after all," said she. "I looked at her this morning when she started for school, and I thought for the first time that there was a little resemblance to the Wheelers."

Grandmother Stark sniffed, but she looked gratified. "I have been noticing it for some time," said she, "but as for looking like the Wheelers, I thought this morning for a minute that I actually saw my poor dear husband looking at me out of that blessed child's eyes."

Grandmother Wheeler smiled her little, aggravating, curved, pink smile.

But even Mrs. Diantha began to notice the change for the better in Amelia. She, however, attributed it to an increase of appetite and a system of deep breathing which she had herself taken up and enjoined Amelia to follow. Amelia was following Lily Jennings instead, but that her mother did not know. Still, she was gratified to see Amelia's little sallow cheeks taking on pretty curves and a soft bloom, and she was more inclined to listen when Grandmother Wheeler ventured to approach the subject of Amelia's attire.

"Amelia would not be so bad-looking if she were better dressed, Diantha," said she.

Diantha lifted her chin, but she paid heed. "Why, does not Amelia dress perfectly well, mother?" she inquired.

"She dresses well enough, but she needs more ribbons and ruffles."

"I do not approve of so many ribbons and ruffles," said Mrs. Diantha. "Amelia has perfectly neat, fresh black or brown ribbons for her hair, and ruffles are not sanitary."

"Ruffles are pretty," said Grandmother Wheeler, "and blue and pink are pretty colors. Now, that Jennings girl looks like a little picture."

But that last speech of Grandmother Wheeler's undid all the previous good. Mrs. Diantha had an unacknowledged—even to herself—disapproval of Mrs. Jennings which dated far back in the past, for a reason which was quite unworthy of her and of her strong mind. When she and Lily's mother had been girls, she had seen Mrs. Jennings look like a picture, and had been perfectly well aware that she herself fell far short of an artist's ideal. Perhaps if Mrs. Stark had believed in ruffles and ribbons, her daughter might have had a different mind when Grandmother Wheeler had finished her little speech.

As it was, Mrs. Diantha surveyed her small, pretty mother-in-law with dignified serenity, which savored only delicately of a snub. "I do not myself approve of the way in which Mrs. Jennings dresses her daughter," said she, "and I do not consider that the child presents to a practical observer as good an appearance as my Amelia."

Grandmother Wheeler had a temper. It was a childish temper and soon over—still, a temper. "Lord," said she, "if you mean to say that you think your poor little snipe of a daughter, dressed like a little maid-of-all-work, can compare with that lovely little Lily Jennings, who is dressed like a doll!—"

"I do not wish that my daughter should be dressed like a doll," said Mrs. Diantha, coolly.

"Well, she certainly isn't," said Grandmother Wheeler. "Nobody would ever take her for a doll as far as looks or dress are concerned. She may be *good* enough. I don't deny that Amelia is a good little girl, but her looks could be improved on."

"Looks matter very little," said Mrs. Diantha.

"They matter very much," said Grandmother Wheeler, pugnaciously, her blue eyes taking on a peculiar opaque glint, as always when she lost her temper, "very much indeed. But looks can't be helped. If poor little Amelia wasn't born with pretty looks, she wasn't. But she wasn't born with such ugly clothes. She might be better dressed."

"I dress my daughter as I consider best," said Mrs. Diantha. Then she left the room.

Grandmother Wheeler sat for a few minutes, her blue eyes opaque, her little pink lips a straight line; then suddenly her eyes lit, and she smiled. "Poor Diantha," said she, "I remember how Henry used to like Lily Jennings's mother before he married Diantha. Sour grapes hang high." But Grandmother Wheeler's beautiful old face was quite soft and gentle. From her heart she pitied the reacher after those high-hanging sour grapes, for Mrs. Diantha had been very good to her.

Then Grandmother Wheeler, who had a mild persistency not evident to a casual observer, began to make plans and lay plots. She was resolved, Diantha or not, that her granddaughter, her son's child, should have some fine feathers. The little conference had taken place in her own room, a large, sunny one, with a little storeroom opening from it. Presently Grandmother Wheeler rose, entered the storeroom, and began rummaging in some old trunks. Then followed days of secret work. Grandmother Wheeler had been noted as a fine needlewoman, and her hand had not yet lost its cunning. She had one of Amelia's ugly little ginghams, purloined from a closet, for size, and she worked two or three dainty wonders. She took Grandmother Stark into her confidence. Sometimes the two ladies, by reason of their age, found it possible to combine with good results.

"Your daughter Diantha is one woman in a thousand," said Grandmother Wheeler, diplomatically, one day, "but she never did care much for clothes."

"Diantha," returned Grandmother Stark, with a suspicious glance, "always realized that clothes were not the things that mattered."

"And, of course, she is right," said Grandmother Wheeler, piously. "Your Diantha is one woman in a thousand. If she cared as much for fine clothes as some women, I don't know where we should all be. It would spoil poor little Amelia."

"Yes, it would," assented Grandmother Stark. "Nothing spoils a little girl more than always to be thinking about her clothes."

"Yes, I was looking at Amelia the other day, and thinking how much more sensible she appeared in

2   17

her plain gingham than Lily Jennings in all her ruffles and ribbons. Even if people were all noticing Lily, and praising her, thinks I to myself, 'How little difference such things really make. Even if our dear Amelia does stand to one side, and nobody notices her, what real matter is it?'" Grandmother Wheeler was inwardly chuckling as she spoke.

Grandmother Stark was at once alert. "Do you mean to say that Amelia is really not taken so much notice of because she dresses plainly?" said she.

"You don't mean that you don't know it, as observant as you are?" replied Grandmother Wheeler.

"Diantha ought not to let it go as far as that," said Grandmother Stark. Grandmother Wheeler looked at her queerly. "Why do you look at me like that?"

"Well, I did something I feared I ought not to have done. And I didn't know what to do, but your speaking so makes me wonder—"

"Wonder what?"

Then Grandmother Wheeler went to her little storeroom and emerged bearing a box. She displayed the contents—three charming little white frocks fluffy with lace and embroidery.

"Did you make them?"

"Yes, I did. I couldn't help it. I thought if the dear child never wore them, it would be some comfort to know they were in the house."

"That one needs a broad blue sash," said Grandmother Stark.

Grandmother Wheeler laughed. She took her impecuniosity easily. "I had to use what I had," said she.

"I will get a blue sash for that one," said Grand-

mother Stark, "and a pink sash for that, and a flowered one for that."

"Of course they will make all the difference,"
said Grandmother Wheeler. "Those beautiful sashes
will really make the dresses."

"I will get them," said Grandmother Stark, with
decision. "I will go right down to Mann Brothers'
store now and get them."

"Then I will make the bows, and sew them on,"
replied Grandmother Wheeler, happily.

It thus happened that little Amelia Wheeler was
possessed of three beautiful dresses, although she
did not know it.

For a long time neither of the two conspiring
grandmothers dared divulge the secret. Mrs. Diantha was a very determined woman, and even her
own mother stood somewhat in awe of her. Therefore, little Amelia went to school during the spring
term soberly clad as ever, and even on the festive
last day wore nothing better than a new blue gingham, made too long, to allow for shrinkage, and new
blue hair-ribbons. The two grandmothers almost
wept in secret conclave over the lovely frocks which
were not worn.

"I respect Diantha," said Grandmother Wheeler.
"You know that. She is one woman in a thousand,
but I do hate to have that poor child go to school
to-day with so many to look at her, and she dressed
so unlike all the other little girls."

"Diantha has got so much sense, it makes her
blind and deaf," declared Grandmother Stark. "I
call it a shame, if she is my daughter."

"Then you don't venture—"

Grandmother Stark reddened. She did not like to own to awe of her daughter. "I *venture*, if that is all," said she, tartly. "You don't suppose I am afraid of Diantha?—but she would not let Amelia wear one of the dresses, anyway, and I don't want the child made any unhappier than she is."

"Well, I will admit," replied Grandmother Wheeler, "if poor Amelia knew she had these beautiful dresses and could not wear them she might feel worse about wearing that homely gingham."

"Gingham!" fairly snorted Grandmother Stark. "I cannot see why Diantha thinks so much of gingham. It shrinks, anyway."

Poor little Amelia did undoubtedly suffer on that last day, when she sat among the others gaily clad, and looked down at her own common little skirts. She was very glad, however, that she had not been chosen to do any of the special things which would have necessitated her appearance upon the little flower-decorated platform. She did not know of the conversation between Madame and her two assistants.

"I would have Amelia recite a little verse or two," said Madame, "but how can I?" Madame adored dress, and had a lovely new one of sheer dull-blue stuff, with touches of silver, for the last day.

"Yes," agreed Miss Parmalee, "that poor child is sensitive, and for her to stand on the platform in one of those plain ginghams would be too cruel."

"Then, too," said Miss Acton, "she would recite her verses exactly like Lily Jennings. She can make her voice exactly like Lily's now. Then everybody would laugh, and Amelia would not know why. She would think they were laughing at her dress, and that would be dreadful."

If Amelia's mother could have heard that conversation everything would have been different, although it is puzzling to decide in what way.

It was the last of the summer vacation in early September, just before school began, that a climax came to Amelia's idolatry and imitation of Lily. The Jenningses had not gone away that summer, so the two little girls had been thrown together a good deal. Mrs. Diantha never went away during a summer. She considered it her duty to remain at home, and she was quite pitiless to herself when it came to a matter of duty.

However, as a result she was quite ill during the last of August and the first of September. The season had been unusually hot, and Mrs. Diantha had not spared herself from her duty on account of the heat. She would have scorned herself if she had done so. But she could not, strong-minded as she was, avert something like a heat prostration after a long walk under a burning sun, nor weeks of confinement and idleness in her room afterward.

When September came, and a night or two of comparative coolness, she felt stronger; still she was compelled by most unusual weakness to refrain from her energetic trot in her duty-path; and then it was that something happened.

One afternoon Lily fluttered over to Amelia's, and Amelia, ever on the watch, spied her.

"May I go out and see Lily?" she asked Grandmother Stark.

"Yes, but don't talk under the windows; your mother is asleep."

Amelia ran out.

"I declare," said Grandmother Stark to Grandmother Wheeler, "I was half a mind to tell that child to wait a minute and slip on one of those pretty dresses. I hate to have her go on the street in that old gingham, with that Jennings girl dressed up like a wax doll."

"I know it."

"And now poor Diantha is so weak—and asleep —it would not have annoyed her."

"I know it."

Grandmother Stark looked at Grandmother Wheeler. Of the two she possessed a greater share of original sin compared with the size of her soul. Moreover, she felt herself at liberty to circumvent her own daughter. Whispering, she unfolded a daring scheme to the other grandmother, who stared at her aghast a second out of her lovely blue eyes, then laughed softly.

"Very well," said she, "if you dare."

"I rather think I dare!" said Grandmother Stark. "Isn't Diantha Wheeler my own daughter?" Grandmother Stark had grown much bolder since Mrs. Diantha had been ill.

Meantime Lily and Amelia walked down the street until they came to a certain vacant lot intersected by a foot-path between tall, feathery grasses and goldenrod and asters and milkweed. They entered the foot-path, and swarms of little butterflies rose around them, and once in a while a protesting bumblebee.

"I am afraid we will be stung by the bees," said Amelia.

"Bumblebees never sting," said Lily; and Amelia believed her.

When the foot-path ended, there was the river-bank. The two little girls sat down under a clump of brook willows and talked, while the river, full of green and blue and golden lights, slipped past them and never stopped.

Then Lily proceeded to unfold a plan, which was not philosophical, but naughtily ingenious. By this time Lily knew very well that Amelia admired her, and imitated her as successfully as possible, considering the drawback of dress and looks.

When she had finished Amelia was quite pale. "I am afraid, I am afraid, Lily," said she.

"What of?"

"My mother will find out; besides, I am afraid it isn't right."

"Who ever told you it was wrong?"

"Nobody ever did," admitted Amelia.

"Well, then you haven't any reason to think it is," said Lily, triumphantly. "And how is your mother ever going to find it out?"

"I don't know."

"Isn't she ill in her room? And does she ever come to kiss you good night, the way my mother does, when she is well?"

"No," admitted Amelia.

"And neither of your grandmothers?"

"Grandmother Stark would think it was silly, like mother, and Grandmother Wheeler can't go up and down stairs very well."

"I can't see but you are perfectly safe. I am the only one that runs any risk at all. I run a great deal of risk, but I am willing to take it," said Lily with a virtuous air. Lily had a small but rather involved scheme simply for her own ends, which did not seem to call for much virtue, but rather the contrary.

Lily had overheard Arnold Carruth and Johnny Trumbull and Lee Westminster and another boy, Jim Patterson, planning a most delightful affair, which even in the cases of the boys was fraught with danger, secrecy, and doubtful rectitude. Not one of the four boys had had a vacation from the village that summer, and their young minds had become charged, as it were, with the seeds of revolution and rebellion. Jim Patterson, the son of the rector, and of them all the most venturesome, had planned to take—he called it "take"; he meant to pay for it, anyway, he said, as soon as he could shake enough money out of his nickel savings-bank—one of his father's Plymouth Rock chickens and have a chicken-roast in the woods back of Dr. Trumbull's. He had planned for Johnny to take some ears of corn suitable for roasting from his father's garden; for Lee to take some cookies out of a stone jar in his mother's pantry; and for Arnold to take some potatoes. Then they four would steal forth under cover of night, build a camp-fire, roast their spoils, and feast.

24

LILY PROCEEDED TO UNFOLD A PLAN NAUGHTILY INGENIOUS

Lily had resolved to be of the party. She resorted to no open methods; the stones of the fighting suffragettes were not for her, little honey-sweet, curled, and ruffled darling; rather the time-worn, if not time-sanctified, weapons of her sex, little instruments of wiles, and tiny dodges, and tiny subterfuges, which would serve her best.

"You know," she said to Amelia, "you don't look like me. Of course you know that, and that can't be helped; but you do walk like me, and talk like me, you know that, because they call you 'Copy-Cat.'"

"Yes, I know," said poor Amelia.

"I don't mind if they do call you 'Copy-Cat,'" said Lily, magnanimously. "I don't mind a bit. But, you see, my mother always comes up-stairs to kiss me good night after I have gone to bed, and tomorrow night she has a dinner-party, and she will surely be a little late, and I can't manage unless you help me. I will get one of my white dresses for you, and all you have to do is to climb out of your window into that cedar-tree—you know you can climb down that, because you are so afraid of burglars climbing up—and you can slip on my dress; you had better throw it out of the window and not try to climb in it, because my dresses tear awful easy, and we might get caught that way. Then you just sneak down to our house, and I shall be outdoors; and when you go up-stairs, if the doors should be open, and anybody should call, you can answer just like me; and I have found that light curly wig Aunt Laura wore when she had her head shaved after she had a fever, and you just put that on and go to bed, and mother will never know when she kisses you good night. Then after the roast I will go to your house, and climb up that tree, and go to bed in your room. And I will have one of your gingham dresses to wear, and very early in the morning I will get up, and you get up, and we both of us can get down the back stairs without being seen, and run home."

Amelia was almost weeping. It was her worshiped Lily's plan, but she was horribly scared. "I don't know," she faltered.

"Don't know! You've got to! You don't love me one single bit or you wouldn't stop to think about whether you didn't know." It was the world-old argument which floors love. Amelia succumbed.

The next evening a frightened little girl clad in one of Lily Jennings's white embroidered frocks was racing to the Jenningses' house, and another little girl, not at all frightened, but enjoying the stimulus of mischief and unwontedness, was racing to the wood behind Dr. Trumbull's house, and that little girl was clad in one of Amelia Wheeler's ginghams. But the plan went all awry.

Lily waited, snuggled up behind an alder-bush, and the boys came, one by one, and she heard this whispered, although there was no necessity for whispering, "Jim Patterson, where's that hen?"

"Couldn't get her. Grabbed her, and all her tail-feathers came out in a bunch right in my hand, and she squawked so, father heard. He was in his study writing his sermon, and he came out, and if I hadn't hid behind the chicken-coop and then run I couldn't have got here. But I can't see as you've got any corn, Johnny Trumbull."

"Couldn't. Every single ear was cooked for dinner."

"I couldn't bring any cookies, either," said Lee Westminster; "there weren't any cookies in the jar."

"And I couldn't bring the potatoes, because the outside cellar door was locked," said Arnold Carruth. "I had to go down the back stairs and out the south door, and the inside cellar door opens out of our dining-room, and I daren't go in there."

"Then we might as well go home," said Johnny Trumbull. "If I had been you, Jim Patterson, I would have brought that old hen if her tail-feathers had come out. Seems to me you scare awful easy."

"Guess if you had heard her squawk!" said Jim, resentfully. "If you want to try to lick me, come on, Johnny Trumbull. Guess you don't darse call me scared again."

Johnny eyed him standing there in the gloom. Jim was not large, but very wiry, and the ground was not suited for combat. Johnny, although a victor, would probably go home considerably the worse in appearance; and he could anticipate the consequences were his father to encounter him.

"Shucks!" said Johnny Trumbull, of the fine old Trumbull family and Madame's exclusive school. "Shucks! who wants your old hen? We had chicken for dinner, anyway."

"So did we," said Arnold Carruth.

"We did, and corn," said Lee.

"We did," said Jim.

27

THE COPY-CAT

Lily stepped forth from the alder-bush. "If," said she, "I were a boy, and had started to have a chicken-roast, I would have *had* a chicken-roast."

But every boy, even the valiant Johnny Trumbull, was gone in a mad scutter. This sudden apparition of a girl was too much for their nerves. They never even knew who the girl was, although little Arnold Carruth said she had looked to him like "Copy-Cat," but the others scouted the idea.

Lily Jennings made the best of her way out of the wood across lots to the road. She was not in a particularly enviable case. Amelia Wheeler was presumably in her bed, and she saw nothing for it but to take the difficult way to Amelia's.

Lily tore a great rent in the gingham going up the cedar-tree, but that was nothing to what followed. She entered through Amelia's window, her prim little room, to find herself confronted by Amelia's mother in a wrapper, and her two grandmothers. Grandmother Stark had over her arm a beautiful white embroidered dress. The two old ladies had entered the room in order to lay the white dress on a chair and take away Amelia's gingham, and there was no Amelia. Mrs. Diantha had heard the commotion, and had risen, thrown on her wrapper, and come. Her mother had turned upon her.

"It is all your fault, Diantha," she had declared.

"My fault?" echoed Mrs. Diantha, bewildered. "Where is Amelia?"

"We don't know," said Grandmother Stark, "but you have probably driven her away from home by your cruelty."

28

"Cruelty?"

"Yes, cruelty. What right had you to make that poor child look like a fright, so people laughed at her? We have made her some dresses that look decent, and had come here to leave them, and to take away those old gingham things that look as if she lived in the almshouse, and leave these, so she would either have to wear them or go without, when we found she had gone."

It was at that crucial moment that Lily entered by way of the window.

"Here she is now," shrieked Grandmother Stark. "Amelia, where—" Then she stopped short.

Everybody stared at Lily's beautiful face suddenly gone white. For once Lily was frightened. She lost all self-control. She began to sob. She could scarcely tell the absurd story for sobs, but she told, every word.

Then, with a sudden boldness, she too turned on Mrs. Diantha. "They call poor Amelia 'Copy-Cat,'" said she, "and I don't believe she would ever have tried so hard to look like me only my mother dresses me so I look nice, and you send Amelia to school looking awfully." Then Lily sobbed again.

"My Amelia is at your house, as I understand?" said Mrs. Diantha, in an awful voice.

"Ye-es, ma-am."

"Let me go," said Mrs. Diantha, violently, to Grandmother Stark, who tried to restrain her. Mrs. Diantha dressed herself and marched down the street, dragging Lily after her. The little girl had to trot to keep up with the tall woman's strides, and all the way she wept.

It was to Lily's mother's everlasting discredit, in Mrs. Diantha's opinion, but to Lily's wonderful relief, that when she heard the story, standing in the hall in her lovely dinner dress, with the strains of music floating from the drawing-room, and cigar smoke floating from the dining-room, she laughed. When Lily said, "And there wasn't even any chicken-roast, mother," she nearly had hysterics.

"If you think this is a laughing matter, Mrs. Jennings, I do not," said Mrs. Diantha, and again her dislike and sorrow at the sight of that sweet, mirthful face was over her. It was a face to be loved, and hers was not.

"Why, I went up-stairs and kissed the child good night, and never suspected," laughed Lily's mother.

"I got Aunt Laura's curly, light wig for her," explained Lily, and Mrs. Jennings laughed again.

It was not long before Amelia, in her gingham, went home, led by her mother—her mother, who was trembling with weakness now. Mrs. Diantha did not scold. She did not speak, but Amelia felt with wonder her little hand held very tenderly by her mother's long fingers.

When at last she was undressed and in bed, Mrs. Diantha, looking very pale, kissed her, and so did both grandmothers.

Amelia, being very young and very tired, went to sleep. She did not know that that night was to mark a sharp turn in her whole life. Thereafter she went to school "dressed like the best," and her mother petted her as nobody had ever known her mother could pet.

It was not so very long afterward that Amelia, out of her own improvement in appearance, developed a little stamp of individuality.

One day Lily wore a white frock with blue ribbons, and Amelia wore one with coral pink. It was a particular day in school; there was company, and tea was served.

"I told you I was going to wear blue ribbons," Lily whispered to Amelia. Amelia smiled lovingly back at her.

"Yes, I know, but I thought I would wear pink."

THE COCK OF THE WALK

THE COCK OF THE WALK

DOWN the road, kicking up the dust until he marched, soldier-wise, in a cloud of it, that rose and grimed his moist face and added to the heavy, brown powder upon the wayside weeds and flowers, whistling a queer, tuneless thing, which yet contained definite sequences—the whistle of a bird rather than a boy—approached Johnny Trumbull, aged ten, small of his age, but accounted by his mates mighty.

Johnny came of the best and oldest family in the village, but it was in some respects an undesirable family for a boy. In it survived, as fossils survive in ancient nooks and crannies of the earth, old traits of race, unchanged by time and environment. Living in a house lighted by electricity, the mental conception of it was to the Trumbulls as the conception of candles; with telephones at hand, they unconsciously still conceived of messages delivered with the old saying, "Ride, ride," etc., and relays of post-horses. They locked their doors, but still had latch-strings in mind. Johnny's father was a physician, adopting modern methods of surgery and prescription, yet his mind harked back to cupping and calomel, and now and then he swerved aside from

35

his path across the field of the present into the future and plunged headlong, as if for fresh air, into the traditional past, and often with brilliant results.

Johnny's mother was a college graduate. She was the president of the woman's club. She read papers savoring of such feminine leaps ahead that they were like gymnastics, but she walked homeward with the gait of her great-grandmother, and inwardly regarded her husband as her lord and master. She minced genteelly, lifting her quite fashionable skirts high above very slender ankles, which were hereditary. Not a woman of her race had ever gone home on thick ankles, and they had all gone home. They had all been at home, even if abroad—at home in the truest sense. At the club, reading her inflammatory paper, Cora Trumbull's real self remained at home intent upon her mending, her dusting, her house economics. It was something remarkably like her astral body which presided at the club.

As for her unmarried sister Janet, who was older and had graduated from a young ladies' seminary instead of a college, whose early fancy had been guided into the lady-like ways of antimacassars and pincushions and wax flowers under glass shades, she was a straighter proposition. No astral pretensions had Janet. She stayed, body and soul together, in the old ways, and did not even project her shadow out of them. There is seldom room enough for one's shadow in one's earliest way of life, but there was plenty for Janet's. There had been a Janet unmarried in every Trumbull family for generations. That in some subtle fashion accounted for her remaining single. There had also been an unmarried Jonathan Trumbull, and that accounted for Johnny's old bachelor uncle Jonathan. Jonathan was a retired clergyman. He had retired before he had preached long, because of doctrinal doubts, which were hereditary. He had a little, dark study in Johnny's father's house, which was the old Trumbull homestead, and he passed much of his time there, debating within himself that matter of doctrines.

Presently Johnny, assiduously kicking up dust, met his uncle Jonathan, who passed without the slightest notice. Johnny did not mind at all. He was used to it. Presently his own father appeared, driving along in his buggy the bay mare at a steady jog, with the next professional call quite clearly upon her equine mind. And Johnny's father did not see him. Johnny did not mind that, either. He expected nothing different.

Then Johnny saw his mother approaching. She was coming from the club meeting. She held up her silk skirts high, as usual, and carried a nice little parcel of papers tied with ribbon. She also did not notice Johnny, who, however, out of sweet respect for his mother's nice silk dress, stopped kicking up dust. Mrs. Trumbull on the village street was really at home preparing a shortcake for supper.

Johnny eyed his mother's faded but rather beautiful face under the rose-trimmed bonnet with admiration and entire absence of resentment. Then he walked on and kicked up the dust again. He loved to kick up the dust in summer, the fallen leaves in autumn, and the snow in winter. Johnny was not a typical Trumbull. None of them had ever cared for simple amusements like that. Looking back for generations on his father's and mother's side (both had been Trumbulls, but very distantly related), none could be discovered who in the least resembled Johnny. No dim blue eye of retrospection and reflection had Johnny; no tendency to tall slenderness which would later bow beneath the greater weight of the soul. Johnny was small, but wiry of build, and looked able to bear any amount of mental development without a lasting bend of his physical shoulders. Johnny had, at the early age of ten, whopped nearly every boy in school, but that was a secret of honor. It was well known in the school that, once the Trumbulls heard of it, Johnny could never whop again. "You fellows know," Johnny had declared once, standing over his prostrate and whimpering foe, "that I don't mind getting whopped at home, but they might send me away to another school, and then I could never whop any of you fellows."

Johnny Trumbull kicking up the dust, himself dust-covered, his shoes, his little queerly fitting dun suit, his cropped head, all thickly powdered, loved it. He sniffed in that dust like a grateful incense. He did not stop dust-kicking when he saw his aunt Janet coming, for, as he considered, her old black gown was not worth the sacrifice. It was true that she might see him. She sometimes did, if she were not reading a book as she walked. It had always been a habit with the Janet Trumbulls to read improving books when they walked abroad. To-day Johnny saw, with a quick glance of those sharp, black eyes, so unlike the Trumbulls', that his aunt Janet was reading. He therefore expected her to pass him without recognition, and marched on kicking up the dust. But suddenly, as he grew nearer the spry little figure, he was aware of a pair of gray eyes, before which waved protectingly a hand clad in a black silk glove with dangling finger-tips, because it was too long, and it dawned swiftly upon him that Aunt Janet was trying to shield her face from the moving column of brown motes. He stopped kicking, but it was too late. Aunt Janet had him by the collar and was vigorously shaking him with nervous strength.

"You are a very naughty little boy," declared Aunt Janet. "You should know better than to walk along the street raising so much dust. No well-brought-up child ever does such things. Who are your parents, little boy?"

Johnny perceived that Aunt Janet did not recognize him, which was easily explained. She wore her reading-spectacles and not her far-seeing ones; besides, her reading spectacles were obscured by dust and her nephew's face was nearly obliterated. Also as she shook him his face was not much in evidence. Johnny disliked, naturally, to tell his aunt Janet that her own sister and brother-in-law were the parents of such a wicked little boy. He therefore kept quiet and submitted to the shaking, making himself as limp as a rag. This, however, exasperated Aunt Janet, who found herself encumbered

39

by a dead weight of a little boy to be shaken, and suddenly Johnny Trumbull, the fighting champion of the town, the cock of the walk of the school, found himself being ignominiously spanked. That was too much. Johnny's fighting blood was up. He lost all consideration for circumstances, he forgot that Aunt Janet was not a boy, that she was quite near being an old lady. She had overstepped the bounds of privilege of age and sex, and an alarming state of equality ensued. Quickly the tables were turned. The boy became far from limp. He stiffened, then bounded and rebounded like wire. He butted, he parried, he observed all his famous tactics of battle, and poor Aunt Janet sat down in the dust, black dress, bonnet, glasses (but the glasses were off and lost), little improving book, black silk gloves, and all; and Johnny, hopeless, awful, irreverent, sat upon his Aunt Janet's plunging knees, which seemed the most lively part of her. He kept his face twisted away from her, but it was not from cowardice. Johnny was afraid lest Aunt Janet should be too much overcome by the discovery of his identity. He felt that it was his duty to spare her that. So he sat still, triumphant but inwardly aghast.

It was fast dawning upon him that his aunt was not a little boy. He was not afraid of any punishment which might be meted out to him, but he was simply horrified. He himself had violated all the honorable conditions of warfare. He felt a little dizzy and ill, and he felt worse when he ventured a hurried glance at Aunt Janet's face. She was very pale through the dust, and her eyes were closed. Johnny thought then that he had killed her.

He got up—the nervous knees were no longer plunging; then he heard a voice, a little-girl voice, always shrill, but now high pitched to a squeak with terror. It was the voice of Lily Jennings. She stood near and yet aloof, a lovely little flower of a girl, all white-scalloped frills and ribbons, with a big white-frilled hat shading a pale little face and covering the top of a head decorated with wonderful yellow curls. She stood behind a big baby-carriage with a pink-lined muslin canopy and containing a nest of pink and white, but an empty nest. Lily's little brother's carriage had a spring broken, and she had been to borrow her aunt's baby-carriage, so that nurse could wheel little brother up and down the veranda. Nurse had a headache, and the maids were busy, and Lily, who was a kind little soul and, moreover, imaginative, and who liked the idea of pushing an empty baby-carriage, had volunteered to go for it. All the way she had been dreaming of what was not in the carriage. She had come directly out of a dream of doll twins when she chanced upon the tragedy in the road.

"What have you been doing now, Johnny Trumbull?" said she. She was tremulous, white with horror, but she stood her ground. It was curious, but Johnny Trumbull, with all his bravery, was always cowed before Lily. Once she had turned and stared at him when he had emerged triumphant but with bleeding nose from a fight; then she had sniffed delicately and gone her way. It had only taken a second, but in that second the victor had met moral defeat.

He looked now at her pale, really scared face, and his own was as pale. He stood and kicked the dust until the swirling column of it reached his head.

"That's right," said Lily; "stand and kick up dust all over me. *What* have you been doing?"

Johnny was trembling so he could hardly stand. He stopped kicking dust.

"Have you killed your aunt?" demanded Lily. It was monstrous, but she had a very dramatic imagination, and there was a faint hint of enjoyment in her tragic voice.

"Guess she's just choked by dust," volunteered Johnny, hoarsely. He kicked the dust again.

"That's right," said Lily. "If she's choked to death by dust, stand there and choke her some more. You are a murderer, Johnny Trumbull, and my mamma will never allow me to speak to you again, and Madame will not allow you to come to school. *And*—I see your papa driving up the street, and there is the chief policeman's buggy just behind." Lily acquiesced entirely in the extraordinary coincidence of the father and the chief of police appearing upon the scene. The unlikely seemed to her the likely. "*Now*," said she, cheerfully, "you will be put in state prison and locked up, and then you will be put to death by a very strong telephone."

Johnny's father was leaning out of his buggy, looking back at the chief of police in his, and the mare was jogging very slowly in a perfect reek of dust. Lily, who was, in spite of her terrific imagination,

human and a girl, rose suddenly to heights of pity
and succor. "They shall never take you, Johnny
Trumbull," said she. "I will save you."

Johnny by this time was utterly forgetful of his
high status as champion (behind her back) of Madame's very select school for select children of a
somewhat select village. He was forgetful of the
fact that a champion never cries. He cried; he
blubbered; tears rolled over his dusty cheeks, making furrows like plowshares of grief. He feared lest
he might have killed his aunt Janet. Women, and
not very young women, might presumably be unable to survive such rough usage as very tough
and at the same time very limber little boys, and
he loved his poor aunt Janet. He grieved because
of his aunt, his parents, his uncle, and rather more
particularly because of himself. He was quite sure
that the policeman was coming for him. Logic had
no place in his frenzied conclusions. He did not
consider how the tragedy had taken place entirely
out of sight of a house, that Lily Jennings was the
only person who had any knowledge of it. He looked
at the masterful, fair-haired little girl like a baby.
"How?" sniffed he.

For answer, Lily pointed to the empty baby-carriage. "Get right in," she ordered.

Even in this dire extremity Johnny hesitated.
"Can't."

"Yes, you can. It is extra large. Aunt Laura's
baby was a twin when he first came; now he's just
an ordinary baby, but his carriage is big enough for
two. There's plenty of room. Besides, you're a

very small boy, very small of your age, even if you do knock all the other boys down and have murdered your aunt. Get in. In a minute they will see you."

There was in reality no time to lose. Johnny did get in. In spite of the provisions for twins, there was none too much room.

Lily covered him up with the fluffy pink-and-lace things, and scowled. "You hump up awfully," she muttered. Then she reached beneath him and snatched out the pillow on which he lay, the baby's little bed. She gave it a swift toss over the fringe of wayside bushes into a field. "Aunt Laura's nice embroidered pillow," said she. "Make yourself just as flat as you can, Johnny Trumbull."

Johnny obeyed, but he was obliged to double himself up like a jack-knife. However, there was no sign of him visible when the two buggies drew up. There stood a pale and frightened little girl, with a baby-carriage canopied with rose and lace and heaped up with rosy and lacy coverlets, presumably sheltering a sleeping infant. Lily was a very keen little girl. She had sense enough not to run. The two men, at the sight of Aunt Janet prostrate in the road, leaped out of their buggies. The doctor's horse stood still; the policeman's trotted away, to Lily's great relief. She could not imagine Johnny's own father haling him away to state prison and the stern Arm of Justice. She stood the fire of bewildered questions in the best and safest fashion. She wept bitterly, and her tears were not assumed. Poor little Lily was all of a sudden crushed under the weight of facts. There was Aunt Janet, she had no doubt, killed by her own nephew, and she was hiding the guilty murderer. She had visions of state prison for herself. She watched fearfully while the two men bent over the prostrate woman, who very soon began to sputter and gasp and try to sit up.

"What on earth is the matter, Janet?" inquired Dr. Trumbull, who was paler than his sister-in-law. In fact, she was unable to look very pale on account of dust.

"Ow!" sputtered Aunt Janet, coughing violently, "get me up out of this dust, John. Ow!"

"What was the matter?"

"Yes, what has happened, madam?" demanded the chief of police, sternly.

"Nothing," replied Aunt Janet, to Lily's and Johnny's amazement. "What do you think has happened? I fell down in all this nasty dust. Ow!"

"What did you eat for luncheon, Janet?" inquired Dr. Trumbull, as he assisted his sister-in-law to her feet.

"What I was a fool to eat," replied Janet Trumbull, promptly. "Cucumber salad and lemon jelly with whipped cream."

"Enough to make anybody have indigestion," said Dr. Trumbull. "You have had one of these attacks before, too, Janet. You remember the time you ate strawberry shortcake and ice-cream?"

Janet nodded meekly. Then she coughed again. "Ow, this dust!" gasped she. "For goodness' sake, John, get me home where I can get some water and take off these dusty clothes or I shall choke to death."

"How does your stomach feel?" inquired Dr. Trumbull.

"Stomach is all right now, but I am just choking to death with the dust." Janet turned sharply toward the policeman. "You have sense enough to keep still, I hope," said she. "I don't want the whole town ringing with my being such an idiot as to eat cucumbers and cream together and being found this way." Janet looked like an animated creation of dust as she faced the chief of police.

"Yes, ma'am," he replied, bowing and scraping one foot and raising more dust.

He and Dr. Trumbull assisted Aunt Janet into the buggy, and they drove off. Then the chief of police discovered that his own horse had gone. "Did you see which way he went, sis?" he inquired of Lily, and she pointed down the road, and sobbed as she did so.

The policeman said something bad under his breath, then advised Lily to run home to her ma, and started down the road.

When he was out of sight, Lily drew back the pink-and-white things from Johnny's face. "Well, you didn't kill her this time," said she.

"Why do you s'pose she didn't tell all about it?" said Johnny, gaping at her.

"How do I know? I suppose she was ashamed to tell how she had been fighting, maybe."

"No, that was not why," said Johnny in a deep voice.

46

"Why was it, then?"

"*She knew.*"

Johnny began to climb out of the baby-carriage.

"What will she do next, then?" asked Lily.

"I don't know," Johnny replied, gloomily.

He was out of the carriage then, and Lily was readjusting the pillows and things. "Get that nice embroidered pillow I threw over the bushes," she ordered, crossly. Johnny obeyed. When she had finished putting the baby-carriage to rights she turned upon poor little Johnny Trumbull, and her face wore the expression of a queen of tragedy. "Well," said Lily Jennings, "I suppose I shall have to marry you when I am grown up, after all this."

Johnny gasped. He thought Lily the most beautiful girl he knew, but to be confronted with murder and marriage within a few minutes was almost too much. He flushed a burning red. He laughed foolishly. He said nothing.

"It will be very hard on me," stated Lily, "to marry a boy who tried to murder his nice aunt."

Johnny revived a bit under this feminine disdain. "I didn't try to murder her," he said in a weak voice.

"You might have, throwing her down in all that awful dust, a nice, clean lady. Ladies are not like boys. It might kill them very quickly to be knocked down on a dusty road."

"I didn't mean to kill her."

"You might have."

"Well, I didn't, and—she—"

"What?"

47

"She spanked me."

"Pooh! That doesn't amount to anything," sniffed Lily.

"It does if you are a boy."

"I don't see why."

"Well, I can't help it if you don't. It does."

"Why shouldn't a boy be spanked when he's naughty, just as well as a girl, I would like to know?"

"Because he's a boy."

Lily looked at Johnny Trumbull. The great fact did remain. He had been spanked, he had thrown his own aunt down in the dust. He had taken advantage of her little-girl protection, but he was a boy. Lily did not understand his why at all, but she bowed before it. However, that she would not admit. She made a rapid change of base. "What," said she, "are you going to do next?"

Johnny stared at her. It was a puzzle.

"If," said Lily, distinctly, "you are afraid to go home, if you think your aunt will tell, I will let you get into Aunt Laura's baby-carriage again, and I will wheel you a little way."

Johnny would have liked at that moment to knock Lily down, as he had his aunt Janet. Lily looked at him shrewdly. "Oh yes," said she, "you can knock me down in the dust there if you want to, and spoil my nice clean dress. You will be a boy, just the same."

"I will never marry you, anyway," declared Johnny.

"Aren't you afraid I'll tell on you and get you another spanking if you don't?"

"Tell if you want to. I'd enough sight rather be spanked than marry you."

A gleam of respect came into the little girl's wisely regarding blue eyes. She, with the swiftness of her sex, recognized in forlorn little Johnny the making of a man. "Oh, well," said she, loftily, "I never was a telltale, and, anyway, we are not grown up, and there will be my trousseau to get, and a lot of other things to do first. I shall go to Europe before I am married, too, and I might meet a boy much nicer than you on the steamer."

"Meet him if you want to."

Lily looked at Johnny Trumbull with more than respect—with admiration—but she kept guard over her little tongue. "Well, you can leave that for the future," said she with a grown-up air.

"I ain't going to leave it. It's settled for good and all now," growled Johnny.

To his immense surprise, Lily curved her white embroidered sleeve over her face and began to weep.

"What's the matter now?" asked Johnny, sulkily, after a minute.

"I think you are a real horrid boy," sobbed Lily.

Lily looked like nothing but a very frilly, sweet, white flower. Johnny could not see her face. There was nothing to be seen except that delicate fluff of white, supported on dainty white-socked, white-slippered limbs.

"Say," said Johnny.

"You are real cruel, when I—I saved your—li-fe," wailed Lily.

"Say," said Johnny, "maybe if I don't see any

4   49

other girl I like better I will marry you when I am grown up, but I won't if you don't stop that howling."

Lily stopped immediately. She peeped at him, a blue peep from under the flopping, embroidered brim of her hat. "Are you in earnest?" She smiled faintly. Her blue eyes, wet with tears, were lovely; so was her hesitating smile.

"Yes, if you don't act silly," said Johnny. "Now you had better run home, or your mother will wonder where that baby-carriage is."

Lily walked away, smiling over her shoulder, the smile of the happily subjugated. "I won't tell anybody, Johnny," she called back in her flute-like voice.

"Don't care if you do," returned Johnny, looking at her with chin in the air and shoulders square, and Lily wondered at his bravery.

But Johnny was not so brave and he did care. He knew that his best course was an immediate return home, but he did not know what he might have to face. He could not in the least understand why his aunt Janet had not told at once. He was sure that she knew. Then he thought of a possible reason for her silence; she might have feared his arrest at the hands of the chief of police. Johnny quailed. He knew his aunt Janet to be rather a brave sort of woman. If she had fears, she must have had reason for them. He might even now be arrested. Suppose Lily did tell. He had a theory that girls usually told. He began to speculate concerning the horrors of prison. Of course he would not be executed, since his aunt was obviously very far from being killed, but he might be imprisoned for a long term.

Johnny went home. He did not kick the dust any more. He walked very steadily and staidly. When he came in sight of the old Colonial mansion, with its massive veranda pillars, he felt chilly. However, he went on. He passed around to the south door and entered and smelled shortcake. It would have smelled delicious had he not had so much on his mind. He looked through the hall, and had a glimpse of his uncle Jonathan in the study, writing. At the right of the door was his father's office. The door of that was open, and Johnny saw his father pouring things from bottles. He did not look at Johnny. His mother crossed the hall. She had on a long white apron, which she wore when making her famous cream shortcakes. She saw Johnny, but merely observed, "Go and wash your face and hands, Johnny; it is nearly supper-time."

Johnny went up-stairs. At the upper landing he found his aunt Janet waiting for him. "Come here," she whispered, and Johnny followed her, trembling, into her own room. It was a large room, rather crowded with heavy, old-fashioned furniture. Aunt Janet had freed herself from dust and was arrayed in a purple silk gown. Her hair was looped loosely on either side of her long face. She was a handsome woman, after a certain type.

"Stand here, Johnny," said she. She had closed the door, and Johnny was stationed before her. She did not seem in the least injured nor the worse for her experience. On the contrary, there was a bright-red flush on her cheeks, and her eyes shone as Johnny had never seen them. She looked eagerly at Johnny.

"Why did you do that?" she said, but there was no anger in her voice.

"I forgot," began Johnny.

"Forgot what?" Her voice was strained with eagerness.

"That you were not another boy," said Johnny.

"Tell me," said Aunt Janet. "No, you need not tell me, because if you did it might be my duty to inform your parents. I know there is no need of your telling. You *must* be in the habit of fighting with the other boys."

"Except the little ones," admitted Johnny.

To Johnny's wild astonishment, Aunt Janet seized him by the shoulders and looked him in the eyes with a look of adoration and immense approval. "Thank goodness," said she, "at last there is going to be a fighter in the Trumbull family. Your uncle would never fight, and your father would not. Your grandfather would. Your uncle and your father are good men, though; you must try to be like them, Johnny."

"Yes, ma'am," replied Johnny, bewildered.

"I think they would be called better men than your grandfather and my father," said Aunt Janet.

"Yes, ma'am."

"I think it is time for you to have your grand-father's watch," said Aunt Janet. "I think you are man enough to take care of it." Aunt Janet had all the time been holding a black leather case. Now she opened it, and Johnny saw the great gold watch which he had seen many times before and had always understood was to be his some day, when he was a man. "Here," said Aunt Janet. "Take good care of it. You must try to be as good as your uncle and father, but you must remember one thing—you will wear a watch which belonged to a man who never allowed other men to crowd him out of the way he elected to go."

"Yes, ma'am," said Johnny. He took the watch.

"What do you say?" inquired his aunt, sharply.

"Thank you."

"That's right. I thought you had forgotten your manners. Your grandfather never did."

"I am sorry, Aunt Janet," muttered Johnny, "that I—"

"You need never say anything about that," his aunt returned, quickly. "I did not see who you were at first. You are too old to be spanked by a woman, but you ought to be whipped by a man, and I wish your grandfather were alive to do it."

"Yes, ma'am," said Johnny. He looked at her bravely. "He could if he wanted to," said he.

Aunt Janet smiled at him proudly. "Of course," said she, "a boy like you never gets the worst of it fighting with other boys."

"No, ma'am," said Johnny.

Aunt Janet smiled again. "Now run and wash your face and hands," said she; "you must not keep supper waiting. Your mother has a paper to write for her club, and I have promised to help her."

THE COPY-CAT

"Yes, ma'am," said Johnny. He walked out, carrying the great gold timepiece, bewildered, embarrassed, modest beneath his honors, but little cock of the walk, whether he would or no, for reasons entirely and forever beyond his ken.

JOHNNY-IN-THE-WOODS

JOHNNY-IN-THE-WOODS

JOHNNY TRUMBULL, he who had demonstrated his claim to be Cock of the Walk by a most impious hand-to-hand fight with his own aunt, Miss Janet Trumbull, in which he had been decisively victorious, and won his spurs, consisting of his late grandfather's immense, solemnly ticking watch, was to take a new path of action. Johnny suddenly developed the prominent Trumbull trait, but in his case it was inverted. Johnny, as became a boy of his race, took an excursion into the past, but instead of applying the present to the past, as was the tendency of the other Trumbulls, he forcibly applied the past to the present. He fairly plastered the past over the exigencies of his day and generation like a penetrating poultice of mustard, and the results were peculiar.

Johnny, being bidden of a rainy day during the midsummer vacation to remain in the house, to keep quiet, read a book, and be a good boy, obeyed, but his obedience was of a doubtful measure of wisdom.

Johnny got a book out of his uncle Jonathan Trumbull's dark little library while Jonathan was walking sedately to the post-office, holding his dripping umbrella at a wonderful slant of exactness, without regard to the wind, thereby getting the soft drive of the rain full in his face, which became, as it were, bedewed with tears, entirely outside any cause of his own emotions.

Johnny probably got the only book of an anti-orthodox trend in his uncle's library. He found tucked away in a snug corner an ancient collection of *Border Ballads*, and he read therein of many unmoral romances and pretty fancies, which, since he was a small boy, held little meaning for him, or charm, beyond a delight in the swing of the rhythm, for Johnny had a feeling for music. It was when he read of Robin Hood, the bold Robin Hood, with his dubious ethics but his certain and unquenchable interest, that Johnny Trumbull became intent. He had the volume in his own room, being somewhat doubtful as to whether it might be of the sort included in the good-boy rôle. He sat beside a rain-washed window, which commanded a view of the wide field between the Trumbull mansion and Jim Simmons's house, and he read about Robin Hood and his Greenwood adventures, his forcible setting the wrong right; and for the first time his imagination awoke, and his ambition. Johnny Trumbull, hitherto hero of nothing except little material fist-fights, wished now to become a hero of true romance.

In fact, Johnny considered seriously the possi-bility of reincarnating, in his own person, Robin Hood. He eyed the wide green field dreamily through his rain-blurred window. It was a pretty field, waving with feathery grasses and starred with daisies and buttercups, and it was very fortunate that it happened to be so wide. Jim Simmons's house was not a desirable feature of the landscape, and looked much better several acres away. It was a neglected, squalid structure, and considered a disgrace to the whole village. Jim was also a disgrace, and an unsolved problem. He owned that house, and somehow contrived to pay the taxes thereon. He also lived and throve in bodily health in spite of evil ways, and his children were many. There seemed no way to dispose finally of Jim Simmons and his house except by murder and arson, and the village was a peaceful one, and such measures were entirely too strenuous.

Presently Johnny, staring dreamily out of his window, saw approaching a rusty-black umbrella held at precisely the wrong angle in respect of the storm, but held with the unvarying stiffness with which a soldier might hold a bayonet, and knew it for his uncle Jonathan's umbrella. Soon he beheld also his uncle's serious, rain-drenched face and his long ambling body and legs. Jonathan was coming home from the post-office, whither he repaired every morning. He never got a letter, never anything except religious newspapers, but the visit to the post-office was part of his daily routine. Rain or shine, Jonathan Trumbull went for the morning mail, and gained thereby a queer negative enjoyment of a perfectly useless duty performed. Johnny watched his uncle draw near to the house, and cruelly reflected how unlike Robin Hood he must be. He even wondered if his uncle could possibly have read

Robin Hood and still show absolutely no result in his own personal appearance. He knew that he, Johnny, could not walk to the post-office and back, even with the drawback of a dripping old umbrella instead of a bow and arrow, without looking a bit like Robin Hood, especially when fresh from reading about him.

Then suddenly something distracted his thoughts from Uncle Jonathan. The long, feathery grass in the field moved with a motion distinct from that caused by the wind and rain. Johnny saw a tiger-striped back emerge, covering long leaps of terror. Johnny knew the creature for a cat afraid of Uncle Jonathan. Then he saw the grass move behind the first leaping, striped back, and he knew there were more cats afraid of Uncle Jonathan. There were even motions caused by unseen things, and he reasoned, "Kittens afraid of Uncle Jonathan." Then Johnny reflected with a great glow of indignation that the Simmonses kept an outrageous number of half-starved cats and kittens, besides a quota of children popularly supposed to be none too well nourished, let alone properly clothed. Then it was that Johnny Trumbull's active, firm imagination slapped the past of old romance like a most thorough mustard poultice over the present. There could be no Lincoln Green, no following of brave outlaws (that is, in the strictest sense), no bows and arrows, no sojourning under greenwood trees and the rest, but something he could, and would, do and be. That rainy day when Johnny Trumbull was a good boy, and stayed in the house, and read a book, marked an epoch.

JOHNNY-IN-THE-WOODS

That night when Johnny went into his aunt Janet's room she looked curiously at his face, which seemed a little strange to her. Johnny, since he had come into possession of his grandfather's watch, went every night, on his way to bed, to his aunt's room for the purpose of winding up that ancient timepiece, Janet having a firm impression that it might not be done properly unless under her supervision. Johnny stood before his aunt and wound up the watch with its ponderous key, and she watched him.

"What have you been doing all day, John?" said she.

"Stayed in the house and—read."

"What did you read, John?"

"A book."

"Do you mean to be impertinent, John?"

"No, ma'am," replied Johnny, and with perfect truth. He had not the slightest idea of the title of the book.

"What was the book?"

"A poetry book."

"Where did you find it?"

"In Uncle Jonathan's library."

"Poetry in Uncle Jonathan's library?" said Janet, in a mystified way. She had a general impression of Jonathan's library as of century-old preserves, altogether dried up and quite indistinguishable one from the other except by labels. Poetry she could not imagine as being there at all. Finally she thought of the early Victorians, and Spenser and Chaucer. The library might include them, but she had an idea that Spenser and Chaucer were not fit reading for a little boy. However, as she remembered Spenser and Chaucer, she doubted if Johnny could understand much of them. Probably he had gotten hold of an early Victorian, and she looked rather contemptuous.

"I don't think much of a boy like you reading poetry," said Janet. "Couldn't you find anything else to read?"

"No, ma'am." That also was truth. Johnny, before exploring his uncle's theological library, had peered at his father's old medical books and his mother's bookcases, which contained quite terrifying uniform editions of standard things written by women.

"I don't suppose there *are* many books written for boys," said Aunt Janet, reflectively.

"No, ma'am," said Johnny. He finished winding the watch, and gave, as was the custom, the key to Aunt Janet, lest he lose it.

"I will see if I cannot find some books of travels for you, John," said Janet. "I think travels would be good reading for a boy. Good night, John."

"Good night, Aunt Janet," replied Johnny. His aunt never kissed him good night, which was one reason why he liked her.

On his way to bed he had to pass his mother's room, whose door stood open. She was busy writing at her desk. She glanced at Johnny.

"Are you going to bed?" said she.

"Yes, ma'am."

Johnny entered the room and let his mother kiss his

forehead, parting his curly hair to do so. He loved his mother, but did not care at all to have her kiss him. He did not object, because he thought she liked to do it, and she was a woman, and it was a very little thing in which he could oblige her.

"Were you a good boy, and did you find a good book to read?" asked she.

"Yes, ma'am."

"What was the book?" Cora Trumbull inquired, absently, writing as she spoke.

"Poetry."

Cora laughed. "Poetry is odd for a boy," said she. "You should have read a book of travels or history. Good night, Johnny."

"Good night, mother."

Then Johnny met his father, smelling strongly of medicines, coming up from his study. But his father did not see him. And Johnny went to bed, having imbibed from that old tale of Robin Hood more of history and more knowledge of excursions into realms of old romance than his elders had ever known during much longer lives than his.

Johnny confided in nobody at first. His feeling nearly led him astray in the matter of Lily Jennings; he thought of her, for one sentimental minute, as Robin Hood's Maid Marion. Then he dismissed the idea peremptorily. Lily Jennings would simply laugh. He knew her. Moreover, she was a girl, and not to be trusted. Johnny felt the need of another boy who would be a kindred spirit; he wished for more than one boy. He wished for a following of heroic and lawless souls, even as Robin

Hood's. But he could think of nobody, after considerable study, except one boy, younger than himself. He was a beautiful little boy, whose mother had never allowed him to have his golden curls cut, although he had been in trousers for quite a while. However, the trousers were foolish, being knickerbockers, and accompanied by low socks, which revealed pretty, dimpled, babyish legs. The boy's name was Arnold Carruth, and that was against him, as being long, and his mother firm about allowing no nickname. Nicknames in any case were not allowed in the very exclusive private school which Johnny attended.

Arnold Carruth, in spite of his being such a beautiful little boy, would have had no standing at all in the school as far as popularity was concerned had it not been for a strain of mischief which triumphed over curls, socks, and pink cheeks and a much-kissed rosebud of a mouth. Arnold Carruth, as one of the teachers permitted herself to state when relaxed in the bosom of her own family, was "as choke-full of mischief as a pod of peas. And the worst of it all is," quoth the teacher, Miss Agnes Rector, who was a pretty young girl, with a hidden sympathy for mischief herself—"the worst of it is, that child looks so like a cherub on a rosy cloud that even if he should be caught nobody would believe it. They would be much more likely to accuse poor little Andrew Jackson Green, because he has a snub nose and is a bit cross-eyed, and I never knew that poor child to do anything except obey rules and learn his lessons. He is almost too good. And another worst of it is, nobody can help loving that little imp of a Carruth boy, mischief and all. I believe the scamp knows it and takes advantage of it."

It is quite possible that Arnold Carruth did profit unworthily by his beauty and engagingness, albeit without calculation. He was so young, it was monstrous to believe him capable of calculation, of deliberate trading upon his assets of birth and beauty and fascination. However, Johnny Trumbull, who was wide awake and a year older, was alive to the situation. He told Arnold Carruth, and Arnold Carruth only, about Robin Hood and his great scheme.

"You can help," said this wise Johnny; "you can be in it, because nobody thinks you can be in anything, on account of your wearing curls."

Arnold Carruth flushed and gave an angry tug at one golden curl which the wind blew over a shoulder. The two boys were in a secluded corner of Madame's lawn, behind a clump of Japanese cedars, during an intermission.

"I can't help it because I wear curls," declared Arnold with angry shame.

"Who said you could? No need of getting mad."

"Mamma and Aunt Flora and grandmamma won't let me have these old curls cut off," said Arnold. "You needn't think I want to have curls like a girl, Johnny Trumbull."

"Who said you did? And I know you don't like to wear those short stockings, either."

"Like to!" Arnold gave a spiteful kick, first of one half-bared, dimpled leg, then of the other.

5 65

"First thing you know I'll steal mamma's or Aunt Flora's stockings and throw these in the furnace— I will. Do you s'pose a feller wants to wear these baby things? I guess not. Women are awful queer, Johnny Trumbull. My mamma and my aunt Flora are awful nice, but they are queer about some things."

"Most women are queer," agreed Johnny, "but my aunt Janet isn't as queer as some. Rather guess if she saw me with curls like a little girl she'd cut 'em off herself."

"Wish she was my aunt," said Arnold Carruth with a sigh. "A feller needs a woman like that till he's grown up. Do you s'pose she'd cut off my curls if I was to go to your house, Johnny?"

"I'm afraid she wouldn't think it was right unless your mother said she might. She has to be real careful about doing right, because my uncle Jonathan used to preach, you know."

Arnold Carruth grinned savagely, as if he endured pain. "Well, I s'pose I'll have to stand the curls and little baby stockings awhile longer," said he. "What was it you were going to tell me, Johnny?"

"I am going to tell you because I know you aren't too good, if you do wear curls and little stockings."

"No, I ain't too good," declared Arnold Carruth, proudly; "I ain't—*honest*, Johnny."

"That's why I'm going to tell you. But if you tell any of the other boys—or girls—"

"Tell girls!" sniffed Arnold.

"If you tell anybody, I'll lick you."

"Guess I ain't afraid."

"Guess you'd be afraid to go home after you'd been licked."

"Guess my mamma would give it to you."

"Run home and tell mamma you'd been whopped, would you, then?"

Little Arnold, beautiful baby boy, straightened himself with a quick remembrance that he was born a man. "You know I wouldn't tell, Johnny Trumbull."

"Guess you wouldn't. Well, here it is—" Johnny spoke in emphatic whispers, Arnold's curly head close to his mouth: "There are a good many things in this town have got to be set right," said Johnny.

Little Arnold stared at him. Then fire shone in his lovely blue eyes under the golden shadow of his curls, a fire which had shone in the eyes of some ancestors of his, for there was good fighting blood in the Carruth family, as well as in the Trumbull, although this small descendant did go about curled and kissed and barelegged.

"How'll we begin?" said Arnold, in a strenuous whisper.

"We've got to begin right away with Jim Simmons's cats and kittens."

"With Jim Simmons's cats and kittens?" repeated Arnold.

"That was what I said, exactly. We've got to begin right there. It is an awful little beginning, but I can't think of anything else. If you can, I'm willing to listen."

"I guess I can't," admitted Arnold, helplessly.

"Of course we can't go around taking away money

67

from rich people and giving it to poor folks. One reason is, most of the poor folks in this town are lazy, and don't get money because they don't want to work for it. And when they are not lazy, they drink. If we gave rich people's money to poor folks like that, we shouldn't do a mite of good. The rich folks would be poor, and the poor folks wouldn't stay rich; they would be lazier, and get more drink. I don't see any sense in doing things like that in this town. There are a few poor folks I have been thinking we might take some money for and do good, but not many."

"Who?" inquired Arnold Carruth, in awed tones.

"Well, there is poor old Mrs. Sam Little. She's awful poor. Folks help her, I know, but she can't be real pleased being helped. She'd rather have the money herself. I have been wondering if we couldn't get some of your father's money away and give it to her, for one."

"Get away papa's money!"

"You don't mean to tell me you are as stingy as that, Arnold Carruth?"

"I guess papa wouldn't like it."

"Of course he wouldn't. But that is not the point. It is not what your father would like; it is what that poor old lady would like."

It was too much for Arnold. He gaped at Johnny.

"If you are going to be mean and stingy, we may as well stop before we begin," said Johnny.

Then Arnold Carruth recovered himself. "Old Mr. Webster Payne is awful poor," said he. "We might take some of your father's money and give it to him."

Johnny snorted, fairly snorted. "If," said he, "you think my father keeps his money where we can get it, you are mistaken, Arnold Carruth. My father's money is all in papers that are not worth much now and that he has to keep in the bank till they are."

Arnold smiled hopefully. "Guess that's the way my papa keeps *his* money."

"It's the way most rich people are mean enough to," said Johnny, severely. "I don't care if it's your father or mine, it's mean. And that's why we've got to begin with Jim Simmons's cats and kittens."

"Are you going to give old Mrs. Sam Little cats?" inquired Arnold.

Johnny sniffed. "Don't be silly," said he. "Though I do think a nice cat with a few kittens might cheer her up a little, and we could steal enough milk, by getting up early and tagging after the milk-man, to feed them. But I wasn't thinking of giving her or old Mr. Payne cats and kittens. I wasn't thinking of folks; I was thinking of all those poor cats and kittens that Mr. Jim Simmons has and doesn't half feed, and that have to go hunting around folks' back doors in the rain, when cats hate water, too, and pick things up that must be bad for their stomachs, when they ought to have their milk regularly in nice, clean saucers. No, Arnold Carruth, what we have got to do is to steal Mr. Jim Simmons's cats and get them in nice homes where they can earn their living catching mice and be well cared for."

"Steal cats?" said Arnold.

"Yes, steal cats, in order to do right," said Johnny Trumbull, and his expression was heroic, even exalted.

It was then that a sweet treble, faltering yet exultant, rang in their ears.

"If," said the treble voice, "you are going to steal dear little kitty cats and get nice homes for them, I'm going to help."

The voice belonged to Lily Jennings, who had stood on the other side of the Japanese cedars and heard every word.

Both boys started in righteous wrath, but Arnold Carruth was the angrier of the two. "Mean little cat yourself, listening," said he. His curls seemed to rise like a crest of rage.

Johnny, remembering some things, was not so outspoken. "You hadn't any right to listen, Lily Jennings," he said, with masculine severity.

"I didn't start to listen," said Lily. "I was looking for cones on these trees. Miss Parmalee wanted us to bring some object of nature into the class, and I wondered whether I could find a queer Japanese cone on one of these trees, and then I heard you boys talking, and I couldn't help listening. You spoke very loud, and I couldn't give up looking for that cone. I couldn't find any, and I heard all about the Simmonses' cats, and I know lots of other cats that haven't got good homes, and—I am going to be in it."

"You *ain't*," declared Arnold Carruth.

"We can't have girls in it," said Johnny the mindful, more politely.

"You've got to have me. You had better have me, Johnny Trumbull," she added with meaning.

Johnny flinched. It was a species of blackmail, but what could he do? Suppose Lily told how she had hidden him—him, Johnny Trumbull, the champion of the school—in that empty baby-carriage! He would have more to contend against than Arnold Carruth with socks and curls. He did not think Lily would tell. Somehow Lily, although a little, befrilled girl, gave an impression of having a knowledge of a square deal almost as much as a boy would; but what boy could tell with a certainty what such an uncertain creature as a girl might or might not do? Moreover, Johnny had a weakness, a hidden, Spartanly hidden, weakness for Lily. He rather wished to have her act as partner in his great enterprise. He therefore gruffly assented.

"All right," he said, "you can be in it. But just you look out. You'll see what happens if you tell."

"She can't be in it; she's nothing but a girl," said Arnold Carruth, fiercely.

Lily Jennings lifted her chin and surveyed him with queenly scorn. "And what are you?" said she. "A little boy with curls and baby socks."

Arnold colored with shame and fury, and subsided. "Mind you don't tell," he said, taking Johnny's cue.

"I sha'n't tell," replied Lily, with majesty. "But you'll tell yourselves if you talk one side of trees without looking on the other."

THE COPY-CAT

There was then only a few moments before Madame's musical Japanese gong which announced the close of intermission should sound, but three determined souls in conspiracy can accomplish much in a few moments. The first move was planned in detail before that gong sounded, and the two boys raced to the house, and Lily followed, carrying a toadstool, which she had hurriedly caught up from the lawn for her object of nature to be taken into class.

It was a poisonous toadstool, and Lily was quite a heroine in the class. That fact doubtless gave her a more dauntless air when, after school, the two boys caught up with her walking gracefully down the road, flirting her skirts and now and then giving her head a toss, which made her fluff of hair fly into a golden foam under her daisy-trimmed straw hat.

"To-night," Johnny whispered, as he sped past.

"At half past nine, between your house and the Simmonses'," replied Lily, without even looking at him. She was a past-mistress of dissimulation.

Lily's mother had guests at dinner that night, and the guests remarked sometimes, within the little girl's hearing, what a darling she was.

"She never gives me a second's anxiety," Lily's mother whispered to a lady beside her. "You cannot imagine what a perfectly good, dependable child she is."

"Now my Christina is a good child in the grain," said the lady, "but she is full of mischief. I never can tell what Christina will do next."

"*I* can always tell," said Lily's mother, in a voice of maternal triumph.

72

"Now only the other night, when I thought Christina was in bed, that absurd child got up and dressed and ran over to see her aunt Bella. Tom came home with her, and of course there was nothing very bad about it. Christina was very bright; she said, 'Mother, you never told me I must not get up and go to see Aunt Bella,' which was, of course, true. I could not gainsay that."

"I cannot," said Lily's mother, "imagine my Lily's doing such a thing."

If Lily had heard that last speech of her mother's, whom she dearly loved, she might have wavered. That pathetic trust in herself might have caused her to justify it. But she had finished her dinner and had been excused, and was undressing for bed, with the firm determination to rise betimes and dress and join Johnny Trumbull and Arnold Carruth. Johnny had the easiest time of them all. He simply had to bid his aunt Janet good night and have the watch wound, and take a fleeting glimpse of his mother at her desk and his father in his office, and go whistling to his room, and sit in the summer darkness and wait until the time came.

Arnold Carruth had the hardest struggle. His mother had an old school friend visiting her, and Arnold, very much dressed up, with his curls falling in a shining fleece upon a real lace collar, had to be shown off and show off. He had to play one little piece which he had learned upon the piano. He had to recite a little poem. He had to be asked how old he was, and if he liked to go to school, and how many teachers he had, and if he loved them, and if he loved his little mates, and which of them he loved best; and he had to be asked if he loved his aunt Dorothy, who was the school friend and not his aunt at all, and would he not like to come and live with her, because she had not any dear little boy; and he was obliged to submit to having his curls twisted around feminine fingers, and to being kissed and hugged, and a whole chapter of ordeals, before he was finally in bed, with his mother's kiss moist upon his lips, and free to assert himself.

That night Arnold Carruth realized himself as having an actual horror of his helpless state of pampered childhood. The man stirred in the soul of the boy, and it was a little rebel with sulky pout of lips and frown of childish brows who stole out of bed, got into some queer clothes, and crept down the back stairs. He heard his aunt Dorothy, who was not his aunt, singing an Italian song in the parlor, he heard the clink of silver and china from the butler's pantry, where the maids were washing the dinner dishes. He smelt his father's cigar, and he gave a little leap of joy on the grass of the lawn. At last he was out at night alone, and—he wore long stockings! That noon he had secreted a pair of his mother's toward that end. When he came home to luncheon he pulled them out of the darning-bag, which he had spied through a closet door that had been left ajar. One of the stockings was green silk, and the other was black, and both had holes in them, but all that mattered was the length. Arnold wore also his father's riding-breeches, which came over his shoes and which were enormously large,

and one of his father's silk shirts. He had resolved
to dress consistently for such a great occasion. His
clothes hampered him, but he felt happy as he sped
clumsily down the road.

However, both Johnny Trumbull and Lily Jennings, who were waiting for him at the rendezvous,
were startled by his appearance. Both began to
run, Johnny pulling Lily after him by the hand,
but Arnold's cautious hallo arrested them. Johnny
and Lily returned slowly, peering through the darkness.

"It's me," said Arnold, with gay disregard of
grammar.

"You looked," said Lily, "like a real fat old man.
What *have* you got on, Arnold Carruth?"

Arnold slouched before his companions, ridiculous
but triumphant. He hitched up a leg of the riding-
breeches and displayed a long, green silk stocking.
Both Johnny and Lily doubled up with laughter.

"What you laughing at?" inquired Arnold, crossly.

"Oh, nothing at all," said Lily. "Only you do
look like a scarecrow broken loose. Doesn't he,
Johnny?"

"I am going home," stated Arnold with dignity.
He turned, but Johnny caught him in his little iron
grip.

"Oh, shucks, Arnold Carruth!" said he. "Don't
be a baby. Come on." And Arnold Carruth with
difficulty came on.

People in the village, as a rule, retired early. Many
lights were out when the affair began, many went
out while it was in progress. All three of the band

steered as clear of lighted houses as possible, and dodged behind trees and hedges when shadowy figures appeared on the road or carriage-wheels were heard in the distance. At their special destination they were sure to be entirely safe. Old Mr. Peter Van Ness always retired very early. To be sure, he did not go to sleep until late, and read in bed, but his room was in the rear of the house on the second floor, and all the windows, besides, were dark. Mr. Peter Van Ness was a very wealthy elderly gentleman, very benevolent. He had given the village a beautiful stone church with memorial windows, a soldiers' monument, a park, and a home for aged couples, called "The Van Ness Home." Mr. Van Ness lived alone with the exception of a housekeeper and a number of old, very well-disciplined servants. The servants always retired early, and Mr. Van Ness required the house to be quiet for his late reading. He was a very studious old gentleman.

To the Van Ness house, set back from the street in the midst of a well-kept lawn, the three repaired, but not as noiselessly as they could have wished. In fact, a light flared in an up-stairs window, which was wide open, and one woman's voice was heard in conclave with another.

"I should think," said the first, "that the lawn was full of cats. Did you ever hear such a mewing, Jane?"

That was the housekeeper's voice. The three, each of whom carried a squirming burlap potato-bag from the Trumbull cellar, stood close to a clump of stately pines full of windy songs, and trembled.

"It do sound like cats, ma'am," said another voice, which was Jane's, the maid, who had brought Mrs. Meeks, the housekeeper, a cup of hot water and peppermint, because her dinner had disagreed with her.

"Just listen," said Mrs. Meeks.

"Yes, ma'am, I should think there was hundreds of cats and little kittens."

"I am so afraid Mr. Van Ness will be disturbed."

"Yes, ma'am."

"You might go out and look, Jane."

"Oh, ma'am, they might be burglars!"

"How can they be burglars when they are cats?" demanded Mrs. Meeks, testily.

Arnold Carruth snickered, and Johnny on one side, and Lily on the other, prodded him with an elbow. They were close under the window.

"Burglars is up to all sorts of queer tricks, ma'am," said Jane. "They may mew like cats to tell one another what door to go in."

"Jane, you talk like an idiot," said Mrs. Meeks. "Burglars talking like cats! Who ever heard of such a thing? It sounds right under that window. Open my closet door and get those heavy old shoes and throw them out."

It was an awful moment. The three dared not move. The cats and kittens in the bags—not so many, after all—seemed to have turned into multiplication-tables. They were positively alarming in their determination to get out, their wrath with one another, and their vociferous discontent with the whole situation.

"I can't hold my bag much longer," said poor little Arnold Carruth.

"Hush up, cry-baby!" whispered Lily, fiercely, in spite of a clawing paw emerging from her own bag and threatening her bare arm.

Then came the shoes. One struck Arnold squarely on the shoulder, nearly knocking him down and making him lose hold of his bag. The other struck Lily's bag, and conditions became worse; but she held on despite a scratch. Lily had pluck.

Then Jane's voice sounded very near, as she leaned out of the window. "I guess they have went, ma'am," said she. "I seen something run."

"I can hear them," said Mrs. Meeks, querulously.

"I seen them run," persisted Jane, who was tired and wished to be gone.

"Well, close that window, anyway, for I know I hear them, even if they have gone," said Mrs. Meeks. The three heard with relief the window slammed down.

The light flashed out, and simultaneously Lily Jennings and Johnny Trumbull turned indignantly upon Arnold Carruth.

"There, you have gone and let all those poor cats go," said Johnny.

"And spoilt everything," said Lily.

Arnold rubbed his shoulder. "You would have let go if you had been hit right on the shoulder by a great shoe," said he, rather loudly.

78

"Hush up!" said Lily. "I wouldn't have let my cats go if I had been killed by a shoe; so there."

"Serves us right for taking a boy with curls," said Johnny Trumbull.

But he spoke unadvisedly. Arnold Carruth was no match whatever for Johnny Trumbull, and had never been allowed the honor of a combat with him; but surprise takes even a great champion at a disadvantage. Arnold turned upon Johnny like a flash, out shot a little white fist, up struck a dimpled leg clad in cloth and leather, and down sat Johnny Trumbull; and, worse, open flew his bag, and there was a yowling exodus.

"There go your cats, too, Johnny Trumbull," said Lily, in a perfectly calm whisper. At that moment both boys, victor and vanquished, felt a simultaneous throb of masculine wrath at Lily. Who was she to gloat over the misfortunes of men? But retribution came swiftly to Lily. That viciously clawing little paw shot out farther, and there was a limit to Spartanism in a little girl born so far from that heroic land. Lily let go of her bag and with difficulty stifled a shriek of pain.

"Whose cats are gone now?" demanded Johnny, rising.

"Yes, whose cats are gone now?" said Arnold.

Then Johnny promptly turned upon him and knocked him down and sat on him.

Lily looked at them, standing, a stately little figure in the darkness. "I am going home." said she. "My mother does not allow me to go with fighting boys."

Johnny rose, and so did Arnold, whimpering slightly. His shoulder ached considerably.

"He knocked me down," said Johnny.

Even as he whimpered and as he suffered, Arnold felt a thrill of triumph. "Always knew I could if I had a chance," said he.

"You couldn't if I had been expecting it," said Johnny.

"Folks get knocked down when they ain't expecting it most of the time," declared Arnold, with more philosophy than he realized.

"I don't think it makes much difference about the knocking down," said Lily. "All those poor cats and kittens that we were going to give a good home, where they wouldn't be starved, have got away, and they will run straight back to Mr. Jim Simmons's."

"If they haven't any more sense than to run back to a place where they don't get enough to eat and are kicked about by a lot of children, let them run," said Johnny.

"That's so," said Arnold. "I never did see what we were doing such a thing for, anyway—stealing Mr. Simmons's cats and giving them to Mr. Van Ness."

It was the girl alone who stood by her guns of righteousness. "I saw and I see," she declared, with dangerously loud emphasis. "It was only our duty to try to rescue poor helpless animals who don't know any better than to stay where they are badly treated. And Mr. Van Ness has so much money he doesn't know what to do with it; he would have been real pleased to give those cats a home and buy milk and liver for them. But it's all spoiled now. I will never undertake to do good again, with a lot of boys in the way, as long as I live; so there!" Lily turned about.

"Going to tell your mother!" said Johnny, with scorn which veiled anxiety.

"No, I'm *not*. I don't tell tales."

Lily marched off, and in her wake went Johnny and Arnold, two poor little disillusioned would-be knights of old romance in a wretchedly commonplace future, not far enough from their horizons for any glamour.

They went home, and of the three Johnny Trumbull was the only one who was discovered. For him his aunt Janet lay in wait and forced a confession. She listened grimly, but her eyes twinkled.

"You have learned to fight, John Trumbull," said she, when he had finished. "Now the very next thing you have to learn, and make yourself worthy of your grandfather Trumbull, is not to be a fool."

"Yes, Aunt Janet," said Johnny.

The next noon, when he came home from school, old Maria, who had been with the family ever since he could remember and long before, called him into the kitchen. There, greedily lapping milk from a saucer, were two very lean, tall kittens."

"See those nice little tommy-cats," said Maria, beaming upon Johnny, whom she loved and whom she sometimes fancied deprived of boyish joys. "Your aunt Janet sent me over to the Simmonses' for them this morning. They are overrun with cats

6   81

—such poor, shiftless folks always be—and you can have them. We shall have to watch for a little while till they get wonted, so they won't run home."

Johnny gazed at the kittens, fast distending with the new milk, and felt presumably much as dear Robin Hood may have felt after one of his successful raids in the fair, poetic past.

"Pretty, ain't they?" said Maria. "They have drank up a whole saucer of milk. 'Most starved, I s'pose."

Johnny gathered up the two forlorn kittens and sat down in a kitchen chair, with one on each shoulder, hard, boyish cheeks pressed against furry, purring sides, and the little fighting Cock of the Walk felt his heart glad and tender with the love of the strong for the weak.

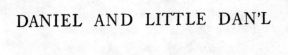

DANIEL AND LITTLE DAN'L

DANIEL AND LITTLE DAN'L

THE Wise homestead dated back more than a
century, yet it had nothing imposing about it
except its site. It was a simple, glaringly white cottage. There was a center front door with two windows on each side; there was a low slant of roof,
pierced by unpicturesque dormers. On the left of
the house was an ell, which had formerly been used
as a shoemaker's shop, but now served as a kitchen.
In the low attic of the ell was stored the shoemaker's
bench, whereon David Wise's grandfather had sat
for nearly eighty years of working days; after him
his eldest son, Daniel's father, had occupied the same
hollow seat of patient toil. Daniel had sat there for
twenty-odd years, then had suddenly realized both
the lack of necessity and the lack of customers, since
the great shoe-plant had been built down in the village. Then Daniel had retired—although he did
not use that expression. Daniel said to his friends
and his niece Dora that he had "quit work." But
he told himself, without the least bitterness, that
work had quit him.

After Daniel had retired, his one physiological
peculiarity assumed enormous proportions. It had
always been with him, but steady work had held it,

85

THE COPY-CAT

to a great extent, at bay. Daniel was a moral coward before physical conditions. He was as one who suffers, not so much from agony of the flesh as from agony of the mind induced thereby. Daniel was a coward before one of the simplest, most inevitable happenings of earthly life. He was a coward before summer heat. All winter he dreaded summer. Summer poisoned the spring for him. Only during the autumn did he experience anything of peace. Summer was then over, and between him and another summer stretched the blessed perspective of winter. Then Daniel Wise drew a long breath and looked about him, and spelled out the beauty of the earth in his simple primer of understanding. Daniel had in his garden behind the house a prolific grape-vine. He ate the grapes, full of the savor of the dead summer, with the gusto of a poet who can at last enjoy triumph over his enemy.

Possibly it was the vein of poetry in Daniel which made him a coward—which made him so vulnerable. During the autumn he reveled in the tints of the landscape which his sitting-room windows commanded. There were many maples and oaks. Day by day the roofs of the houses in the village became more evident, as the maples shed their crimson and gold and purple rags of summer. The oaks remained, great shaggy masses of dark gold and burning russet; later they took on soft hues, making clearer the blue firmament between the boughs. Daniel watched the autumn trees with pure delight. "He will go to-day," he said of a flaming maple after a night of frost which had crisped the white

86

arches of the grass in his dooryard. All day he sat and watched the maple cast its glory, and did not bother much with his simple meals. The Wise house was erected on three terraces. Always through the dry summer the grass was burned to an ugly negation of color. Later, when rain came, the grass was a brilliant green, patched with rosy sorrel and golden stars of arnica. Then later still came the diamond brilliance of the frost. So dry were the terraces in summer-time that no flowers would flourish. When Daniel's mother had come to the house as a bride she had planted under a window a blush-rose bush, but always the blush-roses were few and covered with insects. It was not until the autumn, when it was time for the flowers to die, that the sorrel blessing of waste lands flushed rosily and the arnica showed its stars of slender threads of gold, and there might even be a slight glimpse of purple aster and a dusty spray or two of goldenrod. Then Daniel did not shrink from the sight of the terraces. In summer-time the awful negative glare of them under the afternoon sun maddened him.

In winter he often visited his brother John in the village. He was very fond of John, and John's wife, and their only daughter, Dora. When John died, and later his wife, he would have gone to live with Dora, but she married. Then her husband also died, and Dora took up dressmaking, supporting herself and her delicate little girl-baby. Daniel adored this child. She had been named for him, although her mother had been aghast before the proposition. "Name a girl Daniel, uncle!" she had cried.

"She is going to have what I own after I have done with it, anyway," declared Daniel, gazing with awe and rapture at the tiny flannel bundle in his niece's arms. "That won't make any difference, but I do wish you could make up your mind to call her after me, Dora."

Dora Lee was soft-hearted. She named her girl-baby Daniel, and called her Danny, which was not, after all, so bad, and her old uncle loved the child as if she had been his own. Little Daniel—he always called her Daniel, or, rather, "Dan'l"—was the only reason for his descending into the village on summer days when the weather was hot. Daniel, when he visited the village in summer-time, wore always a green leaf inside his hat and carried an umbrella and a palm-leaf fan. This caused the village boys to shout, "Hullo, grandma!" after him. Daniel, being a little hard of hearing, was oblivious, but he would have been in any case. His whole mind was concentrated in getting along that dusty glare of street, stopping at the store for a paper bag of candy, and finally ending in Dora's little dark parlor, holding his beloved namesake on his knee, watching her blissfully suck a barley stick while he waved his palm-leaf fan. Dora would be fitting gowns in the next room. He would hear the hum of feminine chatter over strictly feminine topics. He felt very much aloof, even while holding the little girl on his knee. Daniel had never married—had never even had a sweetheart. The marriageable women he had seen had not been of the type to attract a dreamer like Daniel Wise. Many of those women thought him "a little off."

DANIEL AND LITTLE DAN'L

Dora Lee, his niece, privately wondered if her uncle had his full allotment of understanding. He seemed much more at home with her little daughter than with herself, and Dora considered herself a very good business woman, with possibly an unusual endowment of common sense. She was such a good business woman that when she died suddenly she left her child with quite a sum in the bank, besides the house. Daniel did not hesitate for a moment. He engaged Miss Sarah Dean for a housekeeper, and took the little girl (hardly more than a baby) to his own home. Dora had left a will, in which she appointed Daniel guardian in spite of her doubt concerning his measure of understanding. There was much comment in the village when Daniel took his little namesake to live in his lonely house on the terrace. "A man and an old maid to bring up that poor child!" they said. But Daniel called Dr. Trumbull to his support. "It is much better for that delicate child to be out of this village, which drains the south hill," Dr. Trumbull declared. "That child needs pure air. It is hot enough in summer all around here, and hot enough at Daniel's, but the air is pure there."

There was no gossip about Daniel and Miss Sarah Dean. Gossip would have seemed about as foolish concerning him and a dry blade of field-grass. Sarah Dean looked like that. She wore rusty black gowns, and her gray-blond hair was swept curtain-wise over her ears on either side of her very thin, mildly severe wedge of a face. Sarah was a notable housekeeper and a good cook. She could make an

89

endless variety of cakes and puddings and pies, and her biscuits were marvels. Daniel had long catered for himself, and a rasher of bacon, with an egg, suited him much better for supper than hot biscuits, preserves, and five kinds of cake. Still, he did not complain, and did not understand that Sarah's fare was not suitable for the child, until Dr. Trumbull told him so.

"Don't you let that child live on that kind of food if you want her to live at all," said Dr. Trumbull. "Lord! what are the women made of, and the men they feed, for that matter? Why, Daniel, there are many people in this place, and hard-working people, too, who eat a quantity of food, yet don't get enough nourishment for a litter of kittens."

"What shall I do?" asked Daniel in a puzzled way.

"Do? You can cook a beefsteak yourself, can't you? Sarah Dean would fry one as hard as sole-leather."

"Yes, I can cook a beefsteak real nice," said Daniel.

"Do it, then; and cook some chops, too, and plenty of eggs."

"I don't exactly hanker after quite so much sweet stuff," said Daniel. "I wonder if Sarah's feelings will be hurt."

"It is much better for feelings to be hurt than stomachs," declared Dr. Trumbull, "but Sarah's feelings will not be hurt. I know her. She is a wiry woman. Give her a knock and she springs back into place. Don't worry about her, Daniel."

When Daniel went home that night he carried a

juicy steak, and he cooked it, and he and little Dan'l had a square meal. Sarah refused the steak with a slight air of hauteur, but she behaved very well. When she set away her untasted layer-cakes and pies and cookies, she eyed them somewhat anxiously. Her standard of values seemed toppling before her mental vision. "They will starve to death if they live on such victuals as beefsteak, instead of good nourishing hot biscuits and cake," she thought. After the supper dishes were cleared away she went into the sitting-room where Daniel Wise sat beside a window, waiting in a sort of stern patience for a whiff of air. It was a very close evening. The sun was red in the low west, but a heaving sea of mist was rising over the lowlands.

Sarah sat down opposite Daniel. "Close, ain't it?" said she. She began knitting her lace edging.

"Pretty close," replied Daniel. He spoke with an effect of forced politeness. Although he had such a horror of extreme heat, he was always chary of boldly expressing his mind concerning it, for he had a feeling that he might be guilty of blasphemy, since he regarded the weather as being due to an Almighty mandate. Therefore, although he suffered, he was extremely polite.

"It is awful up-stairs in little Dan'l's room," said Sarah. "I have got all the windows open except the one that's right on the bed, and I told her she needn't keep more than the sheet and one comfortable over her."

Daniel looked anxious. "Children ain't ever overcome when they are in bed, in the house, are they?"

"Land, no! I never heard of such a thing. And, anyway, little Dan'l's so thin it ain't likely she feels the heat as much as some."

"I hope she don't."

Daniel continued to sit hunched up on himself, gazing with a sort of mournful irritation out of the window upon the landscape over which the misty shadows vaguely wavered.

Sarah knitted. She could knit in the dark. After a while she rose and said she guessed she would go to bed, as to-morrow was her sweeping-day.

Sarah went, and Daniel sat alone.

Presently a little pale figure stole to him through the dusk—the child, in her straight white night-gown, padding softly on tiny naked feet.

"Is that you, Dan'l?"

"Yes, Uncle Dan'l."

"Is it too hot to sleep up in your room?"

"I didn't feel so very hot, Uncle Dan'l, but skeeters were biting me, and a great big black thing just flew in my window!"

"A bat, most likely."

"A bat!" Little Dan'l shuddered. She began a little stifled wail. "I'm afeard of bats," she lamented.

Daniel gathered the tiny creature up. "You can jest set here with Uncle Dan'l," said he. "It is jest a little cooler here, I guess. Once in a while there comes a little whiff of wind."

"Won't any bats come?"

"Lord, no! Your Uncle Dan'l won't let any bats come within a gun-shot."

DANIEL AND LITTLE DAN'L

The little creature settled down contentedly in the old man's lap. Her fair, thin locks fell over his shirt-sleeved arm, her upturned profile was sweetly pure and clear even in the dusk. She was so delicately small that he might have been holding a fairy, from the slight roundness of the childish limbs and figure. Poor little girl!—Dan'l was much too small and thin. Old man Daniel gazed down at her anxiously.

"Jest as soon as the nice fall weather comes," said he, "uncle is going to take you down to the village real often, and you can get acquainted with some other nice little girls and play with them, and that will do uncle's little Dan'l good."

"I saw little Lucy Rose," piped the child, "and she looked at me real pleasant, and Lily Jennings wore a pretty dress. Would they play with me, uncle?"

"Of course they would. You don't feel quite so hot, here, do you?"

"I wasn't so hot, anyway; I was afeard of bats."

"There ain't any bats here."

"And skeeters."

"Uncle don't believe there's any skeeters, neither."

"I don't hear any sing," agreed little Dan'l in a weak voice. Very soon she was fast asleep. The old man sat holding her, and loving her with a simple crystalline intensity which was fairly heavenly. He himself almost disregarded the heat, being raised above it by sheer exaltation of spirit. All the love which had lain latent in his heart leaped to life before the helplessness of this little child in his arms.

He realized himself as much greater and of more importance upon the face of the earth than he had ever been before. He became paternity incarnate and superblessed. It was a long time before he carried the little child back to her room and laid her, still as inert with sleep as a lily, upon her bed. He bent over her with a curious waving motion of his old shoulders as if they bore wings of love and protection; then he crept back down-stairs.

On nights like that he did not go to bed. All the bedrooms were under the slant of the roof and were hot. He preferred to sit until dawn beside his open window, and doze when he could, and wait with despairing patience for the infrequent puffs of cool air breathing blessedly of wet swamp places, which, even when the burning sun arose, would only show dewy eyes of cool reflection. Daniel Wise, as he sat there through the sultry night, even prayed for courage, as a devout sentinel might have prayed at his post. The imagination of the deserter was not in the man. He never even dreamed of appropriating to his own needs any portion of his savings, and going for a brief respite to the deep shadows of mountainous places, or to a cool coast, where the great waves broke in foam upon the sand, breathing out the mighty saving breath of the sea. It never occurred to him that he could do anything but remain at his post and suffer in body and soul and mind, and not complain.

The next morning was terrible. The summer had been one of unusually fervid heat, but that one day was its climax. David went panting up-stairs to

94

his room at dawn. He did not wish Sarah Dean to know that he had sat up all night. He opened his bed, tidily, as was his wont. Through living alone he had acquired many of the habits of an orderly housewife. He went down-stairs, and Sarah was in the kitchen.

"It is a dreadful hot day," said she as Daniel approached the sink to wash his face and hands.

"It does seem a little warm," admitted Daniel, with his studied air of politeness with respect to the weather as an ordinance of God.

"Warm!" echoed Sarah Dean. Her thin face blazed a scarlet wedge between the sleek curtains of her dank hair; perspiration stood on her triangle of forehead. "It is the hottest day I ever knew!" she said, defiantly, and there was open rebellion in her tone.

"It *is* sort of warmish, I rather guess," said Daniel.

After breakfast, old Daniel announced his intention of taking little Dan'l out for a walk.

At that Sarah Dean fairly exploded. "Be you gone clean daft, Dan'l?" said she. "Don't you know that it actually ain't safe to take out such a delicate little thing as that on such a day?"

"Dr. Trumbull said to take her outdoors for a walk every day, rain or shine," returned Daniel, obstinately.

"But Dr. Trumbull didn't say to take her out if it rained fire and brimstone, I suppose," said Sarah Dean, viciously.

Daniel looked at her with mild astonishment.

95

"It is as much as that child's life is worth to take her out such a day as this," declared Sarah, viciously.

"Dr. Trumbull said to take no account of the weather," said Daniel with stubborn patience, "and we will walk on the shady side of the road, and go to Bradley's Brook. It's always a little cool there."

"If she faints away before you get there, you bring her right home," said Sarah. She was almost ferocious. "Just because *you* don't feel the heat, to take out that little pindlin' girl such a day!" she exclaimed.

"Dr. Trumbull said to," persisted Daniel, although he looked a little troubled. Sarah Dean did not dream that, for himself, Daniel Wise would have preferred facing an army with banners to going out under that terrible fusillade of sun-rays. She did not dream of the actual heroism which actuated him when he set out with little Dan'l, holding his big umbrella over her little sunbonneted head and waving in his other hand a palm-leaf fan.

Little Dan'l danced with glee as she went out of the yard. The small, anemic creature did not feel the heat except as a stimulant. Daniel had to keep charging her to walk slowly. "Don't go so fast, little Dan'l, or you'll get overhet, and then what will Mis' Dean say?" he continually repeated.

Little Dan'l's thin, pretty face peeped up at him from between the sides of her green sunbonnet. She pointed one dainty finger at a cloud of pale yellow butterflies in the field beside which they were walking. "Want to chase flutterbies," she chirped.

Little Dan'l had a fascinating way of misplacing her consonants in long words.

"No; you'll get overhet. You just walk along slow with Uncle Dan'l, and pretty soon we'll come to the pretty brook," said Daniel.

"Where the lagon-dries live?" asked little Dan'l, meaning dragon-flies.

"Yes," said Daniel. He was conscious, as he spoke, of increasing waves of thready black floating before his eyes. They had floated since dawn, but now they were increasing. Some of the time he could hardly see the narrow sidewalk path between the dusty meadowsweet and hardhack bushes, since those floating black threads wove together into a veritable veil before him. At such times he walked unsteadily, and little Dan'l eyed him curiously.

"Why don't you walk the way you always do?" she queried.

"Uncle Dan'l can't see jest straight, somehow," replied the old man; "guess it's because it's rather warm."

It was in truth a day of terror because of the heat. It was one of those days which break records, which live in men's memories as great catastrophes, which furnish head-lines for newspapers, and are alluded to with shudders at past sufferings. It was one of those days which seem to forecast the Dreadful Day of Revelation wherein no shelter may be found from the judgment of the fiery firmament. On that day men fell in their tracks and died, or were rushed to hospitals to be succored as by a miracle. And on that day the poor old man who had all his life feared

7   97

and dreaded the heat as the most loathly happening of earth, walked afield for love of the little child. As Daniel went on the heat seemed to become palpable—something which could actually be seen. There was now a thin, gaseous horror over the blazing sky, which did not temper the heat, but increased it, giving it the added torment of steam. The clogging moisture seemed to brood over the accursed earth, like some foul bird with deadly menace in wings and beak.

Daniel walked more and more unsteadily. Once he might have fallen had not the child thrown one little arm around a bending knee. "You 'most tumbled down, Uncle Dan'l," said she. Her little voice had a surprised and frightened note in it.

"Don't you be scared," gasped Daniel; "we have got 'most to the brook; then we'll be all right. Don't you be scared, and—you walk real slow and not get overhet."

The brook was near, and it was time. Daniel staggered under the trees beside which the little stream trickled over its bed of stones. It was not much of a brook at best, and the drought had caused it to lose much of its life. However, it was still there, and there were delicious little hollows of coolness between the stones over which it flowed, and large trees stood about with their feet rooted in the blessed damp. Then Daniel sank down. He tried to reach a hand to the water, but could not. The black veil had woven a compact mass before his eyes. There was a terrible throbbing in his head, but his arms were numb.

DANIEL AND LITTLE DAN'L

Little Dan'l stood looking at him, and her lip quivered. With a mighty effort Daniel cleared away the veil and saw the piteous baby face. "Take —Uncle Dan'l's hat and—fetch him—some water," he gasped. "Don't go too—close and—tumble in."

The child obeyed. Daniel tried to take the dripping hat, but failed. Little Dan'l was wise enough to pour the water over the old man's head, but she commenced to weep, the pitiful, despairing wail of a child who sees failing that upon which she has leaned for support.

Daniel rallied again. The water on his head gave him momentary relief, but more than anything else his love for the child nerved him to effort.

"Listen, little Dan'l," he said, and his voice sounded in his own ears like a small voice of a soul thousands of miles away. "You take the—umbrella, and—you take the fan, and you go real slow, so you don't get overhet, and you tell Mis' Dean, and—"

Then old Daniel's tremendous nerve, that he had summoned for the sake of love, failed him, and he sank back. He was quite unconscious—his face, staring blindly up at the terrible sky between the trees, was to little Dan'l like the face of a stranger. She gave one cry, more like the yelp of a trodden animal than a child's voice. Then she took the open umbrella and sped away. The umbrella bobbed wildly—nothing could be seen of poor little Dan'l but her small, speeding feet. She wailed loudly all the way.

She was half-way home when, plodding along in

a cloud of brown dust, a horse appeared in the road. The horse wore a straw bonnet and advanced very slowly. He drew a buggy, and in the buggy were Dr. Trumbull and Johnny, his son. He had called at Daniel's to see the little girl, and, on being told that they had gone to walk, had said something under his breath and turned his horse's head down the road.

"When we meet them, you must get out, Johnny," he said, "and I will take in that poor old man and that baby. I wish I could put common sense in every bottle of medicine. A day like this!"

Dr. Trumbull exclaimed when he saw the great bobbing black umbrella and heard the wails. The straw-bonneted horse stopped abruptly. Dr. Trumbull leaned out of the buggy. "Who are you?" he demanded.

"Uncle Dan'l is gone," shrieked the child.

"Gone where? What do you mean?"

"He—tumbled right down, and then he was—somebody else. He ain't there."

"Where is 'there'? Speak up quick!"

"The brook—Uncle Dan'l went away at the brook."

Dr. Trumbull acted swiftly. He gave Johnny a push. "Get out," he said. "Take that baby into Jim Mann's house there, and tell Mrs. Mann to keep her in the shade and look out for her, and you tell Jim, if he hasn't got his horse in his farm-wagon, to look lively and harness her in and put all the ice they've got in the house in the wagon. Hurry!"

Johnny was over the wheel before his father had

finished speaking, and Jim Mann just then drew up alongside in his farm-wagon.

"What's to pay?" he inquired, breathless. He was a thin, sinewy man, scantily clad in cotton trousers and a shirt wide open at the breast. Green leaves protruded from under the brim of his tilted straw hat.

"Old Daniel Wise is overcome by the heat," answered Dr. Trumbull. "Put all the ice you have in the house in your wagon, and come along. I'll leave my horse and buggy here. Your horse is faster."

Presently the farm-wagon clattered down the road, dust-hidden behind a galloping horse. Mrs. Jim Mann, who was a loving mother of children, was soothing little Dan'l. Johnny Trumbull watched at the gate. When the wagon returned he ran out and hung on behind, while the strong, ungainly farm-horse galloped to the house set high on the sun-baked terraces.

When old Daniel revived he found himself in the best parlor, with ice all about him. Thunder was rolling overhead and hail clattered on the windows. A sudden storm, the heat-breaker, had come up and the dreadful day was vanquished. Daniel looked up and smiled a vague smile of astonishment at Dr. Trumbull and Sarah Dean; then his eyes wandered anxiously about.

"The child is all right," said Dr. Trumbull; "don't you worry, Daniel. Mrs. Jim Mann is taking care of her. Don't you try to talk. You didn't exactly have a sunstroke, but the heat was too much for you."

THE COPY-CAT

But Daniel spoke, in spite of the doctor's mandate. "The heat," said he, in a curiously clear voice, "ain't never goin' to be too much for me again."

"Don't you talk, Daniel," repeated Dr. Trumbull. "You've always been nervous about the heat. Maybe you won't be again, but keep still. When I told you to take that child out every day I didn't mean when the world was like Sodom and Gomorrah. Thank God, it will be cooler now."

Sarah Dean stood beside the doctor. She looked pale and severe, but adequate. She did not even state that she had urged old Daniel not to go out. There was true character in Sarah Dean.

The weather that summer was an unexpected quantity. Instead of the day after the storm being cool, it was hot. However, old Daniel, after his recovery, insisted on going out of doors with little Dan'l after breakfast. The only concession which he would make to Sarah Dean, who was fairly frantic with anxiety, was that he would merely go down the road as far as the big elm-tree, that he would sit down there, and let the child play about within sight.

"You'll be brought home ag'in, sure as preachin'," said Sarah Dean, "and if you're brought home ag'in, you won't get up ag'in."

Old Daniel laughed. "Now don't you worry, Sarah," said he. "I'll set down under that big ellum and keep cool."

Old Daniel, at Sarah's earnest entreaties, took a palm-leaf fan. But he did not use it. He sat peacefully under the cool trail of the great elm all the forenoon, while little Dan'l played with her doll.

DANIEL AND LITTLE DAN'L

The child was rather languid after her shock of the day before, and not disposed to run about. Also, she had a great sense of responsibility about the old man. Sarah Dean had privately charged her not to let Uncle Daniel get "overhet." She continually glanced up at him with loving, anxious, baby eyes.

"Be you overhet, Uncle Dan'l?" she would ask.

"No, little Dan'l, uncle ain't a mite overhet," the old man would assure her. Now and then little Dan'l left her doll, climbed into the old man's lap, and waved the palm-leaf fan before his face.

Old Daniel Wise loved her so that he seemed, to himself, fairly alight with happiness. He made up his mind that he would find some little girl in the village to come now and then and play with little Dan'l. In the cool of that evening he stole out of the back door, covertly, lest Sarah Dean discover him, and walked slowly to the rector's house in the village. The rector's wife was sitting on her cool, vine-shaded veranda. She was alone, and Daniel was glad. He asked her if the little girl who had come to live with her, Content Adams, could not come the next afternoon and see little Dan'l. "Little Dan'l had ought to see other children once in a while, and Sarah Dean makes real nice cookies," he stated, pleadingly.

Sally Patterson laughed good-naturedly. "Of course she can, Mr. Wise," she said.

The next afternoon Sally herself drove the rector's horse, and brought Content to pay a call on little Dan'l. Sally and Sarah Dean visited in the sitting-room, and left the little girls alone in the parlor with a plate of cookies, to get acquainted.

They sat in solemn silence and stared at each other.
Neither spoke. Neither ate a cooky. When Sally
took her leave, she asked little Dan'l if she had had
a nice time with Content, and little Dan'l said,
"Yes, ma'am."

Sarah insisted upon Content's carrying the cookies
home in the dish with a napkin over it.

"When can I go again to see that other little girl?"
asked Content as she and Sally were jogging home.

"Oh, almost any time. I will drive you over—
because it is rather a lonesome walk for you. Did
you like the little girl? She is younger than you."

"Yes'm."

Also little Dan'l inquired of old Daniel when the
other little girl was coming again, and nodded emphatically when asked if she had had a nice time.
Evidently both had enjoyed, after the inscrutable
fashion of childhood, their silent session with each
other. Content came generally once a week, and
old Daniel was invited to take little Dan'l to the
rector's. On that occasion Lucy Rose was present,
and Lily Jennings. The four little girls had tea together at a little table set on the porch, and only
Lily Jennings talked. The rector drove old Daniel
and the child home, and after they had arrived the
child's tongue was loosened and she chattered. She
had seen everything there was to be seen at the rector's. She told of it in her little silver pipe of a voice.
She had to be checked and put to bed, lest she be
tired out.

"I never knew that child could talk so much," Sarah
said to Daniel, after the little girl had gone up-stairs.

HE REALIZED THAT THE FEAR OF HIS WHOLE LIFE WAS OVERCOME
FOR EVER

"She talks quite some when she's alone with me."

"And she seems to see everything."

"Ain't much that child don't see," said Daniel, proudly.

The summer continued unusually hot, but Daniel never again succumbed. When autumn came, for the first time in his old life old Daniel Wise was sorrowful. He dreaded the effect of the frost and the winter upon his precious little Dan'l, whom he put before himself as fondly as any father could have done, and as the season progressed his dread seemed justified. Poor little Dan'l had cold after cold. Content Adams and Lucy Rose came to see her. The rector's wife and the doctor's sent dainties. But the child coughed and pined, and old Daniel began to look forward to spring and summer—the seasons which had been his bugaboos through life —as if they were angels. When the February thaw came, he told little Dan'l, "Jest look at the snow meltin' and the drops hangin' on the trees; that is a sign of summer."

Old Daniel watched for the first green light along the fences and the meadow hollows. When the trees began to cast slightly blurred shadows, because of budding leaves, and the robins hopped over the terraces, and now and then the air was cleft with blue wings, he became jubilant. "Spring is jest about here, and then uncle's little Dan'l will stop coughin', and run out of doors and pick flowers," he told the child beside the window.

Spring came that year with a riotous rush. Blossoms, leaves, birds, and flowers—all arrived pell-

mell, fairly smothering the world with sweetness
and music. In May, about the first of the month,
there was an intensely hot day. It was as hot as
midsummer. Old Daniel with little Dan'l went
afield. It was, to both, as if they fairly saw the car-
nival-arrival of flowers, of green garlands upon tree-
branches, of birds and butterflies. "Spring is right
here!" said old Daniel. "Summer is right here!
Pick them vi'lets in that holler, little Dan'l." The
old man sat on a stone in the meadowland, and
watched the child in the blue-gleaming hollow gather
up violets in her little hands as if they were jewels.
The sun beat upon his head, the air was heavy with
fragrance, laden with moisture. Old Daniel wiped
his forehead. He was heated, but so happy that he
was not aware of it. He saw wonderful new lights
over everything. He had wielded love, the one invincible weapon of the whole earth, and had conquered his intangible and dreadful enemy. When,
for the sake of that little beloved life, his own life
had become as nothing, old Daniel found himself
superior to it. He sat there in the tumultuous heat
of the May day, watching the child picking violets
and gathering strength with every breath of the
young air of the year, and he realized that the fear
of his whole life was overcome for ever. He realized
that never again, though they might bring suffering,
even death, would he dread the summers with their
torrid winds and their burning lights, since, through
love, he had become under-lord of all the conditions
of his life upon earth.

BIG SISTER SOLLY

BIG SISTER SOLLY

IT did seem strange that Sally Patterson, who, according to her own self-estimation, was the least adapted of any woman in the village, should have been the one chosen by a theoretically selective providence to deal with a psychological problem.

It was conceded that little Content Adams was a psychological problem. She was the orphan child of very distant relatives of the rector. When her parents died she had been cared for by a widowed aunt on her mother's side, and this aunt had also borne the reputation of being a creature apart. When the aunt died, in a small village in the indefinite "Out West," the presiding clergyman had notified Edward Patterson of little Content's lonely and helpless estate. The aunt had subsisted upon an annuity which had died with her. The child had inherited nothing except personal property. The aunt's house had been bequeathed to the church over which the clergyman presided, and after her aunt's death he took her to his own home until she could be sent to her relatives, and he and his wife were exceedingly punctilious about every jot and tittle of the aunt's personal belongings. They even purchased two extra trunks for them, which they charged to the rector.

THE COPY-CAT

Little Content, traveling in the care of a lady who had known her aunt and happened to be coming East, had six large trunks, besides a hat-box and two suit-cases and a nailed-up wooden box containing odds and ends. Content made quite a sensation when she arrived and her baggage was piled on the station platform.

Poor Sally Patterson unpacked little Content's trunks. She had sent the little girl to school within a few days after her arrival. Lily Jennings and Amelia Wheeler called for her, and aided her down the street between them, arms interlocked. Content, although Sally had done her best with a pretty ready-made dress and a new hat, was undeniably a peculiar-looking child. In the first place, she had an expression so old that it was fairly uncanny.

"That child has downward curves beside her mouth already, and lines between her eyes, and what she will look like a few years hence is beyond me," Sally told her husband after she had seen the little girl go out of sight between Lily's curls and ruffles and ribbons and Amelia's smooth skirts.

"She doesn't look like a happy child," agreed the rector. "Poor little thing! Her aunt Eudora must have been a queer woman to train a child."

"She is certainly trained," said Sally, ruefully; "too much so. Content acts as if she were afraid to move or speak or even breathe unless somebody signals permission. I pity her."

She was in the storeroom, in the midst of Content's baggage. The rector sat on an old chair, smoking. He had a conviction that it behooved him

110

as a man to stand by his wife during what might prove an ordeal. He had known Content's deceased aunt years before. He had also known the clergyman who had taken charge of her personal property and sent it on with Content.

"Be prepared for finding almost anything, Sally," he observed. "Mr. Zenock Shanksbury, as I remember him, was so conscientious that it amounted to mania. I am sure he has sent simply unspeakable things rather than incur the reproach of that conscience of his with regard to defrauding Content of one jot or tittle of that personal property."

Sally shook out a long, black silk dress, with jet dangling here and there. "Now here is this dress," said she. "I suppose I really must keep this, but when that child is grown up the silk will probably be cracked and entirely worthless."

"You had better take the two trunks and pack them with such things, and take your chances."

"Oh, I suppose so. I suppose I must take chances with everything except furs and wools, which will collect moths. Oh, goodness!" Sally held up an old-fashioned fitch fur tippet. Little vague winged things came from it like dust. "Moths!" said she, tragically. "Moths now. It is full of them. Edward, you need not tell me that clergyman's wife was conscientious. No conscientious woman would have sent an old fur tippet all eaten with moths into another woman's house. She could not."

Sally took flying leaps across the storeroom. She flung open the window and tossed out the mangy tippet. "This is simply awful!" she declared, as she

111

returned. "Edward, don't you think we are justified in having Thomas take all these things out in the back yard and making a bonfire of the whole lot?"

"No, my dear."

"But, Edward, nobody can tell what will come next. If Content's aunt had died of a contagious disease, nothing could induce me to touch another thing."

"Well, dear, you know that she died from the shock of a carriage accident, because she had a weak heart."

"I know it, and of course there is nothing contagious about that." Sally took up an ancient bandbox and opened it. She displayed its contents: a very frivolous bonnet dating back in style a half-century, gay with roses and lace and green strings, and another with a heavy crape veil dependent.

"You certainly do not advise me to keep these?" asked Sally, despondently.

Edward Patterson looked puzzled. "Use your own judgment," he said, finally.

Sally summarily marched across the room and flung the gay bonnet and the mournful one out of the window. Then she took out a bundle of very old underwear which had turned a saffron yellow with age. "People are always coming to me for old linen in case of burns," she said, succinctly. "After these are washed I can supply an *auto da fe*."

Poor Sally worked all that day and several days afterward. The rector deserted her, and she relied upon her own good sense in the disposition of little

Content's legacy. When all was over she told her husband.

"Well, Edward," said she, "there is exactly one trunk half full of things which the child may live to use, but it is highly improbable. We have had six bonfires, and I have given away three suits of old clothes to Thomas's father. The clothes were very large."

"Must have belonged to Eudora's first husband. He was a stout man," said Edward.

"And I have given two small suits of men's clothes to the Aid Society for the next out-West barrel."

"Eudora's second husband's."

"And I gave the washerwoman enough old baking-dishes to last her lifetime, and some cracked dishes. Most of the dishes were broken, but a few were only cracked; and I have given Silas Thomas's wife ten old wool dresses and a shawl and three old cloaks. All the other things which did not go into the bonfires went to the Aid Society. They will go back out West." Sally laughed, a girlish peal, and her husband joined. But suddenly her smooth forehead contracted. "Edward," said she.

"Well, dear?"

"I am terribly puzzled about one thing." The two were sitting in the study. Content had gone to bed. Nobody could hear easily, but Sally Patterson lowered her voice, and her honest, clear blue eyes had a frightened expression.

"What is it, dear?"

"You will think me very silly and cowardly, and I think I have never been cowardly, but this is really

8   113

very strange. Come with me. I am such a goose, I don't dare go alone to that storeroom."

The rector rose. Sally switched on the lights as they went up-stairs to the storeroom.

"Tread very softly," she whispered. "Content is probably asleep."

The two tiptoed up the stairs and entered the storeroom. Sally approached one of the two new trunks which had come with Content from out West. She opened it. She took out a parcel nicely folded in a large towel.

"See here, Edward Patterson."

The rector stared as Sally shook out a dress— a gay, up-to-date dress, a young girl's dress, a very tall young girl's, for the skirts trailed on the floor as Sally held it as high as she could. It was made of a fine white muslin. There was white lace on the bodice, and there were knots of blue ribbon scattered over the whole, knots of blue ribbon confining tiny bunches of rosebuds and daisies. These knots of blue ribbon and the little flowers made it undeniably a young girl's costume. Even in the days of all ages wearing the costumes of all ages, an older woman would have been abashed before those exceedingly youthful knots of blue ribbons and flowers.

The rector looked approvingly at it. "That is very pretty, it seems to me," he said. "That must be worth keeping, Sally."

"Worth keeping! Well, Edward Patterson, just wait. You are a man, and of course you cannot understand how very strange it is about the dress."

The rector looked inquiringly.

"I want to know," said Sally, "if Content's aunt Eudora had any young relative besides Content. I mean had she a grown-up young girl relative who would wear a dress like this?"

"I don't know of anybody. There might have been some relative of Eudora's first husband. No, he was an only child. I don't think it possible that Eudora had any young girl relative."

"If she had," said Sally, firmly, "she would have kept this dress. You are sure there was nobody else living with Content's aunt at the time she died?"

"Nobody except the servants, and they were an old man and his wife."

"Then whose dress was this?"

"I don't know, Sally."

"You don't know, and I don't. It is very strange."

"I suppose," said Edward Patterson, helpless before the feminine problem, "that—Eudora got it in some way."

"In some way," repeated Sally. "That is always a man's way out of a mystery when there is a mystery. There is a mystery. There is a mystery which worries me. I have not told you all yet, Edward."

"What more is there, dear?"

"I—asked Content whose dress this was, and she said— Oh, Edward, I do so despise mysteries."

"What did she say, Sally?"

"She said it was her big sister Solly's dress."

"Her what?"

"Her big sister Solly's dress. Edward, has Content ever had a sister? Has she a sister now?"

"No, she never had a sister, and she has none

now," declared the rector, emphatically. "I knew all her family. What in the world ails the child?"

"She said her big sister Solly, Edward, and the very name is so inane. If she hasn't any big sister Solly, what are we going to do?"

"Why, the child must simply lie," said the rector.

"But, Edward, I don't think she knows she lies. You may laugh, but I think she is quite sure that she has a big sister Solly, and that this is her dress. I have not told you the whole. After she came home from school to-day she went up to her room, and she left the door open, and pretty soon I heard her talking. At first I thought perhaps Lily or Amelia was up there, although I had not seen either of them come in with Content. Then after a while, when I had occasion to go up-stairs, I looked in her room, and she was quite alone, although I had heard her talking as I went up-stairs. Then I said: 'Content, I thought somebody was in your room. I heard you talking.'

"And she said, looking right into my eyes: 'Yes, ma'am, I was talking.'

"'But there is nobody here,' I said.

"'Yes, ma'am,' she said. 'There isn't anybody here now, but my big sister Solly was here, and she is gone. You heard me talking to my big sister Solly.' I felt faint, Edward, and you know it takes a good deal to overcome me. I just sat down in Content's wicker rocking-chair. I looked at her and she looked at me. Her eyes were just as clear and blue, and her forehead looked like truth itself. She is not exactly a pretty child, and she has a peculiar appearance, but she does certainly look truthful and good, and she looked so then. She had tried to fluff her hair over her forehead a little as I had told her, and not pull it back so tight, and she wore her new dress, and her face and hands were as clean, and she stood straight. You know she is a little inclined to stoop, and I have talked to her about it. She stood straight, and looked at me with those blue eyes, and I did feel fairly dizzy."

"What did you say?"

"Well, after a bit I pulled myself together and I said: 'My dear little girl, what is this? What do you mean about your big sister Sarah?' Edward, I could not bring myself to say that idiotic Solly. In fact, I did think I must be mistaken and had not heard correctly. But Content just looked at me as if she thought me very stupid. 'Solly,' said she. 'My sister's name is Solly.'

"'But, my dear,' I said, 'I understand that you had no sister.'

"'Yes,' said she, 'I have my big sister Solly.'

"'But where has she been all the time?' said I.

"Then Content looked at me and smiled, and it was quite a wonderful smile, Edward. She smiled as if she knew so much more than I could ever know, and quite pitied me."

"She did not answer your question?"

"No, only by that smile which seemed to tell whole volumes about that awful Solly's whereabouts, only I was too ignorant to read them.

"'Where is she now, dear?' I said, after a little.

"'She is gone now,' said Content.

"'Gone where?' said I.

"And then the child smiled at me again. Edward, what are we going to do? Is she untruthful, or has she too much imagination? I have heard of such a thing as too much imagination, and children telling lies which were not really lies."

"So have I," agreed the rector, dryly, "but I never believed in it." The rector started to leave the room.

"What are you going to do?" inquired Sally.

"I am going to endeavor to discriminate between lies and imagination," replied the rector.

Sally plucked at his coat-sleeve as they went down-stairs. "My dear," she whispered, "I think she is asleep."

"She will have to wake up."

"But, my dear, she may be nervous. Would it not be better to wait until to-morrow?"

"I think not," said Edward Patterson. Usually an easy-going man, when he was aroused he was determined to extremes. Into Content's room he marched, Sally following. Neither of them saw their small son Jim peeking around his door. He had heard—he could not help it—the conversation earlier in the day between Content and his mother. He had also heard other things. He now felt entirely justified in listening, although he had a good code of honor. He considered himself in a way responsible, knowing what he knew, for the peace of mind of his parents. Therefore he listened, peeking around the doorway of his dark room.

The electric light flashed out from Content's

room, and the little interior was revealed. It was charmingly pretty. Sally had done her best to make this not altogether welcome little stranger's room attractive. There were garlands of rosebuds swung from the top of the white satin-papered walls. There were dainty toilet things, a little dressing-table decked with ivory, a case of books, chairs cushioned with rosebud chintz, windows curtained with the same.

In the little white bed, with a rose-sprinkled cover-lid over her, lay Content. She was not asleep. Directly, when the light flashed out, she looked at the rector and his wife with her clear blue eyes. Her fair hair, braided neatly and tied with pink ribbons, lay in two tails on either side of her small, certainly very good face. Her forehead was beautiful, very white and full, giving her an expression of candor which was even noble. Content, little lonely girl among strangers in a strange place, mutely beseech-ing love and pity, from her whole attitude toward life and the world, looked up at Edward Patterson and Sally, and the rector realized that his determina-tion was giving way. He began to believe in imagi-nation, even to the extent of a sister Solly. He had never had a daughter, and sometimes the thought of one had made his heart tender. His voice was very kind when he spoke.

"Well, little girl," he said, "what is this I hear?"

Sally stared at her husband and stifled a chuckle.

As for Content, she looked at the rector and said nothing. It was obvious that she did not know what he had heard. The rector explained.

"My dear little girl," he said, "your aunt Sally" —they had agreed upon the relationship of uncle and aunt to Content—"tells me that you have been telling her about your—big sister Solly." The rector half gasped as he said Solly. He seemed to himself to be on the driveling verge of idiocy before the pronunciation of that absurdly inane name.

Content's responding voice came from the pink-and-white nest in which she was snuggled, like the fluting pipe of a canary.

"Yes, sir," said she.

"My dear child," said the rector, "you know perfectly well that you have no big sister—Solly." Every time the rector said Solly he swallowed hard.

Content smiled as Sally had described her smiling. She said nothing. The rector felt reproved and looked down upon from enormous heights of innocence and childhood and the wisdom thereof. However, he persisted.

"Content," he said, "what did you mean by telling your aunt Sally what you did?"

"I was talking with my big sister Solly," replied Content, with the calmness of one stating a fundamental truth of nature.

The rector's face grew stern. "Content," he said, "look at me."

Content looked. Looking seemed to be the instinctive action which distinguished her as an individual.

"Have you a big sister—Solly?" asked the rector. His face was stern, but his voice faltered.

"Yes, sir."

"Then—tell me so."

"I have a big sister Solly," said Content. Now she spoke rather wearily, although still sweetly, as if puzzled why she had been disturbed in sleep to be asked such an obvious question.

"Where has she been all the time, that we have known nothing about her?" demanded the rector.

Content smiled. However, she spoke. "Home," said she.

"When did she come here?"

"This morning."

"Where is she now?"

Content smiled and was silent. The rector cast a helpless look at his wife. He now did not care if she did see that he was completely at a loss. How could a great, robust man and a clergyman be harsh to a tender little girl child in a pink-and-white nest of innocent dreams?

Sally pitied him. She spoke more harshly than her husband. "Content Adams," said she, "you know perfectly well that you have no big sister Solly. Now tell me the truth. Tell me you have no big sister Solly."

"I have a big sister Solly," said Content.

"Come, Edward," said Sally. "There is no use in staying and talking to this obstinate little girl any longer." Then she spoke to Content. "Before you go to sleep," said she, "you must say your prayers, if you have not already done so."

"I have said my prayers," replied Content, and her blue eyes were full of horrified astonishment at the suspicion.

"Then," said Sally, "you had better say them over and add something. Pray that you may always tell the truth."

"Yes, ma'am," said Content, in her little canary pipe.

The rector and his wife went out. Sally switched off the light with a snap as she passed. Out in the hall she stopped and held her husband's arms hard. "Hush!" she whispered. They both listened. They heard this, in the faintest plaint of a voice:

"They don't believe you are here, Sister Solly, but I do."

Sally dashed back into the rosebud room and switched on the light. She stared around. She opened a closet door. Then she turned off the light and joined her husband.

"There was nobody there?" he whispered.

"Of course not."

When they were back in the study the rector and his wife looked at each other.

"We will do the best we can," said Sally. "Don't worry, Edward, for you have to write your sermon to-morrow. We will manage some way. I will admit that I rather wish Content had had some other distant relative besides you who could have taken charge of her."

"You poor child!" said the rector. "It is hard on you, Sally, for she is no kith nor kin of yours."

"Indeed I don't mind," said Sally Patterson, "if only I can succeed in bringing her up."

Meantime Jim Patterson, up-stairs, sitting over his next day's algebra lesson, was even more perplexed than were his parents in the study. He paid little attention to his book. "I can manage little Lucy," he reflected, "but if the others have got hold of it, I don't know."

Presently he rose and stole very softly through the hall to Content's door. She was timid, and always left it open so she could see the hall light until she fell asleep. "Content," whispered Jim.

There came the faintest "What?" in response.

"Don't you," said Jim, in a theatrical whisper, "say another word at school to anybody about your big sister Solly. If you do, I'll whop you, if you are a girl."

"Don't care!" was sighed forth from the room.

"And I'll whop your old big sister Solly, too."

There was a tiny sob.

"I will," declared Jim. "Now you mind!"

The next day Jim cornered little Lucy Rose under a cedar-tree before school began. He paid no attention to Bubby Harvey and Tom Simmons, who were openly sniggering at him. Little Lucy gazed up at Jim, and the blue-green shade of the cedar seemed to bring out only more clearly the white-rose softness of her dear little face. Jim bent over her.

"Want you to do something for me," he whispered.

Little Lucy nodded gravely.

"If my new cousin Content ever says anything to you again—I heard her yesterday—about her big sister Solly, don't you ever say a word about it to anybody else. You will promise me, won't you, little Lucy?"

A troubled expression came into little Lucy's kind eyes. "But she told Lily, and Lily told Amelia, and Amelia told her grandmother Wheeler, and her grandmother Wheeler told Miss Parmalee when she met her on the street after school, and Miss Parmalee called on my aunt Martha and told her," said little Lucy.

"Oh, shucks!" said Jim.

"And my aunt Martha told my father that she thought perhaps she ought to ask for her when she called on your mother. She said Arnold Carruth's aunt Flora was going to call, and his aunt Dorothy. I heard Miss Acton tell Miss Parmalee that she thought they ought to ask for her when they called on your mother, too."

"Little Lucy," he said, and lowered his voice, "you must promise me never, as long as you live, to tell what I am going to tell you."

Little Lucy looked frightened.

"Promise!" insisted Jim.

"I promise," said little Lucy, in a weak voice.

"Never, as long as you live, to tell anybody. Promise!"

"I promise."

"Now, you know if you break your promise and tell, you will be guilty of a dreadful lie and be very wicked."

Little Lucy shivered. "I never will."

"Well, my new cousin Content Adams—tells lies."

Little Lucy gasped.

"Yes, she does. She says she has a big sister Solly, and she hasn't got any big sister Solly. She never did have, and she never will have. She makes believe."

"Makes believe?" said little Lucy, in a hopeful voice.

"Making believe is just a real mean way of lying. Now I made Content promise last night never to say one word in school about her big sister Solly, and I am going to tell you this, so you can tell Lily and the others and not lie. Of course, I don't want to lie myself, because my father is rector, and, besides, mother doesn't approve of it; but if anybody is going to lie, I am the one. Now, you mind, little Lucy. Content's big sister Solly has gone away, and she is never coming back. If you tell Lily and the others I said so, I can't see how you will be lying."

Little Lucy gazed at the boy. She looked like truth incarnate. "But," said she, in her adorable stupidity of innocence, "I don't see how she could go away if she was never here, Jim."

"Oh, of course she couldn't. But all you have to do is to say that you heard me say she had gone. Don't you understand?"

"I don't understand how Content's big sister Solly could possibly go away if she was never here."

"Little Lucy, I wouldn't ask you to tell a lie for the world, but if you were just to say that you heard me say—"

"I think it would be a lie," said little Lucy, "because how can I help knowing if she was never here she couldn't—"

"Oh, well, little Lucy," cried Jim, in despair, still with tenderness—how could he be anything but

125

tender with little Lucy?—"all I ask is never to say anything about it."

"If they ask me?"

"Anyway, you can hold your tongue. You know it isn't wicked to hold your tongue."

Little Lucy absurdly stuck out the pointed tip of her little red tongue. Then she shook her head slowly.

"Well," she said, "I will hold my tongue."

This encounter with innocence and logic had left him worsted. Jim could see no way out of the fact that his father, the rector, his mother, the rector's wife, and he, the rector's son, were disgraced by their relationship to such an unsanctified little soul as this queer Content Adams.

And yet he looked at the poor lonely little girl, who was trying very hard to learn her lessons, who suggested in her very pose and movement a little, scared rabbit ready to leap the road for some bush of hiding, and while he was angry with her he pitied her. He had no doubts concerning Content's keeping her promise. He was quite sure that he would now say nothing whatever about that big sister Solly to the others, but he was not prepared for what happened that very afternoon.

When he went home from school his heart stood still to see Miss Martha Rose, and Arnold Carruth's aunt Flora, and his aunt who was not his aunt, Miss Dorothy Vernon, who was visiting her, all walking along in state with their lace-trimmed parasols, their white gloves, and their nice card-cases. Jim jumped a fence and raced across lots home, and gained on them. He burst in on his mother, sitting on the porch, which was inclosed by wire netting overgrown with a budding vine. It was the first warm day of the season.

"Mother," cried Jim Patterson—"mother, they are coming!"

"Who, for goodness' sake, Jim?"

"Why, Arnold's aunt Flora and his aunt Dorothy and little Lucy's aunt Martha. They are coming to call."

Involuntarily Sally's hand went up to smooth her pretty hair. "Well, what of it, Jim?" said she.

"Mother, they will ask for—big sister Solly!"

Sally Patterson turned pale. "How do you know?"

"Mother, Content has been talking at school. A lot know. You will see they will ask for—"

"Run right in and tell Content to stay in her room," whispered Sally, hastily, for the callers, their white-kidded hands holding their card-cases genteelly, were coming up the walk.

Sally advanced, smiling. She put a brave face on the matter, but she realized that she, Sally Patterson, who had never been a coward, was positively afraid before this absurdity. The callers sat with her on the pleasant porch, with the young vine-shadows making networks over their best gowns. Tea was served presently by the maid, and, much to Sally's relief, before the maid appeared came the inquiry. Miss Martha Rose made it.

"We would be pleased to see Miss Solly Adams also," said Miss Martha.

Flora Carruth echoed her. "I was so glad to hear another nice girl had come to the village," said she with enthusiasm. Miss Dorothy Vernon said something indefinite to the same effect.

"I am sorry," replied Sally, with an effort, "but there is no Miss Solly Adams here now." She spoke the truth as nearly as she could manage without unraveling the whole ridiculous affair. The callers sighed with regret, tea was served with little cakes, and they fluttered down the walk, holding their card-cases, and that ordeal was over.

But Sally sought the rector in his study, and she was trembling. "Edward," she cried out, regardless of her husband's sermon, "something must be done now."

"Why, what is the matter, Sally?"

"People are—calling on her."

"Calling on whom?"

"Big sister—Solly!" Sally explained.

"Well, don't worry, dear," said the rector. "Of course we will do something, but we must think it over. Where is the child now?"

"She and Jim are out in the garden. I saw them pass the window just now. Jim is such a dear boy, he tries hard to be nice to her. Edward Patterson, we ought not to wait."

"My dear, we must."

Meantime Jim and Content Adams were out in the garden. Jim had gone to Content's door and tapped and called out, rather rudely: "Content, I say, put on your hat and come along out in the garden. I've got something to tell you."

"Don't want to," protested Content's little voice, faintly.

"You come right along."

And Content came along. She was an obedient child, and she liked Jim, although she stood much in awe of him. She followed him into the garden back of the rectory, and they sat down on the bench beneath the weeping willow. The minute they were seated Jim began to talk.

"Now," said he, "I want to know."

Content glanced up at him, then looked down and turned pale.

"I want to know, honest Injun," said Jim, "what you are telling such awful whoppers about your old big sister Solly for?"

Content was silent. This time she did not smile, a tear trickled out of her right eye and ran over the pale cheek.

"Because you know," said Jim, observant of the tear, but ruthless, "that you haven't any big sister Solly, and never did have. You are getting us all in an awful mess over it, and father is rector here, and mother is his wife, and I am his son, and you are his niece, and it is downright mean. Why do you tell such whoppers? Out with it!"

Content was trembling violently. "I lived with Aunt Eudora," she whispered.

"Well, what of that? Other folks have lived with their aunts and not told whoppers."

"They haven't lived with Aunt Eudora."

"You ought to be ashamed of yourself, Content

Adams, and you the rector's niece, talking that way about dead folks."

"I don't mean to talk about poor Aunt Eudora," fairly sobbed Content. "Aunt Eudora was a real good aunt, but she was grown up. She was a good deal more grown up than your mother; she really was, and when I first went to live with her I was 'most a little baby; I couldn't speak—plain, and I had to go to bed real early, and slept 'way off from everybody, and I used to be afraid—all alone, and so—"

"Well, go on," said Jim, but his voice was softer. It *was* hard lines for a little kid, especially if she was a girl.

"And so," went on the little, plaintive voice, "I got to thinking how nice it would be if I only had a big sister, and I used to cry and say to myself—I couldn't speak plain, you know, I was so little— 'Big sister would be real solly.' And then first thing I knew—she came."

"Who came?"

"Big sister Solly."

"What rot! She didn't come. Content Adams, you know she didn't come."

"She must have come." persisted the little girl, in a frightened whisper. "She must have. Oh, Jim, you don't know. Big sister Solly must have come, or I would have died like my father and mother."

Jim's arm, which was near her, twitched convulsively, but he did not put it around her.

"She did—co-me," sobbed Content. "Big sister Solly did come."

"Well, have it so," said Jim, suddenly. "No use going over that any longer. Have it she came, but she ain't here now, anyway. Content Adams, you can't look me in the face and tell me that."

Content looked at Jim, and her little face was almost terrible, so full of bewilderment and fear it was. "Jim," whispered Content, "I can't have big sister Solly not be here. I can't send her away. What would she think?"

Jim stared. "Think? Why, she isn't alive to think, anyhow!"

"I can't make her—dead," sobbed Content. "She came when I wanted her, and now when I don't so much, when I've got Uncle Edward and Aunt Sally and you, and don't feel so dreadful lonesome, I can't be so bad as to make her dead."

Jim whistled. Then his face brightened up. He looked at Content with a shrewd and cheerful grin. "See here, kid, you say your sister Solly is big, grown up, don't you?" he inquired.

Content nodded pitifully.

"Then why, if she is grown up and pretty, don't she have a beau?"

Content stopped sobbing and gave him a quick glance.

"Then—why doesn't she get married, and go out West to live?"

Jim chuckled. Instead of a sob, a faint echo of his chuckle came from Content.

Jim laughed merrily. "I say, Content," he cried, "let's have it she's married now, and gone?"

"Well," said Content.

Jim put his arm around her very nicely and protectingly. "It's all right, then," said he, "as all
right as it can be for a girl. Say, Content, ain't it
a shame you aren't a boy?"

"I can't help it," said Content, meekly.

"You see," said Jim, thoughtfully, "I don't, as
a rule, care much about girls, but if you could coast
down-hill and skate, and do a few things like that,
you would be almost as good as a boy."

Content surveyed him, and her pessimistic little
face assumed upward curves. "I will," said she.
"I will do anything, Jim. I will fight if you want
me to, just like a boy."

"I don't believe you could lick any of us fellers
unless you get a good deal harder in the muscles,"
said Jim, eying her thoughtfully; "but we'll play
ball, and maybe by and by you can begin with
Arnold Carruth."

"Could lick him now," said Content.

But Jim's face sobered before her readiness. "Oh
no, you mustn't go to fighting right away," said he.
"It wouldn't do. You really are a girl, you know,
and father is rector."

"Then I won't," said Content; "but I *could* knock
down that little boy with curls; I know I could."

"Well, you needn't. I'll like you just as well.
You see, Content"—Jim's voice faltered, for he was
a boy, and on the verge of sentiment before which
he was shamed—"you see, Content, now your big
sister Solly is married and gone out West, why, you
can have me for your brother, and of course a
brother is a good deal better than a sister."

"Yes," said Content, eagerly.

"I am going," said Jim, "to marry Lucy Rose when I grow up, but I haven't got any sister, and I'd like you first rate for one. So I'll be your big brother instead of your cousin."

"Big brother Solly?"

"Say, Content, that is an awful name, but I don't care. You're only a girl. You can call me anything you want to, but you mustn't call me Solly when there is anybody within hearing."

"I won't."

"Because it wouldn't do," said Jim with weight.

"I never will, honest," said Content.

Presently they went into the house. Dr. Trumbull was there; he had been talking seriously to the rector and his wife. He had come over on purpose.

"It is a perfect absurdity," he said, "but I made ten calls this morning, and everywhere I was asked about that little Adams girl's big sister—why you keep her hidden. They have a theory that she is either an idiot or dreadfully disfigured. I had to tell them I know nothing about it."

"There isn't any girl," said the rector, wearily. "Sally, do explain."

Dr. Trumbull listened. "I have known such cases," he said when Sally had finished.

"What did you do for them?" Sally asked, anxiously.

"Nothing. Such cases have to be cured by time. Children get over these fancies when they grow up."

"Do you mean to say that we have to put up with big sister Solly until Content is grown up?" asked

Sally, in a desperate tone. And then Jim came in. Content had run up-stairs.

"It is all right, mother," said Jim.

Sally caught him by the shoulders. "Oh, Jim, has she told you?"

Jim gave briefly, and with many omissions, an account of his conversation with Content.

"Did she say anything about that dress, Jim?" asked his mother.

"She said her aunt had meant it for that out-West rector's daughter Alice to graduate in, but Content wanted it for her big sister Solly, and told the rector's wife it was hers. Content says she knows she was a naughty girl, but after she had said it she was afraid to say it wasn't so. Mother, I think that poor little thing is scared 'most to death."

"Nobody is going to hurt her," said Sally. "Goodness! that rector's wife was so conscientious that she even let that dress go. Well, I can send it right back, and the girl will have it in time for her graduation, after all. Jim dear, call the poor child down. Tell her nobody is going to scold her." Sally's voice was very tender.

Jim returned with Content. She had on a little ruffled pink gown which seemed to reflect color on her cheeks. She wore an inscrutable expression, at once child-like and charming. She looked shy, furtively amused, yet happy. Sally realized that the pessimistic downward lines had disappeared, that Content was really a pretty little girl.

Sally put an arm around the small, pink figure. "So you and Jim have been talking, dear?" she said.

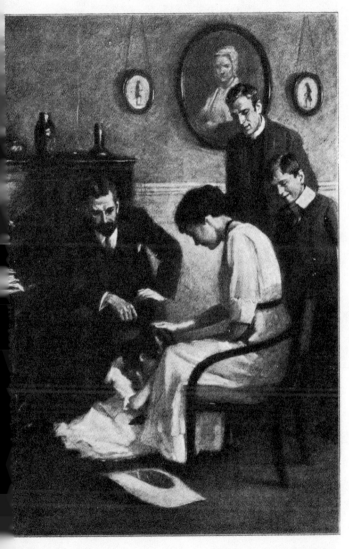

A LITTLE PEAL OF LAUGHTER CAME FROM THE SOFT MUSLIN
FOLDS

"Yes, ma'am," replied little Content. "Jim is my big brother—" She just caught herself before she said Solly.

"And your sister Solly is married and living out West?"

"Yes," said Content, with a long breath. "My sister Solly is married." Smiles broke all over her little face. She hid it in Sally's skirts, and a little peal of laughter like a bird-trill came from the soft muslin folds.

LITTLE LUCY ROSE

LITTLE LUCY ROSE

BACK of the rectory there was a splendid, long hill. The ground receded until the rectory garden was reached, and the hill was guarded on either flank by a thick growth of pines and cedars, and, being a part of the land appertaining to the rectory, was never invaded by the village children. This was considered very fortunate by Mrs. Patterson, Jim's mother, and for an odd reason. The rector's wife was very fond of coasting, as she was of most out-of-door sports, but her dignified position prevented her from enjoying them to the utmost. In many localities the clergyman's wife might have played golf and tennis, have rode and swum and coasted and skated, and nobody thought the worse of her; but in The Village it was different.

Sally had therefore rejoiced at the discovery of that splendid, isolated hill behind the house. It could not have been improved upon for a long, perfectly glorious coast, winding up on the pool of ice in the garden and bumping thrillingly between dry vegetables. Mrs. Patterson steered and Jim made the running pushes, and slid flat on his chest behind his mother. Jim was very proud of his mother. He often wished that he felt at liberty to tell of her feats. He had never been told not to tell, but realized, being rather a sharp boy, that silence was wiser. Jim's mother confided in him, and he respected her confidence. "Oh, Jim dear," she would often say, "there is a mothers' meeting this afternoon, and I would so much rather go coasting with you." Or, "There's a Guild meeting about a fair, and the ice in the garden is really quite smooth."

It was perhaps unbecoming a rector's wife, but Jim loved his mother better because she expressed a preference for the sports he loved, and considered that no other boy had a mother who was quite equal to his. Sally Patterson was small and wiry, with a bright face, and very thick, brown hair, which had a boyish crest over her forehead, and she could run as fast as Jim. Jim's father was much older than his mother, and very dignified, although he had a keen sense of humor. He used to laugh when his wife and son came in after their coasting expeditions.

"Well, boys," he would say, "had a good time?"

Jim was perfectly satisfied and convinced that his mother was the very best and most beautiful person in the village, even in the whole world, until Mr. Cyril Rose came to fill a vacancy of cashier in the bank, and his daughter, little Lucy Rose, as a matter of course, came with him. Little Lucy had no mother. Mr. Cyril's cousin, Martha Rose, kept his house, and there was a colored maid with a bad temper, who was said, however, to be invaluable "help."

Little Lucy attended Madame's school. She came the next Monday after Jim and his friends had planned to have a chicken roast and failed. After Jim saw little Lucy he thought no more of the chicken roast. It seemed to him that he thought no more of anything. He could not by any possibility have learned his lessons had it not been for the desire to appear a good scholar before little Lucy. Jim had never been a self-conscious boy, but that day he was so keenly worried about her opinion of him that his usual easy swing broke into a strut when he crossed the room. He need not have been so troubled, because little Lucy was not looking at him. She was not looking at any boy or girl. She was only trying to learn her lesson. Little Lucy was that rather rare creature, a very gentle, obedient child, with a single eye for her duty. She was so charming that it was sad to think how much her mother had missed, as far as this world was concerned.

The minute Madame saw her a singular light came into her eyes—the light of love of a childless woman for a child. Similar lights were in the eyes of Miss Parmalee and Miss Acton. They looked at one another with a sort of sweet confidence when they were drinking tea together after school in Madame's study.

"Did you ever see such a darling?" said Madame. Miss Parmalee said she never had, and Miss Acton echoed her.

"She is a little angel," said Madame.

"She worked so hard over her geography lesson," said Miss Parmalee, "and she got the Amazon River in New England and the Connecticut in South

America, after all; but she was so sweet about it, she made me want to change the map of the world. Dear little soul, it did seem as if she ought to have rivers and everything else just where she chose."

"And she tried so hard to reach an octave, and her little finger is too short," said Miss Acton; "and she hasn't a bit of an ear for music, but her little voice is so sweet it does not matter."

"I have seen prettier children," said Madame, "but never one quite such a darling."

Miss Parmalee and Miss Acton agreed with Madame, and so did everybody else. Lily Jennings's beauty was quite eclipsed by little Lucy, but Lily did not care; she was herself one of little Lucy's most fervent admirers. She was really Jim Patterson's most formidable rival in the school. "You don't care about great, horrid boys, do you, dear?" Lily said to Lucy, entirely within hearing of Jim and Lee Westminster and Johnny Trumbull and Arnold Carruth and Bubby Harvey and Frank Ellis, and a number of others who glowered at her.

Dear little Lucy hesitated. She did not wish to hurt the feelings of boys, and the question had been loudly put. Finally she said she didn't know. Lack of definite knowledge was little Lucy's rock of refuge in time of need. She would look adorable, and say in her timid little fluty voice, "I don't—know." The last word came always with a sort of gasp which was alluring. All the listening boys were convinced that little Lucy loved them all individually and generally, because of her "I don't—know."

Everybody was convinced of little Lucy's affection for everybody, which was one reason for her charm. She flattered without knowing that she did so. It was impossible for her to look at any living thing except with soft eyes of love. It was impossible for her to speak without every tone conveying the sweetest deference and admiration. The whole atmosphere of Madame's school changed with the advent of the little girl. Everybody tried to live up to little Lucy's supposed ideal, but in reality she had no ideal. Lucy was the simplest of little girls, only intent upon being good, doing as she was told, and winning her father's approval, also her cousin Martha's.

Martha Rose was quite elderly, although still good-looking. She was not popular, because she was very silent. She dressed becomingly, received calls and returned them, but hardly spoke a word. People rather dreaded her coming. Miss Martha Rose would sit composedly in a proffered chair, her gloved hands crossed over her nice, gold-bound card-case, her chin tilted at an angle which never varied, her mouth in a set smile which never wavered, her slender feet in their best shoes toeing out precisely under the smooth sweep of her gray silk skirt. Miss Martha Rose dressed always in gray, a fashion which the village people grudgingly admired. It was undoubtedly becoming and distinguished, but savored ever so slightly of ostentation, as did her custom of always dressing little Lucy in blue. There were different shades and fabrics, but blue it always was. It was the best color for the child, as it revealed the fact that her big, dark eyes were blue.

Shaded as they were by heavy, curly lashes, they would have been called black or brown, but the blue in them leaped to vision above the blue of blue frocks. Little Lucy had the finest, most delicate features, a mist of soft, dark hair, which curled slightly, as mist curls, over sweet, round temples. She was a small, daintily clad child, and she spoke and moved daintily and softly; and when her blue eyes were fixed upon anybody's face, that person straightway saw love and obedience and trust in them, and love met love half-way. Even Miss Martha Rose looked another woman when little Lucy's innocent blue eyes were fixed upon her rather handsome but colorless face between the folds of her silvery hair; Miss Martha's hair had turned prematurely gray. Light would come into Martha Rose's face, light and animation, although she never talked much even to Lucy. She never talked much to her cousin Cyril, but he was rather glad of it. He had a keen mind, but it was easily diverted, and he was engrossed in his business, and concerned lest he be disturbed by such things as feminine chatter, of which he certainly had none in his own home, if he kept aloof from Jenny, the colored maid. Hers was the only female voice ever heard to the point of annoyance in the Rose house.

It was rather wonderful how a child like little Lucy and Miss Martha lived with so little conversation. Martha talked no more at home than abroad; moreover, at home she had not the attitude of waiting for some one to talk to her, which people outside considered trying. Martha did not expect her cousin to talk to her. She seldom asked a question. She almost never volunteered a perfectly useless observation. She made no remarks upon self-evident topics. If the sun shone, she never mentioned it. If there was a heavy rain, she never mentioned that. Miss Martha suited her cousin exactly, and for that reason, aside from the fact that he had been devoted to little Lucy's mother, it never occurred to him to marry again. Little Lucy talked no more than Miss Martha, and nobody dreamed that she sometimes wanted somebody to talk to her. Nobody dreamed that the dear little girl, studying her lessons, learning needlework, trying very futilely to play the piano, was lonely; but she was without knowing it herself. Martha was so kind and so still; and her father was so kind and so still, engrossed in his papers or books, often sitting by himself in his own study. Little Lucy in this peace and stillness was not having her share of childhood. When other little girls came to play with her, Miss Martha enjoined quiet, and even Lily Jennings's bird-like chattering became subdued. It was only at school that Lucy got her chance for the irresponsible delight which was the simple right of her childhood, and there her zeal for her lessons prevented. She was happy at school, however, for there she lived in an atmosphere of demonstrative affection. The teachers were given to seizing her in fond arms and caressing her, and so were her girl companions; while the boys, especially Jim Patterson, looked wistfully on.

Jim Patterson was in love, a charming little poetical

boy-love; but it was love. Everything which he did in those days was with the thought of little Lucy for incentive. He stood better in school than he had ever done before, but it was all for the sake of little Lucy. Jim Patterson had one talent, rather rudimentary, still a talent. He could play by ear. His father owned an old violin. He had been inclined to music in early youth, and Jim got permission to practise on it, and he went by himself in the hot attic and practised. Jim's mother did not care for music, and her son's preliminary scraping tortured her. Jim tucked the old fiddle under one round boy-cheek and played in the hot attic, with wasps buzzing around him; and he spent his pennies for catgut, and he learned to mend fiddle-strings; and finally came a proud Wednesday afternoon when there were visitors in Madame's school, and he stood on the platform, with Miss Acton playing an accompaniment on the baby grand piano, and he managed a feeble but true tune on his violin. It was all for little Lucy, but little Lucy cared no more for music than his mother; and while Jim was playing she was rehearsing in the depths of her mind the little poem which later she was to recite; for this adorable little Lucy was, as a matter of course, to figure in the entertainment. It therefore happened that she heard not one note of Jim Patterson's painfully executed piece, for she was saying to herself in mental singsong a foolish little poem, beginning:

> There was one little flower that bloomed
> Beside a cottage door.

LITTLE LUCY ROSE

When she went forward, little darling blue-clad figure, there was a murmur of admiration; and when she made mistakes straight through the poem, saying,

> There was a little flower that fell
> On my aunt Martha's floor,

for beginning, there was a roar of tender laughter and a clapping of tender, maternal hands, and everybody wanted to catch hold of little Lucy and kiss her. It was one of the irresistible charms of this child that people loved her the more for her mistakes, and she made many, although she tried so very hard to avoid them. Little Lucy was not in the least brilliant, but she held love like a precious vase, and it gave out perfume better than mere knowledge.

Jim Patterson was so deeply in love with her when he went home that night that he confessed to his mother. Mrs. Patterson had led up to the subject by alluding to little Lucy while at the dinner-table. "Edward," she said to her husband—both she and the rector had been present at Madame's school entertainment and the tea-drinking afterward—"did you ever see in all your life such a darling little girl as the new cashier's daughter? She quite makes up for Miss Martha, who sat here one solid hour, holding her card-case, waiting for me to talk to her. That child is simply delicious, and I was so glad she made mistakes."

"Yes, she is a charming child," assented the rector, "despite the fact that she is not a beauty, hardly even pretty."

THE COPY-CAT

"I know it," said Mrs. Patterson, "but she has the worth of beauty."

Jim was quite pale while his father and mother were talking. He swallowed the hot soup so fast that it burnt his tongue. Then he turned very red, but nobody noticed him. When his mother came up-stairs to kiss him good night he told her.

"Mother," said he, "I have something to tell you."

"All right, Jim," replied Sally Patterson, with her boyish air.

"It is very important," said Jim.

Mrs. Patterson did not laugh; she did not even smile. She sat down beside Jim's bed and looked seriously at his eager, rapt, shamed little boy-face on the pillow. "Well?" said she, after a minute which seemed difficult to him.

Jim coughed. Then he spoke with a blurt. "Mother," said Jim, "by and by, of course not quite yet, but by and by, will you have any objection to Miss Lucy Rose as a daughter?"

Even then Sally Patterson did not laugh or even smile. "Are you thinking of marrying her, Jim?" asked she, quite as if her son had been a man.

"Yes, mother," replied Jim. Then he flung up his little arms in pink pajama sleeves, and Sally Patterson took his face between her two hands and kissed him warmly.

"She is a darling, and your choice does you credit, Jim," said she. "Of course you have said nothing to her yet?"

"I thought it was rather too soon."

148

"I really think you are very wise, Jim," said his mother. "It is too soon to put such ideas into the poor child's head. She is younger than you, isn't she, Jim?"

"She is just six months and three days younger," replied Jim, with majesty.

"I thought so. Well, you know, Jim, it would just wear her all out, as young as that, to be obliged to think about her trousseau and housekeeping and going to school, too."

"I know it," said Jim, with a pleased air. "I thought I was right, mother."

"Entirely right; and you, too, really ought to finish school, and take up a profession or a business, before you say anything definite. You would want a nice home for the dear little thing, you know that, Jim."

Jim stared at his mother out of his white pillow. "I thought I would stay with you, and she would stay with her father until we were both very much older," said he. "She has a nice home now, you know, mother."

Sally Patterson's mouth twitched a little, but she spoke quite gravely and reasonably. "Yes, that is very true," said she; "still, I do think you are wise to wait, Jim."

When Sally Patterson had left Jim, she looked in on the rector in his study. "Our son is thinking seriously of marrying, Edward," said she.

The rector stared at her. She had shut the door, and she laughed.

"He is very discreet. He has consulted me as to

my approval of her as daughter and announced his intention to wait a little while."

The rector laughed; then he wrinkled his forehead uneasily. "I don't like the little chap getting such ideas," said he.

"Don't worry, Edward; he hasn't got them," said Sally Patterson.

"I hope not."

"He has made a very wise choice. She is that perfect darling of a Rose girl who couldn't speak her piece, and thought we all loved her when we laughed."

"Well, don't let him get foolish ideas; that is all, my dear," said the rector.

"Don't worry, Edward. I can manage him," said Sally.

But she was mistaken. The very next day Jim proposed in due form to little Lucy. He could not help it. It was during the morning intermission, and he came upon her seated all alone under a haw-thorn hedge, studying her arithmetic anxiously. She was in blue, as usual, and a very perky blue bow sat on her soft, dark hair, like a bluebird. She glanced up at Jim from under her long lashes.

"Do two and seven make eight or ten? If you please, will you tell me?" said she.

"Say, Lucy," said Jim, "will you marry me by and by?"

Lucy stared at him uncomprehendingly.

"Will you?"

"Will I what?"

"Marry me by and by?"

Lucy took refuge in her little harbor of ignorance. "I don't know," said she.

"But you like me, don't you, Lucy?"

"I don't know."

"Don't you like me better than you like Johnny Trumbull?"

"I don't know."

"You like me better than you like Arnold Carruth, don't you? He has curls and wears socks."

"I don't know."

"When do you think you can be sure?"

"I don't know."

Jim stared helplessly at little Lucy. She stared back sweetly.

"Please tell me whether two and seven make six or eleven, Jim," said she.

"They make nine," said Jim.

"I have been counting my fingers and I got it eleven, but I suppose I must have counted one finger twice," said little Lucy. She gazed reflectively at her little baby-hands. A tiny ring with a blue stone shone on one finger.

"I will give you a ring, you know," Jim said, coaxingly.

"I have got a ring my father gave me. Did you say it was ten, please, Jim?"

"Nine," gasped Jim.

"All the way I can remember," said little Lucy, "is for you to pick just so many leaves off the hedge, and I will tie them in my handkerchief, and just before I have to say my lesson I will count those leaves."

Jim obediently picked nine leaves from the hawthorn hedge, and little Lucy tied them into her handkerchief, and then the Japanese gong sounded and they went back to school.

That night after dinner, just before Lucy went to bed, she spoke of her own accord to her father and Miss Martha, a thing which she seldom did. "Jim Patterson asked me to marry him when I asked him what seven and two made in my arithmetic lesson," said she. She looked with the loveliest round eyes of innocence first at her father, then at Miss Martha. Cyril Rose gasped and laid down his newspaper.

"What did you say, little Lucy?" he asked.

"Jim Patterson asked me to marry him when I asked him to tell me how much seven and two made in my arithmetic lesson."

Cyril Rose and his cousin Martha looked at each other.

"Arnold Carruth asked me, too, when a great big wasp flew on my arm and frightened me."

Cyril and Martha continued to look. The little, sweet, uncertain voice went on.

"And Johnny Trumbull asked me when I 'most fell down on the sidewalk; and Lee Westminster asked me when I wasn't doing anything, and so did Bubby Harvey."

"What did you tell them?" asked Miss Martha, in a faint voice.

"I told them I didn't know."

"You had better have the child go to bed now," said Cyril. "Good night, little Lucy. Always tell father everything."

"Yes, father," said little Lucy, and was kissed, and went away with Martha.

When Martha returned, her cousin looked at her severely. He was a fair, gentle-looking man, and severity was impressive when he assumed it.

"Really, Martha," said he, "don't you think you had better have a little closer outlook over that baby?"

"Oh, Cyril, I never dreamed of such a thing," cried Miss Martha.

"You really must speak to Madame," said Cyril. "I cannot have such things put into the child's head."

"Oh, Cyril, how can I?"

"I think it is your duty."

"Cyril, could not—you?"

Cyril grinned. "Do you think," said he, "that I am going to that elegant widow schoolma'am and say, 'Madame, my young daughter has had four proposals of marriage in one day, and I must beg you to put a stop to such proceedings'? No, Martha; it is a woman's place to do such a thing as that. The whole thing is too absurd, indignant as I am about it. Poor little soul!"

So it happened that Miss Martha Rose, the next day being Saturday, called on Madame, but, not being asked any leading question, found herself absolutely unable to deliver herself of her errand, and went away with it unfulfilled.

"Well, I must say," said Madame to Miss Parmalee, as Miss Martha tripped wearily down the front walk—"I must say, of all the educated women

who have really been in the world, she is the strang-
est. You and I have done nothing but ask inane
questions, and she has sat waiting for them, and
chirped back like a canary. I am simply worn out."

"So am I," sighed Miss Parmalee.

But neither of them was so worn out as poor
Miss Martha, anticipating her cousin's reproaches.
However, her wonted silence and reticence stood
her in good stead, for he merely asked, after little
Lucy had gone to bed:

"Well, what did Madame say about Lucy's proposals?"

"She did not say anything," replied Martha.

"Did she promise it would not occur again?"

"She did not promise, but I don't think it will."

The financial page was unusually thrilling that
night, and Cyril Rose, who had come to think rather
lightly of the affair, remarked, absent-mindedly:
"Well, I hope it does not occur again. I cannot have
such ridiculous ideas put into the child's head. If
it does, we get a governess for her and take her away
from Madame's." Then he resumed his reading,
and Martha, guilty but relieved, went on with her
knitting.

It was late spring then, and little Lucy had attended Madame's school several months, and her
popularity had never waned. A picnic was planned
to Dover's Grove, and the romantic little girls had
insisted upon a May queen, and Lucy was unani-
mously elected. The pupils of Madame's school went
to the picnic in the manner known as a "straw-
ride." Miss Parmalee sat with them, her feet

uncomfortably tucked under her. She was the youngest of the teachers, and could not evade the duty. Madame and Miss Acton headed the procession, sitting comfortably in a victoria driven by the colored man Sam, who was employed about the school. Dover's Grove was six miles from the village, and a favorite spot for picnics. The victoria rolled on ahead; Madame carried a black parasol, for the sun was on her side and the day very warm. Both ladies wore thin, dark gowns, and both felt the languor of spring.

The straw-wagon, laden with children seated upon the golden trusses of straw, looked like a wagon-load of blossoms. Fair and dark heads, rosy faces looked forth in charming clusters. They sang, they chattered. It made no difference to them that it was not the season for a straw-ride, that the trusses were musty. They inhaled the fragrance of blooming boughs under which they rode, and were quite oblivious to all discomfort and unpleasantness. Poor Miss Parmalee, with her feet going to sleep, sneezing from time to time from the odor of the old straw, did not obtain the full beauty of the spring day. She had protested against the straw-ride.

"The children really ought to wait until the season for such things," she had told Madame, quite boldly; and Madame had replied that she was well aware of it, but the children wanted something of the sort, and the hay was not cut, and straw, as it happened, was more easily procured.

"It may not be so very musty," said Madame; "and you know, my dear, straw is clean, and I am sorry, but you do seem to be the one to ride with the children on the straw, because"—Madame dropped her voice—"you are really younger, you know, than either Miss Acton or I."

Poor Miss Parmalee could almost have dispensed with her few years of superior youth to have gotten rid of that straw-ride. She had no parasol, and the sun beat upon her head, and the noise of the children got horribly on her nerves. Little Lucy was her one alleviation. Little Lucy sat in the midst of the boisterous throng, perfectly still, crowned with her garland of leaves and flowers, her sweet, pale little face calmly observant. She was the high light of Madame's school, the effect which made the whole. All the others looked at little Lucy, they talked to her, they talked at her; but she remained herself unmoved, as a high light should be. "Dear little soul," Miss Parmalee thought. She also thought that it was a pity that little Lucy could not have worn a white frock in her character as Queen of the May, but there she was mistaken. The blue was of a peculiar shade, of a very soft material, and nothing could have been prettier. Jim Patterson did not often look away from little Lucy; neither did Arnold Carruth; neither did Bubby Harvey; neither did Johnny Trumbull; neither did Lily Jennings; neither did many others.

Amelia Wheeler, however, felt a little jealous as she watched Lily. She thought Lily ought to have been queen; and she, while she did not dream of competing with incomparable little Lucy, wished Lily would not always look at Lucy with such worshipful admiration. Amelia was inconsistent. She knew that she herself could not aspire to being an object of worship, but the state of being a nonentity for Lily was depressing. "Wonder if I jumped out of this old wagon and got killed if she would mind one bit?" she thought, tragically. But Amelia did not jump. She had tragic impulses, or rather imaginations of tragic impulses, but she never carried them out. It was left for little Lucy, flower-crowned and calmly sweet and gentle under honors, to be guilty of a tragedy of which she never dreamed. For that was the day when little Lucy was lost.

When the picnic was over, when the children were climbing into the straw-wagon and Madame and Miss Acton were genteely disposed in the victoria, a lamentable cry arose. Sam drew his reins tight and rolled his inquiring eyes around; Madame and Miss Acton leaned far out on either side of the victoria.

"Oh, what is it?" said Madame. "My dear Miss Acton, do pray get out and see what the trouble is. I begin to feel a little faint."

In fact, Madame got her cut-glass smelling-bottle out of her bag and began to sniff vigorously. Sam gazed backward and paid no attention to her. Madame always felt faint when anything unexpected occurred, and smelled at the pretty bottle, but she never fainted.

Miss Acton got out, lifting her nice skirts clear of the dusty wheel, and she scuttled back to the uproarious straw-wagon, showing her slender ankles and trimly shod feet. Miss Acton was a very wiry, dainty woman, full of nervous energy. When she reached the straw-wagon Miss Parmalee was climbing out, assisted by the driver. Miss Parmalee was very pale and visibly tremulous. The children were all shrieking in dissonance, so it was quite impossible to tell what the burden of their tale of woe was; but obviously something of a tragic nature had happened.

"What is the matter?" asked Miss Acton, teetering like a humming-bird with excitement.

"Little Lucy—" gasped Miss Parmalee.

"What about her?"

"She isn't here."

"Where is she?"

"We don't know. We just missed her."

Then the cry of the children for little Lucy Rose, although sadly wrangled, became intelligible. Madame came, holding up her silk skirt and sniffing at her smelling-bottle, and everybody asked questions of everybody else, and nobody knew any satisfactory answers. Johnny Trumbull was confident that he was the last one to see little Lucy, and so were Lily Jennings and Amelia Wheeler, and so were Jim Patterson and Bubby Harvey and Arnold Carruth and Lee Westminster and many others; but when pinned down to the actual moment everybody disagreed, and only one thing was certain—little Lucy Rose was missing.

"What shall I say to her father?" moaned Madame.

"Of course, we shall find her before we say anything," returned Miss Parmalee, who was sure to rise to an emergency. Madame sank helpless before one. "You had better go and sit under that tree (Sam, take a cushion out of the carriage for Madame) and keep quiet; then Sam must drive to the village and give the alarm, and the straw-wagon had better go, too; and the rest of us will hunt by threes, three always keeping together. Remember, children, three of you keep together, and, whatever you do, be sure and do not separate. We cannot have another lost."

It seemed very sound advice. Madame, pale and frightened, sat on the cushion under the tree and sniffed at her smelling-bottle, and the rest scattered and searched the grove and surrounding underbrush thoroughly. But it was sunset when the groups returned to Madame under her tree, and the straw-wagon with excited people was back, and the victoria with Lucy's father and the rector and his wife, and Dr. Trumbull in his buggy, and other carriages fast arriving. Poor Miss Martha Rose had been out calling when she heard the news, and she was walking to the scene of action. The victoria in which her cousin was seated left her in a cloud of dust. Cyril Rose had not noticed the mincing figure with the card-case and the parasol.

The village searched for little Lucy Rose, but it was Jim Patterson who found her, and in the most unlikely of places. A forlorn pair with a multiplicity of forlorn children lived in a tumble-down house about half a mile from the grove. The man's name was Silas Thomas, and his wife's was Sarah. Poor Sarah had lost a large part of the small wit she had originally owned several years before, when her youngest daughter, aged four, died. All the babies that had arrived since had not consoled her for the death of that little lamb, by name Viola May, nor restored her full measure of under-wit. Poor Sarah Thomas had spied adorable little Lucy separated from her mates by chance for a few minutes, picking wild flowers, and had seized her in forcible but loving arms and carried her home. Had Lucy not been such a silent, docile child, it could never have happened; but she was a mere little limp thing in the grasp of the over-loving, deprived mother who thought she had gotten back her own beloved Viola May.

When Jim Patterson, big-eyed and pale, looked in at the Thomas door, there sat Sarah Thomas, a large, unkempt, wild-visaged, but gentle creature, holding little Lucy and cuddling her, while Lucy, shrinking away as far as she was able, kept her big, dark eyes of wonder and fear upon the woman's face. And all around were clustered the Thomas children, unkempt as their mother, a gentle but degenerate brood, all of them believing what their mother said. Viola May had come home again. Silas Thomas was not there; he was trudging slowly homeward from a job of wood-cutting. Jim saw only the mother, little Lucy, and that poor little flock of children gazing in wonder and awe. Jim rushed in and faced Sarah Thomas. "Give me little Lucy!" said he, as fiercely as any man. But he reckoned without the unreasoning love of a mother. Sarah only held little Lucy faster, and the

VIOLA MAY HAD COME HOME AGAIN

poor little girl rolled appealing eyes at him over that brawny, grasping arm of affection.

Jim raced for help, and it was not long before it came. Little Lucy rode home in the victoria, seated in Sally Patterson's lap. "Mother, you take her," Jim had pleaded; and Sally, in the face and eyes of Madame, had gathered the little trembling creature into her arms. In her heart she had not much of an opinion of any woman who had allowed such a darling little girl out of her sight for a moment. Madame accepted a seat in another carriage and rode home, explaining and sniffing and inwardly resolving never again to have a straw-ride.

Jim stood on the step of the victoria all the way home. They passed poor Miss Martha Rose, still faring toward the grove, and nobody noticed her, for the second time. She did not turn back until the straw-wagon, which formed the tail of the little procession, reached her. That she halted with mad waves of her parasol, and, when told that little Lucy was found, refused a seat on the straw because she did not wish to rumple her best gown and turned about and fared home again.

The rectory was reached before Cyril Rose's house, and Cyril yielded gratefully to Sally Patterson's proposition that she take the little girl with her, give her dinner, see that she was washed and brushed and freed from possible contamination from the Thomases, who were not a cleanly lot, and later brought home in the rector's carriage. However, little Lucy stayed all night at the rectory. She had a bath; her lovely, misty hair was brushed; she

11   161

was fed and petted; and finally Sally Patterson telephoned for permission to keep her overnight. By that time poor Martha had reached home and was busily brushing her best dress.

After dinner, little Lucy, very happy and quite restored, sat in Sally Patterson's lap on the veranda, while Jim hovered near. His innocent boy-love made him feel as if he had wings. But his wings only bore him to failure, before an earlier and mightier force of love than his young heart could yet compass for even such a darling as little Lucy. He sat on the veranda step and gazed eagerly and rapturously at little Lucy on his mother's lap, and the desire to have her away from other loves came over him. He saw the fireflies dancing in swarms on the lawn, and a favorite sport of the children of the village occurred to him.

"Say, little Lucy," said Jim.

Little Lucy looked up with big, dark eyes under her mist of hair, as she nestled against Sally Patterson's shoulder.

"Say, let's chase fireflies, little Lucy."

"Do you want to chase fireflies with Jim, darling?" asked Sally.

Little Lucy nestled closer. "I would rather stay with you," said she in her meek flute of a voice, and she gazed up at Sally with the look which she might have given the mother she had lost.

Sally kissed her and laughed. Then she reached down a fond hand and patted her boy's head. "Never mind, Jim," said Sally. "Mothers have to come first."

NOBLESSE

NOBLESSE

MARGARET LEE encountered in her late middle age the rather singular strait of being entirely alone in the world. She was unmarried, and as far as relatives were concerned, she had none except those connected with her by ties not of blood, but by marriage.

Margaret had not married when her flesh had been comparative; later, when it had become superlative, she had no opportunities to marry. Life would have been hard enough for Margaret under any circumstances, but it was especially hard, living, as she did, with her father's stepdaughter and that daughter's husband.

Margaret's stepmother had been a child in spite of her two marriages, and a very silly, although pretty child. The daughter, Camille, was like her, although not so pretty, and the man whom Camille had married was what Margaret had been taught to regard as "common." His business pursuits were irregular and partook of mystery. He always smoked cigarettes and chewed gum. He wore loud shirts and a diamond scarf-pin which had upon him the appearance of stolen goods. The gem had belonged to Margaret's own mother, but when Camille expressed a desire to present it to Jack Desmond, Margaret had yielded with no outward hesitation, but afterward she wept miserably over its loss when alone in her room. The spirit had gone out of Margaret, the little which she had possessed. She had always been a gentle, sensitive creature, and was almost helpless before the wishes of others.

After all, it had been a long time since Margaret had been able to force the ring even upon her little finger, but she had derived a small pleasure from the reflection that she owned it in its faded velvet box, hidden under laces in her top bureau drawer. She did not like to see it blazing forth from the tie of this very ordinary young man who had married Camille. Margaret had a gentle, high-bred contempt for Jack Desmond, but at the same time a vague fear of him. Jack had a measure of unscrupulous business shrewdness, which spared nothing and nobody, and that in spite of the fact that he had not succeeded.

Margaret owned the old Lee place, which had been magnificent, but of late years the expenditures had been reduced and it had deteriorated. The conservatories had been closed. There was only one horse in the stable. Jack had bought him. He was a worn-out trotter with legs carefully bandaged. Jack drove him at reckless speed, not considering those slender, braceleted legs. Jack had a racing-gig, and when in it, with striped coat, cap on one side, cigarette in mouth, lines held taut, skimming along the roads in clouds of dust, he thought himself the man and true sportsman which he was not. Some of the old Lee silver had paid for that waning trotter.

Camille adored Jack, and cared for no associations, no society, for which he was not suited. Before the trotter was bought she told Margaret that the kind of dinners which she was able to give in Fairhill were awfully slow. "If we could afford to have some men out from the city, some nice fellers that Jack knows, it would be worth while," said she, "but we have grown so hard up we can't do a thing to make it worth their while. Those men haven't got any use for a back-number old place like this. We can't take them round in autos, nor give them a chance at cards, for Jack couldn't pay if he lost, and Jack is awful honorable. We can't have the right kind of folks here for any fun. I don't propose to ask the rector and his wife, and old Mr. Harvey, or people like the Leaches."

"The Leaches are a very good old family," said Margaret, feebly.

"I don't care for good old families when they are so slow," retorted Camille. "The fellers we could have here, if we were rich enough, come from fine families, but they are up-to-date. It's no use hanging on to old silver dishes we never use and that I don't intend to spoil my hands shining. Poor Jack don't have much fun, anyway. If he wants that trotter—he says it's going dirt cheap—I think it's mean he can't have it, instead of your hanging on to a lot of out-of-style old silver; so there."

Two generations ago there had been French blood in Camille's family. She put on her clothes beautifully; she had a dark, rather fine-featured, alert little face, which gave a wrong impression, for she was essentially vulgar. Sometimes poor Margaret Lee wished that Camille had been definitely vicious, if only she might be possessed of more of the characteristics of breeding. Camille so irritated Margaret in those somewhat abstruse traits called sensibilities that she felt as if she were living with a sort of spiritual nutmeg-grater. Seldom did Camille speak that she did not jar Margaret, although unconsciously. Camille meant to be kind to the stout woman, whom she pitied as far as she was capable of pitying without understanding. She realized that it must be horrible to be no longer young, and so stout that one was fairly monstrous, but how horrible she could not with her mentality conceive. Jack also meant to be kind. He was not of the brutal—that is, intentionally brutal—type, but he had a shrewd eye to the betterment of himself, and no realization of the torture he inflicted upon those who opposed that betterment.

For a long time matters had been worse than usual financially in the Lee house. The sisters had been left in charge of the sadly dwindled estate, and had depended upon the judgment, or lack of judgment, of Jack. He approved of taking your chances and striking for larger income. The few good old grandfather securities had been sold, and wild ones from the very jungle of commerce had been substituted. Jack, like most of his type, while shrewd, was as credulous as a child. He lied himself, and expected all men to tell him the truth. Camille at his bidding mortgaged the old place, and Margaret dared not oppose. Taxes were not paid; interest was not paid;

credit was exhausted. Then the house was put up at public auction, and brought little more than sufficient to pay the creditors. Jack took the balance and staked it in a few games of chance, and of course lost. The weary trotter stumbled one day and had to be shot. Jack became desperate. He frightened Camille. He was suddenly morose. He bade Camille pack, and Margaret also, and they obeyed. Camille stowed away her crumpled finery in the bulging old trunks, and Margaret folded daintily her few remnants of past treasures. She had an old silk gown or two, which resisted with their rich honesty the inroads of time, and a few pieces of old lace, which Camille understood no better than she understood their owner.

Then Margaret and the Desmonds went to the city and lived in a horrible, tawdry little flat in a tawdry locality. Jack roared with bitter mirth when he saw poor Margaret forced to enter her tiny room sidewise; Camille laughed also, although she chided Jack gently. "Mean of you to make fun of poor Margaret, Jacky dear," she said.

For a few weeks Margaret's life in that flat was horrible; then it became still worse. Margaret nearly filled with her weary, ridiculous bulk her little room, and she remained there most of the time, although it was sunny and noisy, its one window giving on a courtyard strung with clothes-lines and teeming with boisterous life. Camille and Jack went trolley-riding, and made shift to entertain a little, merry but questionable people, who gave them passes to vaudeville and entertained in their turn until the small hours. Unquestionably these people suggested to Jack Desmond the scheme which spelled tragedy to Margaret.

She always remembered one little dark man with keen eyes who had seen her disappearing through her door of a Sunday night when all these gay, bedraggled birds were at liberty and the fun ran high. "Great Scott!" the man had said, and Margaret had heard him demand of Jack that she be recalled. She obeyed, and the man was introduced, also the other members of the party. Margaret Lee stood in the midst of this throng and heard their repressed titters of mirth at her appearance. Everybody there was in good humor with the exception of Jack, who was still nursing his bad luck, and the little dark man, whom Jack owed. The eyes of Jack and the little dark man made Margaret cold with a terror of something, she knew not what. Before that terror the shame and mortification of her exhibition to that merry company was of no import.

She stood among them, silent, immense, clad in her dark purple silk gown spread over a great hoop-skirt. A real lace collar lay softly over her enormous, billowing shoulders; real lace ruffles lay over her great, shapeless hands. Her face, the delicacy of whose features was veiled with flesh, flushed and paled. Not even flesh could subdue the sad brilliancy of her dark-blue eyes, fixed inward upon her own sad state, unregardful of the company. She made an indefinite murmur of response to the salutations given her, and then retreated. She heard the roar of laughter after she had squeezed through the

door of her room. Then she heard eager conversation, of which she did not catch the real import, but
which terrified her with change expressions. She
was quite sure that she was the subject of that eager
discussion. She was quite sure that it boded her
no good.

In a few days she knew the worst; and the worst
was beyond her utmost imaginings. This was before the days of moving-picture shows; it was the
day of humiliating spectacles of deformities, when
inventions of amusements for the people had not
progressed. It was the day of exhibitions of sad
freaks of nature, calculated to provoke tears rather
than laughter in the healthy-minded, and poor Margaret Lee was a chosen victim. Camille informed
her in a few words of her fate. Camille was sorry
for her, although not in the least understanding why
she was sorry. She realized dimly that Margaret
would be distressed, but she was unable from her
narrow point of view to comprehend fully the whole
tragedy.

"Jack has gone broke," stated Camille. "He
owes Bill Stark a pile, and he can't pay a cent of it;
and Jack's sense of honor about a poker debt is
about the biggest thing in his character. Jack has
got to pay. And Bill has a little circus, going to
travel all summer, and he's offered big money for
you. Jack can pay Bill what he owes him, and we'll
have enough to live on, and have lots of fun going
around. You hadn't ought to make a fuss about it."

Margaret, pale as death, stared at the girl, pertly
slim, and common and pretty, who stared back

laughingly, although still with the glimmer of un-
comprehending pity in her black eyes.

"What does — he — want — me — for?" gasped
Margaret.

"For a show, because you are so big," replied
Camille. "You will make us all rich, Margaret.
Ain't it nice?"

Then Camille screamed, the shrill raucous scream
of the women of her type, for Margaret had fallen
back in a dead faint, her immense bulk inert in her
chair. Jack came running in alarm. Margaret had
suddenly gained value in his shrewd eyes. He was
as pale as she.

Finally Margaret raised her head, opened her
miserable eyes, and regained her consciousness of
herself and what lay before her. There was no course
open but submission. She knew that from the first.
All three faced destitution; she was the one financial
asset, she and her poor flesh. She had to face it,
and with what dignity she could muster.

Margaret had great piety. She kept constantly
before her mental vision the fact in which she believed, that the world which she found so hard, and
which put her to unspeakable torture, was not all.

A week elapsed before the wretched little show
of which she was to be a member went on the road,
and night after night she prayed. She besieged her
God for strength. She never prayed for respite.
Her realization of the situation and her lofty resolution prevented that. The awful, ridiculous combat was before her; there was no evasion; she prayed
only for the strength which leads to victory.

However, when the time came, it was all worse than she had imagined. How could a woman gently born and bred conceive of the horrible ignominy of such a life? She was dragged hither and yon, to this and that little town. She traveled through sweltering heat on jolting trains; she slept in tents; she lived—she, Margaret Lee—on terms of equality with the common and the vulgar. Daily her absurd unwieldiness was exhibited to crowds screaming with laughter. Even her faith wavered. It seemed to her that there was nothing for evermore beyond those staring, jeering faces of silly mirth and delight at sight of her, seated in two chairs, clad in a pink spangled dress, her vast shoulders bare and sparkling with a tawdry necklace, her great, bare arms covered with brass bracelets, her hands incased in short, white kid gloves, over the fingers of which she wore a number of rings—stage properties.

Margaret became a horror to herself. At times it seemed to her that she was in the way of fairly losing her own identity. It mattered little that Camille and Jack were very kind to her, that they showed her the nice things which her terrible earnings had enabled them to have. She sat in her two chairs—the two chairs proved a most successful advertisement—with her two kid-cushiony hands clenched in her pink spangled lap, and she suffered agony of soul, which made her inner self stern and terrible, behind that great pink mask of face. And nobody realized until one sultry day when the show opened at a village in a pocket of green hills—indeed, its name was Greenhill—and Sydney Lord went to see it.

Margaret, who had schooled herself to look upon her audience as if they were not, suddenly comprehended among them another soul who understood her own. She met the eyes of the man, and a wonderful comfort, as of a cool breeze blowing over the face of clear water, came to her. She knew that the man understood. She knew that she had his fullest sympathy. She saw also a comrade in the toils of comic tragedy, for Sydney Lord was in the same case. He was a mountain of flesh. As a matter of fact, had he not been known in Greenhill and respected as a man of weight of character as well as of body, and of an old family, he would have rivaled Margaret. Beside him sat an elderly woman, sweet-faced, slightly bent as to her slender shoulders, as if with a chronic attitude of submission. She was Sydney's widowed sister, Ellen Waters. She lived with her brother and kept his house, and had no will other than his.

Sydney Lord and his sister remained when the rest of the audience had drifted out, after the privileged hand-shakes with the queen of the show. Every time a coarse, rustic hand reached familiarly after Margaret's, Sydney shrank.

He motioned his sister to remain seated when he approached the stage. Jack Desmond, who had been exploiting Margaret, gazed at him with admiring curiosity. Sydney waved him away with a commanding gesture. "I wish to speak to her a moment. Pray leave the tent," he said,

and Jack obeyed.   People always obeyed Sydney
Lord.

Sydney stood before Margaret, and he saw the
clear crystal, which was herself, within all the flesh,
clad in tawdry raiment, and she knew that he saw it.

"Good God!" said Sydney, "you are a lady!"

He continued to gaze at her, and his eyes, large
and brown, became blurred; at the same time his
mouth tightened.

"How came you to be in such a place as this?"
demanded Sydney.   He spoke almost as if he were
angry with her.

Margaret explained briefly.

"It is an outrage," declared Sydney.   He said
it, however, rather absently.   He was reflecting.
"Where do you live?" he asked.

"Here."

"You mean—?"

"They make up a bed for me here, after the people
have gone."

"And I suppose you had—before this—a comfortable house."

"The house which my grandfather Lee owned,
the old Lee mansion-house, before we went to the
city.   It was a very fine old Colonial house," explained Margaret, in her finely modulated voice.

"And you had a good room?"

"The southeast chamber had always been mine.
It was very large, and the furniture was old Spanish
mahogany."

"And now—" said Sydney.

"Yes," said Margaret.   She looked at him, and

her serious blue eyes seemed to see past him. "It will not last," she said.

"What do you mean?"

"I try to learn a lesson. I am a child in the school of God. My lesson is one that always ends in peace."

"Good God!" said Sydney.

He motioned to his sister, and Ellen approached in a frightened fashion. Her brother could do no wrong, but this was the unusual, and alarmed her.

"This lady—" began Sydney.

"Miss Lee," said Margaret. "I was never married. I am Miss Margaret Lee."

"This," said Sydney, "is my sister Ellen, Mrs. Waters. Ellen, I wish you to meet Miss Lee."

Ellen took into her own Margaret's hand, and said feebly that it was a beautiful day and she hoped Miss Lee found Greenhill a pleasant place to—visit.

Sydney moved slowly out of the tent and found Jack Desmond. He was standing near with Camille, who looked her best in a pale-blue summer silk and a black hat trimmed with roses. Jack and Camille never really knew how the great man had managed, but presently Margaret had gone away with him and his sister.

Jack and Camille looked at each other.

"Oh, Jack, ought you to have let her go?" said Camille.

"What made you let her go?" asked Jack.

"I—don't know. I couldn't say anything. That man has a tremendous way with him. Goodness!"

"He is all right here in the place, anyhow," said Jack. "They look up to him. He is a big-bug here.

Comes of a family like Margaret's, though he hasn't got much money. Some chaps were braggin' that they had a bigger show than her right here, and I found out."

"Suppose," said Camille, "Margaret does not come back?"

"He could not keep her without bein' arrested," declared Jack, but he looked uneasy. He had, however, looked uneasy for some time. The fact was, Margaret had been very gradually losing weight. Moreover, she was not well. That very night, after the show was over, Bill Stark, the little dark man, had a talk with the Desmonds about it.

"Truth is, before long, if you don't look out, you'll have to pad her," said Bill; "and giants don't amount to a row of pins after that begins."

Camille looked worried and sulky. "She ain't very well, anyhow," said she. "I ain't going to kill Margaret."

"It's a good thing she's got a chance to have a night's rest in a house," said Bill Stark.

"The fat man has asked her to stay with him and his sister while the show is here," said Jack.

"The sister invited her," said Camille, with a little stiffness. She was common, but she had lived with Lees, and her mother had married a Lee. She knew what was due Margaret, and also due herself.

"The truth is," said Camille, "this is an awful sort of life for a woman like Margaret. She and her folks were never used to anything like it."

"Why didn't you make your beauty husband hustle and take care of her and you, then?" demanded Bill, who admired Camille, and disliked her because she had no eyes for him.

"My husband has been unfortunate. He has done the best he could," responded Camille. "Come, Jack; no use talking about it any longer. Guess Margaret will pick up. Come along. I'm tired out."

That night Margaret Lee slept in a sweet chamber with muslin curtains at the windows, in a massive old mahogany bed, much like hers which had been sacrificed at an auction sale. The bed-linen was linen, and smelled of lavender. Margaret was too happy to sleep. She lay in the cool, fragrant sheets and was happy, and convinced of the presence of the God to whom she had prayed. All night Sydney Lord sat down-stairs in his book-walled sanctum and studied over the situation. It was a crucial one. The great psychological moment of Sydney Lord's life for knight-errantry had arrived. He studied the thing from every point of view. There was no romance about it. These were hard, sordid, tragic, ludicrous facts with which he had to deal. He knew to a nicety the agonies which Margaret suffered. He knew, because of his own capacity for sufferings of like stress. "And she is a woman and a lady," he said, aloud.

If Sydney had been rich enough, the matter would have been simple. He could have paid Jack and Camille enough to quiet them, and Margaret could have lived with him and his sister and their two old servants. But he was not rich; he was even poor. The price to be paid for Margaret's liberty was a bitter one, but it was that or nothing. Sydney faced it. He looked about the room. To him the walls lined with the dull gleams of old books were lovely. There was an oil portrait of his mother over the mantel-shelf. The weather was warm now, and there was no need for a hearth fire, but how exquisitely home-like and dear that room could be when the snow drove outside and there was the leap of flame on the hearth! Sydney was a scholar and a gentleman. He had led a gentle and sequestered life. Here in his native village there were none to gibe and sneer. The contrast of the traveling show would be as great for him as it had been for Margaret, but he was the male of the species, and she the female. Chivalry, racial, harking back to the beginning of nobility in the human, to its earliest dawn, fired Sydney. The pale daylight invaded the study. Sydney, as truly as any knight of old, had girded himself, and with no hope, no thought of reward, for the battle in the eternal service of the strong for the weak, which makes the true worth of the strong.

There was only one way. Sydney Lord took it. His sister was spared the knowledge of the truth for a long while. When she knew, she did not lament; since Sydney had taken the course, it must be right. As for Margaret, not knowing the truth, she yielded. She was really on the verge of illness. Her spirit was of too fine a strain to enable her body to endure long. When she was told that she was to remain with Sydney's sister while Sydney went away on business, she made no objection. A wonderful sense of relief, as of wings of healing being spread under her despair, was upon her. Camille came to bid her good-by.

"I hope you have a nice visit in this lovely house," said Camille, and kissed her. Camille was astute, and to be trusted. She did not betray Sydney's confidence. Sydney used a disguise—a dark wig over his partially bald head and a little make-up—and he traveled about with the show and sat on three chairs, and shook hands with the gaping crowd, and was curiously happy. It was discomfort; it was ignominy; it was maddening to support by the exhibition of his physical deformity a perfectly worthless young couple like Jack and Camille Desmond, but it was all superbly ennobling for the man himself.

Always as he sat on his three chairs, immense, grotesque—the more grotesque for his splendid dignity of bearing—there was in his soul of a gallant gentleman the consciousness of that other, whom he was shielding from a similar ordeal. Compassion and generosity, so great that they comprehended love itself and excelled its highest type, irradiated the whole being of the fat man exposed to the gaze of his inferiors. Chivalry, which rendered him almost god-like, strengthened him for his task. Sydney thought always of Margaret as distinct from her physical self, a sort of crystalline, angelic soul, with no encumbrance of earth. He achieved a purely spiritual conception of her. And Margaret, living again her gentle lady life, was likewise ennobled by a gratitude which transformed her. Always a clear and beautiful soul, she gave out new lights of character like a jewel in the sun. And she also thought of Sydney as distinct from his physical self. The consciousness of the two human beings, one of the other, was a consciousness as of two wonderful lines of good and beauty, moving for ever parallel, separate, and inseparable in an eternal harmony of spirit.

CORONATION

CORONATION

JIM BENNET had never married. He had passed middle life, and possessed considerable property. Susan Adkins kept house for him. She was a widow and a very distant relative. Jim had two nieces, his brother's daughters. One, Alma Beecher, was married; the other, Amanda, was not. The nieces had naïvely grasping views concerning their uncle and his property. They stated freely that they considered him unable to care for it; that a guardian should be appointed and the property be theirs at once. They consulted Lawyer Thomas Hopkinson with regard to it; they discoursed at length upon what they claimed to be an idiosyncrasy of Jim's, denoting failing mental powers.

"He keeps a perfect slew of cats, and has a coal fire for them in the woodshed all winter," said Amanda.

"Why in thunder shouldn't he keep a fire in the woodshed if he wants to?" demanded Hopkinson. "I know of no law against it. And there isn't a law in the country regulating the number of cats a man can keep." Thomas Hopkinson, who was an old friend of Jim's, gave his prominent chin an upward jerk as he sat in his office arm-chair before his clients.

"There is something besides cats," said Alma.

"What?"

"He talks to himself."

"What in creation do you expect the poor man to do? He can't talk to Susan Adkins about a blessed thing except tidies and pincushions. That woman hasn't a thought in her mind outside her soul's salvation and fancy-work. Jim has to talk once in a while to keep himself a man. What if he does talk to himself? I talk to myself. Next thing you will want to be appointed guardian over me, Amanda."

Hopkinson was a bachelor, and Amanda flushed angrily.

"He wasn't what I call even gentlemanly," she told Alma, when the two were on their way home.

"I suppose Tom Hopkinson thought you were setting your cap at him," retorted Alma. She relished the dignity of her married state, and enjoyed giving her spinster sister little claws when occasion called. However, Amanda had a temper of her own, and she could claw back.

"*You* needn't talk," said she. "You only took Joe Beecher when you had given up getting anybody better. You wanted Tom Hopkinson yourself. I haven't forgotten that blue silk dress you got and wore to meeting. You needn't talk. You know you got that dress just to make Tom look at you, and he didn't. You needn't talk."

"I wouldn't have married Tom Hopkinson if he had been the only man on the face of the earth," declared Alma with dignity; but she colored hotly.

Amanda sniffed. "Well, as near as I can find out,

"YOU NEEDN'T TALK. YOU WANTED TOM HOPKINSON YOURSELF"

Uncle Jim can go on talking to himself and keeping cats, and we can't do anything," said she.

When the two women were home, they told Alma's husband, Joe Beecher, about their lack of success. They were quite heated with their walk and excitement. "I call it a shame," said Alma. "Anybody knows that poor Uncle Jim would be better off with a guardian."

"Of course," said Amanda. "What man that had a grain of horse sense would do such a crazy thing as to keep a coal fire in a woodshed?"

"For such a slew of cats, too," said Alma, nodding fiercely.

Alma's husband, Joe Beecher, spoke timidly and undecidedly in the defense. "You know," he said, "that Mrs. Adkins wouldn't have those cats in the house, and cats mostly like to sit round where it's warm."

His wife regarded him. Her nose wrinkled. "I suppose next thing *you'll* be wanting to have a cat round where it's warm, right under my feet, with all I have to do," said she. Her voice had an actual acidity of sound.

Joe gasped. He was a large man with a constant expression of wondering inquiry. It was the expression of his babyhood; he had never lost it, and it was an expression which revealed truly the state of his mind. Always had Joe Beecher wondered, first of all at finding himself in the world at all, then at the various happenings of existence. He probably wondered more about the fact of his marriage with Alma Bennet than anything else, although he never betrayed his wonder. He was always painfully anxious to please his wife, of whom he stood in awe. Now he hastened to reply: "Why, no, Alma; of course I won't."

"Because," said Alma, "I haven't come to my time of life, through all the trials I've had, to be taking any chances of breaking my bones over any miserable, furry, four-footed animal that wouldn't catch a mouse if one run right under her nose."

"I don't want any cat," repeated Joe, miserably. His fear and awe of the two women increased. When his sister-in-law turned upon him he fairly cringed.

"Cats!" said Amanda. Then she sniffed. The sniff was worse than speech.

Joe repeated in a mumble that he didn't want any cats, and went out, closing the door softly after him, as he had been taught. However, he was entirely sure, in the depths of his subjugated masculine mind, that his wife and her sister had no legal authority whatever to interfere with their uncle's right to keep a hundred coal fires in his woodshed, for a thousand cats. He always had an inner sense of glee when he heard the two women talk over the matter. Once Amanda had declared that she did not believe that Tom Hopkinson knew much about law, anyway.

"He seems to stand pretty high," Joe ventured with the utmost mildness.

"Yes, he does," admitted Alma, grudgingly.

"It does not follow he knows law," persisted Amanda, "and it *may* follow that he likes cats.

There was that great Maltese tommy brushing round all the time we were in his office, but I didn't dare shoo him off for fear it might be against the law." Amanda laughed, a very disagreeable little laugh. Joe said nothing, but inwardly he chuckled. It was the cause of man with man. He realized a great, even affectionate, understanding of Jim.

The day after his nieces had visited the lawyer's office, Jim was preparing to call on his friend Edward Hayward, the minister. Before leaving he looked carefully after the fire in the woodshed. The stove was large. Jim piled on the coal, regardless outwardly that the housekeeper, Susan Adkins, had slammed the kitchen door to indicate her contempt. Inwardly Jim felt hurt, but he had felt hurt so long from the same cause that the sensation had become chronic, and was borne with a gentle patience. Moreover, there was something which troubled him more and was the reason for his contemplated call on his friend. He evened the coals on the fire with great care, and replenished from the pail in the ice-box the cats' saucers. There was a circle of clean white saucers around the stove. Jim owned many cats; counting the kittens, there were probably over twenty. Mrs. Adkins counted them in the sixties. "Those sixty-seven cats," she said.

Jim often gave away cats when he was confident of securing good homes, but supply exceeded the demand. Now and then tragedies took place in that woodshed. Susan Adkins came bravely to the front upon these occasions. Quite convinced was Susan Adkins that she had a good home, and it behooved her to keep it, and she did not in the least object to drowning, now and then, a few very young kittens. She did this with neatness and despatch while Jim walked to the store on an errand and was supposed to know nothing about it. There was simply not enough room in his woodshed for the accumulation of cats, although his heart could have held all.

That day, as he poured out the milk, cats of all ages and sizes and colors purred in a softly padding multitude around his feet, and he regarded them with love. There were tiger cats, Maltese cats, black-and-white cats, black cats and white cats, tommies and females, and his heart leaped to meet the pleading mews of all. The saucers were surrounded. Little pink tongues lapped. "Pretty pussy! pretty pussy!" cooed Jim, addressing them in general. He put on his overcoat and hat, which he kept on a peg behind the door. Jim had an arm-chair in the woodshed. He always sat there when he smoked; Susan Adkins demurred at his smoking in the house, which she kept so nice, and Jim did not dream of rebellion. He never questioned the right of a woman to bar tobacco smoke from a house. Before leaving he refilled some of the saucers. He was not sure that all of the cats were there; some might be afield, hunting, and he wished them to find refreshment when they returned. He stroked the splendid striped back of a great tiger tommy which filled his arm-chair. This cat was his special pet. He fastened the outer shed door with a bit of rope in order that it might not blow entirely open, and yet allow his feline friends to pass, should they choose. Then he went out.

The day was clear, with a sharp breath of frost. The fields gleamed with frost, offering to the eye a fine shimmer as of diamond-dust under the brilliant blue sky, overspread in places with a dapple of little white clouds.

"White frost and mackerel sky; going to be falling weather," Jim said, aloud, as he went out of the yard, crunching the crisp grass under heel.

Susan Adkins at a window saw his lips moving. His talking to himself made her nervous, although it did not render her distrustful of his sanity. It was fortunate that Susan had not told Jim that she disliked his habit. In that case he would have deprived himself of that slight solace; he would not have dreamed of opposing Susan's wishes. Jim had a great pity for the nervous whims, as he regarded them, of women—a pity so intense and tender that it verged on respect and veneration. He passed his nieces' house on the way to the minister's, and both were looking out of windows and saw his lips moving.

"There he goes, talking to himself like a crazy loon," said Amanda.

Alma nodded.

Jim went on, blissfully unconscious. He talked in a quiet monotone; only now and then his voice rose; only now and then there were accompanying gestures. Jim had a straight mile down the broad village street to walk before he reached the church and the parsonage beside it.

Jim and the minister had been friends since boyhood. They were graduates and classmates of the same college. Jim had had unusual educational advantages for a man coming from a simple family. The front door of the parsonage flew open when Jim entered the gate, and the minister stood there smiling. He was a tall, thin man with a wide mouth, which either smiled charmingly or was set with severity. He was as brown and dry as a wayside weed which winter had subdued as to bloom but could not entirely prostrate with all its icy storms and compelling blasts. Jim, advancing eagerly toward the warm welcome in the door, was a small man, and bent at that, but he had a handsome old face, with the rose of youth on the cheeks and the light of youth in the blue eyes, and the quick changes of youth, before emotions, about the mouth.

"Hullo, Jim!" cried Dr. Edward Hayward. Hayward, for a doctor of divinity, was considered somewhat lacking in dignity at times; still, he was Dr. Hayward, and the failing was condoned. Moreover, he was a Hayward, and the Haywards had been, from the memory of the oldest inhabitant, the great people of the village. Dr. Hayward's house was presided over by his widowed cousin, a lady of enough dignity to make up for any lack of it in the minister. There were three servants, besides the old butler who had been Hayward's attendant when he had been a young man in college. Village people were proud of their minister, with his degree and what they considered an imposing household retinue.

Hayward led, and Jim followed, to the least pre-

tentious room in the house—not the study proper,
which was lofty, book-lined, and leather-furnished,
curtained with broad sweeps of crimson damask, but
a little shabby place back of it, accessible by a narrow door. The little room was lined with shelves;
they held few books, but a collection of queer and
dusty things—strange weapons, minerals, odds and
ends—which the minister loved and with which his
lady cousin never interfered.

"Louisa," Hayward had told his cousin when she
entered upon her post, "do as you like with the
whole house, but let my little study alone. Let it
look as if it had been stirred up with a garden-rake
—that little room is my territory, and no disgrace
to you, my dear, if the dust rises in clouds at every
step."

Jim was as fond of the little room as his friend.
He entered, and sighed a great sigh of satisfaction
as he sank into the shabby, dusty hollow of a large
chair before the hearth fire. Immediately a black
cat leaped into his lap, gazed at him with green-
jewel eyes, worked her paws, purred, settled into a
coil, and slept. Jim lit his pipe and threw the match
blissfully on the floor. Dr. Hayward set an electric
coffee-urn at its work, for the little room was a
curious mixture of the comfortable old and the
comfortable modern.

"Sam shall serve our luncheon in here," he said,
with a staid glee.

Jim nodded happily.

"Louisa will not mind," said Hayward. "She is
precise, but she has a fine regard for the rights of the

individual, which is most commendable." He seated himself in a companion chair to Jim's, lit his own pipe, and threw the match on the floor. Occasionally, when the minister was out, Sam, without orders so to do, cleared the floor of matches.

Hayward smoked and regarded his friend, who looked troubled despite his comfort. "What is it, Jim?" asked the minister at last.

"I don't know how to do what is right for me to do," replied the little man, and his face, turned toward his friend, had the puzzled earnestness of a child.

Hayward laughed. It was easily seen that his was the keener mind. In natural endowments there had never been equality, although there was great similarity of tastes. Jim, despite his education, often lapsed into the homely vernacular of which he heard so much. An involuntarily imitative man in externals was Jim, but essentially an original. Jim proceeded.

"You know, Edward, I have never been one to complain," he said, with an almost boyish note of apology.

"Never complained half enough; that's the trouble," returned the other.

"Well, I overheard something Mis' Adkins said to Mis' Amos Trimmer the other afternoon. Mis' Trimmer was calling on Mis' Adkins. I couldn't help overhearing unless I went outdoors, and it was snowing and I had a cold. I wasn't listening."

"Had a right to listen if you wanted to," declared Hayward, irascibly.

"Well, I couldn't help it unless I went outdoors. Mis' Adkins she was in the kitchen making light-bread for supper, and Mis' Trimmer had sat right down there with her. Mis' Adkins's kitchen is as clean as a parlor, anyway. Mis' Adkins said to Mis' Trimmer, speaking of me—because Mis' Trimmer had just asked where I was and Mis' Adkins had said I was out in the woodshed sitting with the cats and smoking—Mis' Adkins said, 'He's just a door-mat, that's what he is.' Then Mis' Trimmer says, 'The way he lets folks ride over him beats me.' Then Mis' Adkins says again: 'He's nothing but a door-mat. He lets everybody that wants to just trample on him and grind their dust into him, and he acts real pleased and grateful.'"

Hayward's face flushed. "Did Mrs. Adkins mention that she was one of the people who used you for a door-mat?" he demanded.

Jim threw back his head and laughed like a child, with the sweetest sense of unresentful humor. "Lord bless my soul, Edward," replied Jim, "I don't believe she ever thought of that."

"And at that very minute you, with a hard cold, were sitting out in that draughty shed smoking because she wouldn't allow you to smoke in your own house!"

"I don't mind that, Edward," said Jim, and laughed again.

"Could you see to read your paper out there, with only that little shed window? And don't you like to read your paper while you smoke?"

"Oh yes," admitted Jim; "but my! I don't mind

195

little things like that! Mis' Adkins is only a poor widow woman, and keeping my house nice and not having it smell of tobacco is all she's got. They can talk about women's rights—I feel as if they ought to have them fast enough, if they want them, poor things; a woman has a hard row to hoe, and will have, if she gets all the rights in creation. But I guess the rights they'd find it hardest to give up would be the rights to have men look after them just a little more than they look after other men, just because they are women. When I think of Annie Berry—the girl I was going to marry, you know, if she hadn't died—I feel as if I couldn't do enough for another woman. Lord! I'm glad to sit out in the woodshed and smoke. Mis' Adkins is pretty good-natured to stand all the cats."

Then the coffee boiled, and Hayward poured out some for Jim and himself. He had a little silver service at hand, and willow-ware cups and saucers. Presently Sam appeared, and Hayward gave orders concerning luncheon.

"Tell Miss Louisa we are to have it served here," said he, "and mind, Sam, the chops are to be thick and cooked the way we like them; and don't forget the East India chutney, Sam."

"It does seem rather a pity that you cannot have chutney at home with your chops, when you are so fond of it," remarked Hayward when Sam had gone.

"Mis' Adkins says it will give me liver trouble, and she isn't strong enough to nurse."

"So you have to eat her ketchup?"

"Well, she doesn't put seasoning in it," admitted
196

Jim. "But Mis' Adkins doesn't like seasoning her-self, and I don't mind."

"And I know the chops are never cut thick, the way we like them."

"Mis' Adkins likes her meat well done, and she can't get such thick chops well done. I suppose our chops are rather thin, but I don't mind."

"Beefsteak and chops, both cut thin, and fried up like sole-leather. I know!" said Dr. Hayward, and he stamped his foot with unregenerate force.

"I don't mind a bit, Edward."

"You ought to mind, when it is your own house, and you buy the food and pay your housekeeper. It is an outrage!"

"I don't mind, really, Edward."

Dr. Hayward regarded Jim with a curious ex-pression compounded of love, anger, and contempt. "Any more talk of legal proceedings?" he asked, brusquely.

Jim flushed. "Tom ought not to tell of that."

"Yes, he ought; he ought to tell it all over town. He doesn't, but he ought. It is an outrage! Here you have been all these years supporting your nieces, and they are working away like field-mice, burrowing under your generosity, trying to get a chance to take action and appropriate your property and have you put under a guardian."

"I don't mind a bit," said Jim; "but—"

The other man looked inquiringly at him, and, seeing a pitiful working of his friend's face, he jumped up and got a little jar from a shelf. "We will drop the whole thing until we have had our chops and chutney," said he. "You are right; it is not worth minding. Here is a new brand of tobacco I want you to try. I don't half like it, myself, but you may."

Jim, with a pleased smile, reached out for the tobacco, and the two men smoked until Sam brought the luncheon. It was well cooked and well served on an antique table. Jim was thoroughly happy. It was not until the luncheon was over and another pipe smoked that the troubled, perplexed expression returned to his face.

"Now," said Hayward, "out with it!"

"It is only the old affair about Alma and Amanda, but now it has taken on a sort of new aspect."

"What do you mean by a new aspect?"

"It seems," said Jim, slowly, "as if they were making it so I couldn't do for them."

Hayward stamped his foot. "That does sound new," he said, dryly. "I never thought Alma Beecher or Amanda Bennet ever objected to have you do for them."

"Well," said Jim, "perhaps they don't now, but they want me to do it in their own way. They don't want to feel as if I was giving and they taking; they want it to seem the other way round. You see, if I were to deed over my property to them, and then they allowance me, they would feel as if they were doing the giving."

"Jim, you wouldn't be such a fool as that?"

"No, I wouldn't," replied Jim, simply. "They wouldn't know how to take care of it, and Mis' Adkins would be left to shift for herself. Joe Beecher is real good-hearted, but he always lost every dollar he touched. No, there wouldn't be any sense in that. I don't mean to give in, but I do feel pretty well worked up over it."

"What have they said to you?"

Jim hesitated.

"Out with it, now. One thing you may be sure of: nothing that you can tell me will alter my opinion of your two nieces for the worse. As for poor Joe Beecher, there is no opinion, one way or the other. What did they say?"

Jim regarded his friend with a curiously sweet, far-off expression. "Edward," he said, "sometimes I believe that the greatest thing a man's friends can do for him is to drive him into a corner with God; to be so unjust to him that they make him understand that God is all that mortal man is meant to have, and that is why he finds out that most people, especially the ones he does for, don't care for him."

Hayward looked solemnly and tenderly at the other's almost rapt face. "You are right, I suppose, old man," said he; "but what did they do?"

"They called me in there about a week ago and gave me an awful talking to."

"About what?"

Jim looked at his friend with dignity. "They were two women talking, and they went into little matters not worth repeating," said he. "All is— they seemed to blame me for everything I had ever done for them, and for everything I had ever done, anyway. They seemed to blame me for being born

and living, and, most of all, for doing anything for
them."

"It is an outrage!" declared Hayward. "Can't
you see it?"

"I can't seem to see anything plain about it,"
returned Jim, in a bewildered way. "I always supposed a man had to do something bad to be given
a talking to; but it isn't so much that, and I don't
bear any malice against them. They are only two
women, and they are nervous. What worries me is,
they do need things, and they can't get on and be
comfortable unless I do for them; but if they are
going to feel that way about it, it seems to cut me
off from doing, and that does worry me, Edward."

The other man stamped. "Jim Bennet," he said,
"they have talked, and now I am going to."

"You, Edward?"

"Yes, I am. It is entirely true what those two
women, Susan Adkins and Mrs. Trimmer, said about
you. You *are* a door-mat, and you ought to be
ashamed of yourself for it. A man should be a man,
and not a door-mat. It is the worst thing in the
world for people to walk over him and trample him.
It does them much more harm than it does him. In
the end the trampler is much worse off than the
trampled upon. Jim Bennet, your being a door-
mat may cost other people their souls' salvation.
You are selfish in the grain to be a door-mat."

Jim turned pale. His child-like face looked suddenly old with his mental effort to grasp the other's
meaning. In fact, he was a child—one of the little
ones of the world—although he had lived the span

of a man's life. Now one of the hardest problems of the elders of the world was presented to him. "You mean—" he said, faintly.

"I mean, Jim, that for the sake of other people, if not for your own sake, you ought to stop being a door-mat and be a man in this world of men."

"What do you want me to do?"

"I want you to go straight to those nieces of yours and tell them the truth. You know what your wrongs are as well as I do. You know what those two women are as well as I do. They keep the letter of the Ten Commandments—that is right. They attend my church—that is right. They scour the outside of the platter until it is bright enough to blind those people who don't understand them; but inwardly they are petty, ravening wolves of greed and ingratitude. Go and tell them; they don't know themselves. Show them what they are. It is your Christian duty."

"You don't mean for me to stop doing for them?"

"I certainly do mean just that — for a while, anyway."

"They can't possibly get along, Edward; they will suffer."

"They have a little money, haven't they?"

"Only a little in savings-bank. The interest pays their taxes."

"And you gave them that?"

Jim colored.

"Very well, their taxes are paid for this year; let them use that money. They will not suffer, ex-cept in their feelings, and that is where they ought to suffer. Man, you would spoil all the work of the Lord by your selfish tenderness toward sinners!"

"They aren't sinners."

"Yes, they are—spiritual sinners, the worst kind in the world. Now—"

"You don't mean for me to go now?"

"Yes, I do—now. If you don't go now you never will. Then, afterward, I want you to go home and sit in your best parlor and smoke, and have all your cats in there, too."

Jim gasped. "But, Edward! Mis' Adkins—"

"I don't care about Mrs. Adkins. She isn't as bad as the rest, but she needs her little lesson, too."

"Edward, the way that poor woman works to keep the house nice—and she don't like the smell of tobacco smoke."

"Never mind whether she likes it or not. You smoke."

"And she don't like cats."

"Never mind. Now you go."

Jim stood up. There was a curious change in his rosy, child-like face. There was a species of quickening. He looked at once older and more alert. His friend's words had charged him as with electricity. When he went down the street he looked taller.

Amanda Bennet and Alma Beecher, sitting sewing at their street windows, made this mistake.

"That isn't Uncle Jim," said Amanda. "That man is a head taller, but he looks a little like him."

"It can't be Uncle Jim," agreed Alma. Then both started.

"It is Uncle Jim, and he is coming here," said Amanda.

Jim entered. Nobody except himself, his nieces, and Joe Beecher ever knew exactly what happened, what was the aspect of the door-mat erected to human life, of the worm turned to menace. It must have savored of horror, as do all meek and down-trodden things when they gain, driven to bay, the strength to do battle. It must have savored of the god-like, when the man who had borne with patience, dignity, and sorrow for them the stings of lesser things because they were lesser things, at last arose and revealed himself superior, with a great height of the spirit, with the power to crush.

When Jim stopped talking and went home, two pale, shocked faces of women gazed after him from the windows. Joe Beecher was sobbing like a child. Finally his wife turned her frightened face upon him, glad to have still some one to intimidate.

"For goodness' sake, Joe Beecher, stop crying like a baby," said she, but she spoke in a queer whisper, for her lips were stiff.

Joe stood up and made for the door.

"Where are you going?" asked his wife.

"Going to get a job somewhere," replied Joe, and went. Soon the women saw him driving a neighbor's cart up the street.

"He's going to cart gravel for John Leach's new sidewalk!" gasped Alma.

"Why don't you stop him?" cried her sister. "You can't have your husband driving a tip-cart for John Leach. Stop him, Alma!"

"I can't stop him," moaned Alma. "I don't feel as if I could stop anything."

Her sister gazed at her, and the same expression was on both faces, making them more than sisters of the flesh. Both saw before them a stern boundary wall against which they might press in vain for the rest of their lives, and both saw the same sins of their hearts.

Meantime Jim Bennet was seated in his best parlor and Susan Adkins was whispering to Mrs. Trimmer out in the kitchen.

"I don't know whether he's gone stark, staring mad or not," whispered Susan, "but he's in the parlor smoking his worst old pipe, and that big tiger tommy is sitting in his lap, and he's let in all the other cats, and they're nosing round, and I don't dare drive 'em out. I took up the broom, then I put it away again. I never knew Mr. Bennet to act so. I can't think what's got into him."

"Did he say anything?"

"No, he didn't say much of anything, but he said it in a way that made my flesh fairly creep. Says he, 'As long as this is my house and my furniture and my cats, Mis' Adkins, I think I'll sit down in the parlor, where I can see to read my paper and smoke at the same time.' Then he holds the kitchen door open, and he calls, 'Kitty, kitty, kitty!' and that great tiger tommy comes in with his tail up, rubbing round his legs, and all the other cats followed after. I shut the door before these last ones got into the parlor." Susan Adkins regarded malevolently the three tortoise-shell cats of three generations and vari-

204

ous stages of growth, one Maltese settled in a purring round of comfort with four kittens, and one perfectly black cat, which sat glaring at her with beryl-colored eyes.

"That black cat looks evil," said Mrs. Trimmer.

"Yes, he does. I don't know why I didn't drown him when he was a kitten."

"Why didn't you drown all those Malty kittens?"

"The old cat hid them away until they were too big. Then he wouldn't let me. What do you suppose has come to him? Just smell that awful pipe!"

"Men do take queer streaks every now and then," said Mrs. Trimmer. "My husband used to, and he was as good as they make 'em, poor man. He would eat sugar on his beefsteak, for one thing. The first time I saw him do it I was scared. I thought he was plum crazy, but afterward I found out it was just because he was a man, and his ma hadn't wanted him to eat sugar when he was a boy. Mr. Bennet will get over it."

"He don't act as if he would."

"Oh yes, he will. Jim Bennet never stuck to anything but being Jim Bennet for very long in his life, and this ain't being Jim Bennet."

"He is a very good man," said Susan with a somewhat apologetic tone.

"He's too good."

"He's too good to cats."

"Seems to me he's too good to 'most everybody. Think what he has done for Amanda and Alma, and how they act!"

"Yes, they are ungrateful and real mean to him;
205

and I feel sometimes as if I would like to tell them just what I think of them," said Susan Adkins. "Poor man, there he is, studying all the time what he can do for people, and he don't get very much himself."

Mrs. Trimmer arose to take leave. She had a long, sallow face, capable of a sarcastic smile. "Then," said she, "if I were you I wouldn't begrudge him a chair in the parlor and a chance to read and smoke and hold a pussy-cat."

"Who said I was begrudging it? I can air out the parlor when he's got over the notion."

"Well, he will, so you needn't worry," said Mrs. Trimmer. As she went down the street she could see Jim's profile beside the parlor window, and she smiled her sarcastic smile, which was not altogether unpleasant. "He's stopped smoking, and he ain't reading," she told herself. "It won't be very long before he's Jim Bennet again."

But it was longer than she anticipated, for Jim's will was propped by Edward Hayward's. Edward kept Jim to his standpoint for weeks, until a few days before Christmas. Then came self-assertion, that self-assertion of negation which was all that Jim possessed in such a crisis. He called upon Dr. Hayward; the two were together in the little study for nearly an hour, and talk ran high, then Jim prevailed.

"It's no use, Edward," he said; "a man can't be made over when he's cut and dried in one fashion, the way I am. Maybe I'm doing wrong, but to me it looks like doing right, and there's something in

the Bible about every man having his own right
and wrong. If what you say is true, and I am hin-
dering the Lord Almighty in His work, then it is
for Him to stop me. He can do it. But meantime
I've got to go on doing the way I always have. Joe
has been trying to drive that tip-cart, and the horse
ran away with him twice. Then he let the cart fall
on his foot and mash one of his toes, and he can
hardly get round, and Amanda and Alma don't dare
touch that money in the bank for fear of not having
enough to pay the taxes next year in case I don't
help them. They only had a little money on hand
when I gave them that talking to, and Christmas
is 'most here, and they haven't got things they really
need. Amanda's coat that she wore to meeting last
Sunday didn't look very warm to me, and poor
Alma had her furs chewed up by the Leach dog, and
she's going without any. They need lots of things.
And poor Mis' Adkins is 'most sick with tobacco
smoke. I can see it, though she doesn't say anything,
and the nice parlor curtains are full of it, and cat
hairs are all over things. I can't hold out any longer,
Edward. Maybe I am a door-mat; and if I am, and
it is wicked, may the Lord forgive me, for I've got
to keep right on being a door-mat."

Hayward sighed and lighted his pipe. However,
he had given up and connived with Jim.

On Christmas eve the two men were in hiding
behind a clump of cedars in the front yard of Jim's
nieces' house. They watched the expressman deliver
a great load of boxes and packages. Jim drew a
breath of joyous relief.

"They are taking them in," he whispered—"they are taking them in, Edward!"

Hayward looked down at the dim face of the man beside him, and something akin to fear entered his heart. He saw the face of a lifelong friend, but he saw something in it which he had never recognized before. He saw the face of one of the children of heaven, giving only for the sake of the need of others, and glorifying the gifts with the love and pity of an angel.

"I was afraid they wouldn't take them!" whispered Jim, and his watching face was beautiful, although it was only the face of a little, old man of a little village, with no great gift of intellect. There was a full moon riding high; the ground was covered with a glistening snow-level, over which wavered wonderful shadows, as of wings. One great star prevailed despite the silver might of the moon. To Hayward Jim's face seemed to prevail, as that star, among all the faces of humanity.

Jim crept noiselessly toward a window, Hayward at his heels. The two could see the lighted interior plainly.

"See poor Alma trying on her furs," whispered Jim, in a rapture. "See Amanda with her coat. They have found the money. See Joe heft the turkey." Suddenly he caught Hayward's arm, and the two crept away. Out on the road, Jim fairly sobbed with pure delight. "Oh, Edward," he said, "I am so thankful they took the things! I was so afraid they wouldn't, and they needed them! Oh, Edward, I am so thankful!" Edward pressed his friend's arm.

CORONATION

When they reached Jim's house a great tiger-cat leaped to Jim's shoulder with the silence and swiftness of a shadow. "He's always watching for me," said Jim, proudly. "Pussy! Pussy!" The cat began to purr loudly, and rubbed his splendid head against the man's cheek.

"I suppose," said Hayward, with something of awe in his tone, "that you won't smoke in the parlor to-night?"

"Edward, I really can't. Poor woman, she's got it all aired and beautifully cleaned, and she's so happy over it. There's a good fire in the shed, and I will sit there with the pussy-cats until I go to bed. Oh, Edward, I am so thankful that they took the things!"

"Good night, Jim."

"Good night. You don't blame me, Edward?"

"Who am I to blame you, Jim? Good night."

Hayward watched the little man pass along the path to the shed door. Jim's back was slightly bent, but to his friend it seemed bent beneath a holy burden of love and pity for all humanity, and the inheritance of the meek seemed to crown that drooping old head. The door-mat, again spread freely for the trampling feet of all who got comfort thereby, became a blessed thing. The humble creature, despised and held in contempt like One greater than he, giving for the sake of the needs of others, went along the narrow foot-path through the snow. The minister took off his hat and stood watching until the door was opened and closed and the little window gleamed with golden light.

14

THE AMETHYST COMB

THE AMETHYST COMB

MISS JANE CAREW was at the railroad station waiting for the New York train. She was about to visit her friend, Mrs. Viola Longstreet. With Miss Carew was her maid, Margaret, a middle-aged New England woman, attired in the stiffest and most correct of maid-uniforms. She carried an old, large sole-leather bag, and also a rather large sole-leather jewel-case. The jewel-case, carried openly, was rather an unusual sight at a New England railroad station, but few knew what it was. They concluded it to be Margaret's special hand-bag. Margaret was a very tall, thin woman, unbending as to carriage and expression. The one thing out of absolute plumb about Margaret was her little black bonnet. That was askew. Time had bereft the woman of so much hair that she could fasten no head-gear with security, especially when the wind blew, and that morning there was a stiff gale. Margaret's bonnet was cocked over one eye. Miss Carew noticed it.

"Margaret, your bonnet is crooked," she said.

Margaret straightened her bonnet, but immediately the bonnet veered again to the side, weighted by a stiff jet aigrette. Miss Carew observed the careen of the bonnet, realized that it was inevitable, and did not mention it again. Inwardly she resolved upon the removal of the jet aigrette later on. Miss Carew was slightly older than Margaret, and dressed in a style somewhat beyond her age. Jane Carew had been alert upon the situation of departing youth. She had eschewed gay colors and extreme cuts, and had her bonnets made to order, because there were no longer anything but hats in the millinery shop. The milliner in Wheaton, where Miss Carew lived, had objected, for Jane Carew inspired reverence.

"A bonnet is too old for you, Miss Carew," she said. "Women much older than you wear hats."

"I trust that I know what is becoming to a woman of my years, thank you, Miss Waters," Jane had replied, and the milliner had meekly taken her order.

After Miss Carew had left, the milliner told her girls that she had never seen a woman so perfectly crazy to look her age as Miss Carew. "And she a pretty woman, too," said the milliner; "as straight as an arrer, and slim, and with all that hair, scarcely turned at all."

Miss Carew, with all her haste to assume years, remained a pretty woman, softly slim, with an abundance of dark hair, showing little gray. Sometimes Jane reflected, uneasily, that it ought at her time of life to be entirely gray. She hoped nobody would suspect her of dyeing it. She wore it parted in the middle, folded back smoothly, and braided in a compact mass on the top of her head. The style of her clothes was slightly behind the fashion, just enough to suggest conservatism and age. She carried a little silver-bound bag in one nicely gloved hand; with the other she held daintily out of the dust of the platform her dress-skirt. A glimpse of a silk frilled petticoat, of slender feet, and ankles delicately slim, was visible before the onslaught of the wind. Jane Carew made no futile effort to keep her skirts down before the wind-gusts. She was so much of the gentlewoman that she could be gravely oblivious to the exposure of her ankles. She looked as if she had never heard of ankles when her black silk skirts lashed about them. She rose superbly above the situation. For some abstruse reason Margaret's skirts were not affected by the wind. They might have been weighted with buckram, although it was no longer in general use. She stood, except for her veering bonnet, as stiffly immovable as a wooden doll.

Miss Carew seldom left Wheaton. This visit to New York was an innovation. Quite a crowd gathered about Jane's sole-leather trunk when it was dumped on the platform by the local expressman. "Miss Carew is going to New York," one said to another, with much the same tone as if he had said, "The great elm on the common is going to move into Dr. Jones's front yard."

When the train arrived, Miss Carew, followed by Margaret, stepped aboard with a majestic disregard of ankles. She sat beside a window, and Margaret placed the bag on the floor and held the jewel-case in her lap. The case contained the Carew jewels. They were not especially valuable, although they were rather numerous. There were cameos in brooches and heavy gold bracelets; corals which Miss Carew had not worn since her young girlhood. There were a set of garnets, some badly cut diamonds in ear-rings and rings, some seed-pearl ornaments, and a really beautiful set of amethysts. There were a necklace, two brooches—a bar and a circle—ear-rings, a ring, and a comb. Each piece was charming, set in filigree gold with seed-pearls, but perhaps of them all the comb was the best. It was a very large comb. There was one great amethyst in the center of the top; on either side was an intricate pattern of plums in small amethysts, and seed-pearl grapes, with leaves and stems of gold. Margaret in charge of the jewel-case was imposing. When they arrived in New York she confronted every-body whom she met with a stony stare, which was almost accusative and convictive of guilt, in spite of entire innocence on the part of the person stared at. It was inconceivable that any mortal would have dared lay violent hands upon that jewel-case under that stare. It would have seemed to partake of the nature of grand larceny from Providence.

When the two reached the up-town residence of Viola Longstreet, Viola gave a little scream at the sight of the case.

"My dear Jane Carew, here you are with Margaret carrying that jewel-case out in plain sight. How dare you do such a thing? I really wonder you have not been held up a dozen times."

Miss Carew smiled her gentle but almost stern smile—the Carew smile, which consisted in a widening and slightly upward curving of tightly closed lips.

"I do not think," said she, "that anybody would be apt to interfere with Margaret."

Viola Longstreet laughed, the ringing peal of a child, although she was as old as Miss Carew. "I think you are right, Jane," said she. "I don't believe a crook in New York would dare face that maid of yours. He would as soon encounter Plymouth Rock. I am glad you have brought your delightful old jewels, although you never wear anything except those lovely old pearl sprays and dull diamonds."

"Now," stated Jane, with a little toss of pride, "I have Aunt Felicia's amethysts."

"Oh, sure enough! I remember you did write me last summer that she had died and you had the amethysts at last. She must have been very old."

"Ninety-one."

"She might have given you the amethysts before. You, of course, will wear them; and I—am going to borrow the corals!"

Jane Carew gasped.

"You do not object, do you, dear? I have a new dinner-gown which clamors for corals, and my bank-account is strained, and I could buy none equal to those of yours, anyway."

"Oh, I do not object," said Jane Carew; still she looked aghast.

Viola Longstreet shrieked with laughter. "Oh, I know. You think the corals too young for me. You have not worn them since you left off dotted muslin. My dear, you insisted upon growing old —I insisted upon remaining young. I had two new dotted muslins last summer. As for corals, I would wear them in the face of an opposing army! Do not judge me by yourself, dear. You laid hold of Age and held him, although you had your complexion and your shape and hair. As for me, I had my complexion and kept it. I also had my hair and kept it. My shape has been a struggle, but it was worth while. I, my dear, have held Youth so tight that he has almost choked to death, but held him I have. You cannot deny it. Look at me, Jane Carew, and tell me if, judging by my looks, you can reasonably state that I have no longer the right to wear corals."

Jane Carew looked. She smiled the Carew smile. "You *do* look very young, Viola," said Jane, "but you are not."

"Jane Carew," said Viola, "I am young. May I wear your corals at my dinner to-morrow night?"

"Why, of course, if you think—"

"If I think them suitable. My dear, if there were on this earth ornaments more suitable to extreme youth than corals, I would borrow them if you owned them, but, failing that, the corals will answer. Wait until you see me in that taupe dinner-gown and the corals!"

Jane waited. She visited with Viola, whom she loved, although they had little in common, partly because of leading widely different lives, partly because of constitutional variations. She was dressed for dinner fully an hour before it was necessary, and she sat in the library reading when Viola swept in.

THE AMETHYST COMB

Viola was really entrancing. It was a pity that Jane Carew had such an unswerving eye for the essential truth that it could not be appeased by actual effect. Viola had doubtless, as she had said, struggled to keep her slim shape, but she had kept it, and, what was more, kept it without evidence of struggle. If she was in the least hampered by tight lacing and length of undergarment, she gave no evidence of it as she curled herself up in a big chair and (Jane wondered how she could bring herself to do it) crossed her legs, revealing one delicate foot and ankle, silk-stockinged with taupe, and shod with a coral satin slipper with a silver heel and a great silver buckle. On Viola's fair round neck the Carew corals lay bloomingly; her beautiful arms were clasped with them; a great coral brooch with wonderful carving confined a graceful fold of the taupe over one hip, a coral comb surmounted the shining waves of Viola's hair. Viola was an ash-blonde, her complexion was as roses, and the corals were ideal for her. As Jane regarded her friend's beauty, however, the fact that Viola was not young, that she was as old as herself, hid it and overshadowed it.

"Well, Jane, don't you think I look well in the corals, after all?" asked Viola, and there was something pitiful in her voice.

When a man or a woman holds fast to youth, even if successfully, there is something of the pitiful and the tragic involved. It is the everlasting struggle of the soul to retain the joy of earth, whose fleeting distinguishes it from heaven, and whose retention is not accomplished without an inner knowledge of its futility.

"I suppose you do, Viola," replied Jane Carew, with the inflexibility of fate, "but I really think that only very young girls ought to wear corals."

Viola laughed, but the laugh had a minor cadence. "But I *am* a young girl, Jane," she said. "I *must* be a young girl. I never had any girlhood when I should have had. You know that."

Viola had married, when very young, a man old enough to be her father, and her wedded life had been a sad affair, to which, however, she seldom alluded. Viola had much pride with regard to the inevitable past.

"Yes," agreed Jane. Then she added, feeling that more might be expected, "Of course I suppose that marrying so very young does make a difference."

"Yes," said Viola, "it does. In fact, it makes of one's girlhood an anti-climax, of which many dispute the wisdom, as you do. But have it I will. Jane, your amethysts are beautiful."

Jane regarded the clear purple gleam of a stone on her arm. "Yes," she agreed, "Aunt Felicia's amethysts have always been considered very beautiful."

"And such a full set," said Viola.

"Yes," said Jane. She colored a little, but Viola did not know why. At the last moment Jane had decided not to wear the amethyst comb, because it seemed to her altogether too decorative for a woman of her age, and she was afraid to mention it to Viola. She was sure that Viola would laugh at her and insist upon her wearing it.

"The ear-rings are lovely," said Viola. "My dear, I don't see how you ever consented to have your ears pierced."

"I was very young, and my mother wished me to," replied Jane, blushing.

The door-bell rang. Viola had been covertly listening for it all the time. Soon a very beautiful young man came with a curious dancing step into the room. Harold Lind always gave the effect of dancing when he walked. He always, moreover, gave the effect of extreme youth and of the utmost joy and mirth in life itself. He regarded everything and everybody with a smile as of humorous appreciation, and yet the appreciation was so good-natured that it offended nobody.

"Look at me—I am absurd and happy; look at yourself, also absurd and happy; look at everybody else likewise; look at life—a jest so delicious that it is quite worth one's while dying to be made acquainted with it." That is what Harold Lind seemed to say. Viola Longstreet became even more youthful under his gaze; even Jane Carew regretted that she had not worn her amethyst comb and began to doubt its unsuitability. Viola very soon called the young man's attention to Jane's amethysts, and Jane always wondered why she did not then mention the comb. She removed a brooch and a bracelet for him to inspect.

"They are really wonderful," he declared. "I have never seen greater depth of color in amethysts."

"Mr. Lind is an authority on jewels," declared Viola. The young man shot a curious glance at her, which Jane remembered long afterward. It was one of those glances which are as keystones to situations.

Harold looked at the purple stones with the expression of a child with a toy. There was much of the child in the young man's whole appearance, but of a mischievous and beautiful child, of whom his mother might observe, with adoration and ill-concealed boastfulness, "I can never tell what that child will do next!"

Harold returned the bracelet and brooch to Jane, and smiled at her as if amethysts were a lovely purple joke between her and himself, uniting them by a peculiar bond of fine understanding. "Exquisite, Miss Carew," he said. Then he looked at Viola. "Those corals suit you wonderfully, Mrs. Longstreet," he observed, "but amethysts would also suit you."

"Not with this gown," replied Viola, rather pitifully. There was something in the young man's gaze and tone which she did not understand, but which she vaguely quivered before.

Harold certainly thought the corals were too young for Viola. Jane understood, and felt an unworthy triumph. Harold, who was young enough in actual years to be Viola's son, and was younger still by reason of his disposition, was amused by the sight of her in corals, although he did not intend to betray his amusement. He considered Viola in corals as too rude a jest to share with her. Had poor Viola once grasped Harold Lind's estimation of her she would have as soon gazed upon herself in her coffin. Harold's comprehension of the essentials was beyond Jane Carew's. It was fairly ghastly, partaking of the nature of X-rays, but it never disturbed Harold Lind. He went along his dance-track undisturbed, his blue eyes never losing their high lights of glee, his lips never losing their inscrutable smile at some happy understanding between life and himself. Harold had fair hair, which was very smooth and glossy. His skin was like a girl's. He was so beautiful that he showed cleverness in an affectation of carelessness in dress. He did not like to wear evening clothes, because they had necessarily to be immaculate. That evening Jane regarded him with an inward criticism that he was too handsome for a man. She told Viola so when the dinner was over and he and the other guests had gone.

"He is very handsome," she said, "but I never like to see a man quite so handsome."

"You will change your mind when you see him in tweeds," returned Viola. "He loathes evening clothes."

Jane regarded her anxiously. There was something in Viola's tone which disturbed and shocked her. It was inconceivable that Viola should be in love with that youth, and yet— "He looks very young," said Jane in a prim voice.

"He *is* young," admitted Viola; "still, not quite so young as he looks. Sometimes I tell him he will look like a boy if he lives to be eighty."

"Well, he must be very young," persisted Jane.

"Yes," said Viola, but she did not say how young. Viola herself, now that the excitement was over, did not look so young as at the beginning of the evening. She removed the corals, and Jane considered that she looked much better without them.

"Thank you for your corals, dear," said Viola. "Where is Margaret?"

Margaret answered for herself by a tap on the door. She and Viola's maid, Louisa, had been sitting on an upper landing, out of sight, watching the guests down-stairs. Margaret took the corals and placed them in their nest in the jewel-case, also the amethysts, after Viola had gone. The jewel-case was a curious old affair with many compartments. The amethysts required two. The comb was so large that it had one for itself. That was the reason why Margaret did not discover that evening that it was gone. Nobody discovered it for three days, when Viola had a little card-party. There was a whist-table for Jane, who had never given up the reserved and stately game. There were six tables in Viola's pretty living-room, with a little conservatory at one end and a leaping hearth fire at the other. Jane's partner was a stout old gentleman whose wife was shrieking with merriment at an auction-bridge table. The other whist-players were a stupid, very small young man who was aimlessly willing to play anything, and an amiable young woman who believed in self-denial. Jane played conscientiously. She returned trump leads, and played second hand low, and third high, and it was not until the third rubber was over that she saw. It had been in full evidence from the first. Jane would have seen it before the guests arrived, but Viola had not put it in her hair until the last moment. Viola was wild with delight, yet shamefaced and a trifle uneasy. In a soft, white gown, with violets at her waist, she was playing with Harold Lind, and in her ash-blond hair was Jane Carew's amethyst comb. Jane gasped and paled. The amiable young woman who was her opponent stared at her. Finally she spoke in a low voice.

"Aren't you well, Miss Carew?" she asked.

The men, in their turn, stared. The stout one rose fussily. "Let me get a glass of water," he said. The stupid small man stood up and waved his hands with nervousness.

"Aren't you well?" asked the amiable young lady again.

Then Jane Carew recovered her poise. It was seldom that she lost it. "I am quite well, thank you, Miss Murdock," she replied. "I believe diamonds are trumps."

They all settled again to the play, but the young lady and the two men continued glancing at Miss Carew. She had recovered her dignity of manner, but not her color. Moreover, she had a bewildered expression. Resolutely she abstained from glancing again at her amethyst comb in Viola Longstreet's ash-blond hair, and gradually, by a course of subconscious reasoning as she carefully played her cards, she arrived at a conclusion which caused her color to return and the bewildered expression to disappear. When refreshments were served, the amiable young lady said, kindly:

"You look quite yourself, now, dear Miss Carew,

15   225

but at one time while we were playing I was really alarmed. You were very pale."

"I did not feel in the least ill," replied Jane Carew. She smiled her Carew smile at the young lady. Jane had settled it with herself that of course Viola had borrowed that amethyst comb, appealing to Margaret. Viola ought not to have done that; she should have asked her, Miss Carew; and Jane wondered, because Viola was very well bred; but of course that was what had happened. Jane had come down before Viola, leaving Margaret in her room, and Viola had asked her. Jane did not then remember that Viola had not even been told that there was an amethyst comb in existence. She remembered when Margaret, whose face was as pale and bewildered as her own, mentioned it, when she was brushing her hair.

"I saw it, first thing, Miss Jane," said Margaret. "Louisa and I were on the landing, and I looked down and saw your amethyst comb in Mrs. Longstreet's hair."

"She had asked you for it, because I had gone down-stairs?" asked Jane, feebly.

"No, Miss Jane. I had not seen her. I went out right after you did. Louisa had finished Mrs. Longstreet, and she and I went down to the mailbox to post a letter, and then we sat on the landing, and—I saw your comb."

"Have you," asked Jane, "looked in the jewel-case?"

"Yes, Miss Jane."

"And it is not there?"

226

THE AMETHYST COMB

"It is not there, Miss Jane." Margaret spoke with a sort of solemn intoning. She recognized what the situation implied, and she, who fitted squarely and entirely into her humble state, was aghast before a hitherto unimagined occurrence. She could not, even with the evidence of her senses against a lady and her mistress's old friend, believe in them. Had Jane told her firmly that she had not seen that comb in that ash-blond hair she might have been hypnotized into agreement. But Jane simply stared at her, and the Carew dignity was more shaken than she had ever seen it.

"Bring the jewel-case here, Margaret," ordered Jane in a gasp.

Margaret brought the jewel-case, and everything was taken out; all the compartments were opened, but the amethyst comb was not there. Jane could not sleep that night. At dawn she herself doubted the evidence of her senses. The jewel-case was thoroughly overlooked again, and still Jane was incredulous that she would ever see her comb in Viola's hair again. But that evening, although there were no guests except Harold Lind, who dined at the house, Viola appeared in a pink-tinted gown, with a knot of violets at her waist, and—she wore the amethyst comb. She said not one word concerning it; nobody did. Harold Lind was in wild spirits. The conviction grew upon Jane that the irresponsible, beautiful youth was covertly amusing himself at her, at Viola's, at everybody's expense. Perhaps he included himself. He talked incessantly, not in reality brilliantly, but with an effect of sparkling

227

effervescence which was fairly dazzling. Viola's servants restrained with difficulty their laughter at his sallies. Viola regarded Harold with ill-concealed tenderness and admiration. She herself looked even younger than usual, as if the innate youth in her leaped to meet this charming comrade.

Jane felt sickened by it all. She could not understand her friend. Not for one minute did she dream that there could be any serious outcome of the situation; that Viola would marry this mad youth, who, she knew, was making such covert fun at her expense; but she was bewildered and indignant. She wished that she had not come. That evening when she went to her room she directed Margaret to pack, as she intended to return home the next day. Margaret began folding gowns with alacrity. She was as conservative as her mistress and she severely disapproved of many things. However, the matter of the amethyst comb was uppermost in her mind. She was wild with curiosity. She hardly dared inquire, but finally she did.

"About the amethyst comb, ma'am?" she said, with a delicate cough.

"What about it, Margaret?" returned Jane, severely.

"I thought perhaps Mrs. Longstreet had told you how she happened to have it."

Poor Jane Carew had nobody in whom to confide. For once she spoke her mind to her maid. "She has not said one word. And, oh, Margaret, I don't know what to think of it."

Margaret pursed her lips.

THE AMETHYST COMB

"What do *you* think, Margaret?"

"I don't know, Miss Jane."

"I don't."

"I did not mention it to Louisa," said Margaret.

"Oh, I hope not!" cried Jane.

"But she did to me," said Margaret. "She asked had I seen Miss Viola's new comb, and then she laughed, and I thought from the way she acted that—" Margaret hesitated.

"That what?"

"That she meant Mr. Lind had given Miss Viola the comb."

Jane started violently. "Absolutely impossible!" she cried. "That, of course, is nonsense. There must be some explanation. Probably Mrs. Longstreet will explain before we go."

Mrs. Longstreet did not explain. She wondered and expostulated when Jane announced her firm determination to leave, but she seemed utterly at a loss for the reason. She did not mention the comb.

When Jane Carew took leave of her old friend she was entirely sure in her own mind that she would never visit her again—might never even see her again.

Jane was unutterably thankful to be back in her own peaceful home, over which no shadow of absurd mystery brooded; only a calm afternoon light of life, which disclosed gently but did not conceal or betray. Jane settled back into her pleasant life, and the days passed, and the weeks, and the months, and the years. She heard nothing whatever from or about Viola Longstreet for three years. Then, one day, Margaret returned from the city, and she had met Viola's old maid Louisa in a department store, and she had news. Jane wished for strength to refuse to listen, but she could not muster it. She listened while Margaret brushed her hair.

"Louisa has not been with Miss Viola for a long time," said Margaret. "She is living with somebody else. Miss Viola lost her money, and had to give up her house and her servants, and Louisa said she cried when she said good-by."

Jane made an effort. "What became of—" she began.

Margaret answered the unfinished sentence. She was excited by gossip as by a stimulant. Her thin cheeks burned, her eyes blazed. "Mr. Lind," said Margaret, "Louisa told me, had turned out to be real bad. He got into some money trouble, and then"—Margaret lowered her voice—"he was arrested for taking a lot of money which didn't belong to him. Louisa said he had been in some business where he handled a lot of other folks' money, and he cheated the men who were in the business with him, and he was tried, and Miss Viola, Louisa thinks, hid away somewhere so they wouldn't call her to testify, and then he had to go to prison; but—" Margaret hesitated.

"What is it?" asked Jane.

"Louisa thinks he died about a year and a half ago. She heard the lady where she lives now talking about it. The lady used to know Miss Viola, and she heard the lady say Mr. Lind had died in prison, that he couldn't stand the hard life, and that Miss

Viola had lost all her money through him, and then"
—Margaret hesitated again, and her mistress prodded
sharply—"Louisa said that she heard the lady say
that she had thought Miss Viola would marry him,
but she hadn't, and she had more sense than she
had thought."

"Mrs. Longstreet would never for one moment
have entertained the thought of marrying Mr. Lind;
he was young enough to be her grandson," said
Jane, severely.

"Yes, ma'am," said Margaret.

It so happened that Jane went to New York
that day week, and at a jewelry counter in one of
the shops she discovered the amethyst comb. There
were on sale a number of bits of antique jewelry,
the precious flotsam and jetsam of old and wealthy
families which had drifted, nobody knew before
what currents of adversity, into that harbor of
sale for all the world to see. Jane made no inquiries;
the saleswoman volunteered simply the information
that the comb was a real antique, and the stones
were real amethysts and pearls, and the setting was
solid gold, and the price was thirty dollars; and
Jane bought it. She carried her old amethyst comb
home, but she did not show it to anybody. She
replaced it in its old compartment in her jewel-
case and thought of it with wonder, with a hint of
joy at regaining it, and with much sadness. She
was still fond of Viola Longstreet. Jane did not
easily part with her loves. She did not know where
Viola was. Margaret had inquired of Louisa, who
did not know. Poor Viola had probably drifted

into some obscure harbor of life wherein she was hiding until life was over.

And then Jane met Viola one spring day on Fifth Avenue.

"It is a very long time since I have seen you," said Jane with a reproachful accent, but her eyes were tenderly inquiring.

"Yes," agreed Viola. Then she added, "I have seen nobody. Do you know what a change has come in my life?" she asked.

"Yes, dear," replied Jane, gently. "My Margaret met Louisa once and she told her."

"Oh yes—Louisa," said Viola. "I had to discharge her. My money is about gone. I have only just enough to keep the wolf from entering the door of a hall bedroom in a respectable boarding-house. However, I often hear him howl, but I do not mind at all. In fact, the howling has become company for me. I rather like it. It is queer what things one can learn to like. There are a few left yet, like the awful heat in summer, and the food, which I do not fancy, but that is simply a matter of time."

Viola's laugh was like a bird's song—a part of her —and nothing except death could silence it for long.

"Then," said Jane, "you stay in New York all summer?"

Viola laughed again. "My dear," she replied, "of course. It is all very simple. If I left New York, and paid board anywhere, I would never have enough money to buy my return fare, and certainly not to keep that wolf from my hall-bedroom door."

"Then," said Jane, "you are going home with me."

THE AMETHYST COMB

"I cannot consent to accept charity, Jane," said Viola. "Don't ask me."

Then, for the first time in her life, Viola Longstreet saw Jane Carew's eyes blaze with anger. "You dare to call it charity coming from me to you?" she said, and Viola gave in.

When Jane saw the little room where Viola lived, she marveled, with the exceedingly great marveling of a woman to whom love of a man has never come, at a woman who could give so much and with no return.

Little enough to pack had Viola. Jane understood with a shudder of horror that it was almost destitution, not poverty, to which her old friend was reduced.

"You shall have that northeast room which you always liked," she told Viola when they were on the train.

"The one with the old-fashioned peacock paper, and the pine-tree growing close to one window?" said Viola, happily.

Jane and Viola settled down to life together, and Viola, despite the tragedy which she had known, realized a peace and happiness beyond her imagination. In reality, although she still looked so youthful, she was old enough to enjoy the pleasures of later life. Enjoy them she did to the utmost. She and Jane made calls together, entertained friends at small and stately dinners, and gave little teas. They drove about in the old Carew carriage. Viola had some new clothes. She played very well on Jane's old piano. She embroidered, she gardened. She lived the sweet, placid life of an older lady in a little village, and loved it. She never mentioned Harold Lind.

Not among the vicious of the earth was poor Harold Lind; rather among those of such beauty and charm that the earth spoils them, making them, in their own estimation, free guests at all its tables of bounty. Moreover, the young man had, deeply rooted in his character, the traits of a mischievous child, rejoicing in his mischief more from a sense of humor so keen that it verged on cruelty than from any intention to harm others. Over that affair of the amethyst comb, for instance, his irresponsible, selfish, childish soul had fairly reveled in glee. He had not been fond of Viola, but he liked her fondness for himself. He had made sport of her, but only for his own entertainment—never for the entertainment of others. He was a beautiful creature, seeking out paths of pleasure and folly for himself alone, which ended as do all paths of earthly pleasure and folly. Harold had admired Viola, but from the same point of view as Jane Carew's. Viola had, when she looked her youngest and best, always seemed so old as to be venerable to him. He had at times compunctions, as if he were making a jest of his grandmother. Viola never knew the truth about the amethyst comb. He had considered that one of the best frolics of his life. He had simply purloined it and presented it to Viola, and merrily left matters to settle themselves.

Viola and Jane had lived together a month before the comb was mentioned. Then one day Viola was in Jane's room and the jewel-case was out, and she began examining its contents. When she found the amethyst comb she gave a little cry. Jane, who had been seated at her desk and had not seen what was going on, turned around.

Viola stood holding the comb, and her cheeks were burning. She fondled the trinket as if it had been a baby. Jane watched her. She began to understand the bare facts of the mystery of the disappearance of her amethyst comb, but the subtlety of it was forever beyond her. Had the other woman explained what was in her mind, in her heart—how that reckless young man whom she had loved had given her the treasure because he had heard her admire Jane's amethysts, and she, all unconscious of any wrong-doing, had ever regarded it as the one evidence of his thoughtful tenderness, it being the one gift she had ever received from him; how she parted with it, as she had parted with her other jewels, in order to obtain money to purchase comforts for him while he was in prison—Jane could not have understood. The fact of an older woman being fond of a young man, almost a boy, was beyond her mental grasp. She had no imagination with which to comprehend that innocent, pathetic, almost terrible love of one who has trodden the earth long for one who has just set dancing feet upon it. It was noble of Jane Carew that, lacking all such imagination, she acted as she did: that, although she did not, could not, formulate it to herself, she would no more have deprived the other woman and the dead man of that one little unscathed bond of tender goodness than she would have robbed his grave of flowers.

Viola looked at her. "I cannot tell you all about it; you would laugh at me," she whispered; "but this was mine once."

"It is yours now, dear," said Jane.

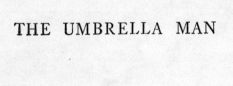

THE UMBRELLA MAN

THE UMBRELLA MAN

IT was an insolent day. There are days which, to imaginative minds, at least, possess strangely human qualities. Their atmospheres predispose people to crime or virtue, to the calm of good will, to sneaking vice, or fierce, unprovoked aggression. The day was of the last description. A beast, or a human being in whose veins coursed undisciplined blood, might, as involuntarily as the boughs of trees lash before storms, perform wild and wicked deeds after inhaling that hot air, evil with the sweat of sin-evoked toil, with nitrogen stored from festering sores of nature and the loathsome emanations of suffering life.

It had not rained for weeks, but the humidity was great. The clouds of dust which arose beneath the man's feet had a horrible damp stickiness. His face and hands were grimy, as were his shoes, his cheap, ready-made suit, and his straw hat. However, the man felt a pride in his clothes, for they were at least the garb of freedom. He had come out of prison the day before, and had scorned the suit proffered him by the officials. He had given it away, and bought a new one with a goodly part of his small stock of money. This suit was of a small-checked pattern.

Nobody could tell from it that the wearer had just left jail. He had been there for several years for one of the minor offenses against the law. His term would probably have been shorter, but the judge had been careless, and he had no friends. Stebbins had never been the sort to make many friends, although he had never cherished animosity toward any human being. Even some injustice in his sentence had not caused him to feel any rancor.

During his stay in the prison he had not been really unhappy. He had accepted the inevitable— the yoke of the strong for the weak—with a patience which brought almost a sense of enjoyment. But, now that he was free, he had suddenly become alert, watchful of chances for his betterment. From being a mere kenneled creature he had become as a hound on the scent, the keenest on earth—that of self-interest. He was changed, while yet living, from a being outside the world to one with the world before him. He felt young, although he was a middle-aged, almost elderly man. He had in his pocket only a few dollars. He might have had more had he not purchased the checked suit and had he not given much away. There was another man whose term would be up in a week, and he had a sickly wife and several children. Stebbins, partly from native kindness and generosity, partly from a sentiment which almost amounted to superstition, had given him of his slender store. He had been deprived of his freedom because of money; he said to himself that his return to it should be heralded by the music of it scattered abroad for the good of another.

THE UMBRELLA MAN

Now and then as he walked Stebbins removed his new straw hat, wiped his forehead with a stiff new handkerchief, looked with some concern at the grime left upon it, then felt anxiously of his short crop of grizzled hair. He would be glad when it grew only a little, for it was at present a telltale to observant eyes. Also now and then he took from another pocket a small mirror which he had just purchased, and scrutinized his face. Every time he did so he rubbed his cheeks violently, then viewed with satisfaction the hard glow which replaced the yellow prison pallor. Every now and then, too, he remembered to throw his shoulders back, hold his chin high, and swing out his right leg more freely. At such times he almost swaggered, he became fairly insolent with his new sense of freedom. He felt himself the equal if not the peer of all creation. Whenever a carriage or a motor-car passed him on the country road he assumed, with the skill of an actor, the air of a business man hastening to an important engagement. However, always his mind was working over a hard problem. He knew that his store of money was scanty, that it would not last long even with the strictest economy; he had no friends; a prison record is sure to leak out when a man seeks a job. He was facing the problem of bare existence.

Although the day was so hot, it was late summer; soon would come the frost and the winter. He wished to live to enjoy his freedom, and all he had for assets was that freedom; which was paradoxical, for it did not signify the ability to obtain work, which was the power of life. Outside the stone wall of the prison he was now inclosed by a subtle, intangible, yet infinitely more unyielding one—the prejudice of his kind against the released prisoner. He was to all intents and purposes a prisoner still, for all his spurts of swagger and the youthful leap of his pulses, and while he did not admit that to himself, yet always, since he had the hard sense of the land of his birth—New England—he pondered that problem of existence. He felt instinctively that it would be a useless proceeding for him to approach any human being for employment. He knew that even the freedom, which he realized through all his senses like an essential perfume, could not yet overpower the reek of the prison. As he walked through the clogging dust he thought of one after another whom he had known before he had gone out of the world of free men and had bent his back under the hand of the law. There were, of course, people in his little native village, people who had been friends and neighbors, but there were none who had ever loved him sufficiently for him to conquer his resolve to never ask aid of them. He had no relatives except cousins more or less removed, and they would have nothing to do with him.

There had been a woman whom he had meant to marry, and he had been sure that she would marry him; but after he had been a year in prison the news had come to him in a roundabout fashion that she had married another suitor. Even had she remained single he could not have approached her, least of all for aid. Then, too, through all his term she had made no sign, there had been no letter, no message; and he had received at first letters and flowers and messages from sentimental women. There had been nothing from her. He had accepted nothing, with the curious patience, carrying an odd pleasure with it, which had come to him when the prison door first closed upon him. He had not forgotten her, but he had not consciously mourned her. His loss, his ruin, had been so tremendous that she had been swallowed up in it. When one's whole system needs to be steeled to trouble and pain, single pricks lose importance. He thought of her that day without any sense of sadness. He imagined her in a pretty, well-ordered home with her husband and children. Perhaps she had grown stout. She had been a slender woman. He tried idly to imagine how she would look stout, then by the sequence of self-preservation the imagination of stoutness in another led to the problem of keeping the covering of flesh and fatness upon his own bones. The question now was not of the woman; she had passed out of his life. The question was of the keeping that life itself, the life which involved everything else, in a hard world, which would remorselessly as a steel trap grudge him life and snap upon him, now he was become its prey.

He walked and walked, and it was high noon, and he was hungry. He had in his pocket a small loaf of bread and two frankfurters, and he heard the splashing ripple of a brook. At that juncture the road was bordered by thick woodland. He followed, pushing his way through the trees and undergrowth, the sound of the brook, and sat down in a cool, green solitude with a sigh of relief. He bent over the clear run, made a cup of his hand, and drank, then he fell to eating. Close beside him grew some wintergreen, and when he had finished his bread and frankfurters he began plucking the glossy, aromatic leaves and chewing them automatically. The savor reached his palate, and his memory awakened before it as before a pleasant tingling of a spur. As a boy how he had loved this little green low-growing plant! It had been one of the luxuries of his youth. Now, as he tasted it, joy and pathos stirred in his very soul. What a wonder youth had been, what a splendor, what an immensity to be rejoiced over and regretted! The man lounging beside the brook, chewing wintergreen leaves, seemed to realize antipodes. He lived for the moment in the past, and the immutable future, which might contain the past in the revolution of time. He smiled, and his face fell into boyish, almost childish, contours. He plucked another glossy leaf with his hard, veinous old hands. His hands would not change to suit his mood, but his limbs relaxed like those of a boy. He stared at the brook gurgling past in brown ripples, shot with dim prismatic lights, showing here clear green water lines, here inky depths, and he thought of the possibility of trout. He wished for fishing-tackle.

Then suddenly out of a mass of green looked two girls, with wide, startled eyes, and rounded mouths of terror which gave vent to screams. There was a scuttling, then silence. The man wondered why the girls were so silly, why they ran. He did not dream of the possibility of their terror of him. He ate another wintergreen leaf, and thought of the woman he had expected to marry when he was arrested and imprisoned. She did not go back to his childish memories. He had met her when first youth had passed, and yet, somehow, the savor of the wintergreen leaves brought her face before him. It is strange how the excitement of one sense will sometimes act as stimulant for the awakening of another. Now the sense of taste brought into full activity that of sight. He saw the woman just as she had looked when he had last seen her. She had not been pretty, but she was exceedingly dainty, and possessed of a certain elegance of carriage which attracted. He saw quite distinctly her small, irregular face and the satin-smooth coils of dark hair around her head; he saw her slender, dusky hands with the well-cared-for nails and the too prominent veins; he saw the gleam of the diamond which he had given her. She had sent it to him just after his arrest, and he had returned it. He wondered idly whether she still owned it and wore it, and what her husband thought of it. He speculated childishly— somehow imprisonment had encouraged the return of childish speculations—as to whether the woman's husband had given her a larger and costlier diamond than his, and he felt a pang of jealousy. He refused to see another diamond than his own upon that slender, dark hand. He saw her in a black silk gown which had been her best. There had been some red about it, and a glitter of jet. He had thought it a magnificent gown, and the woman in it like a princess. He could see her leaning back, in her long slim grace, in a corner of a sofa, and the soft dark folds starry with jet sweeping over her knees and just allowing a glimpse of one little foot. Her feet had been charming, very small and highly arched. Then he remembered that that evening they had been to a concert in the town hall, and that afterward they had partaken of an oyster stew in a little restaurant. Then back his mind traveled to the problem of his own existence, his food and shelter and clothes. He dismissed the woman from his thought. He was concerned now with the primal conditions of life itself. How was he to eat when his little stock of money was gone? He sat staring at the brook; he chewed wintergreen leaves no longer. Instead he drew from his pocket an old pipe and a paper of tobacco. He filled his pipe with care—tobacco was precious; then he began to smoke, but his face now looked old and brooding through the rank blue vapor. Winter was coming, and he had not a shelter. He had not money enough to keep him long from starvation. He knew not how to obtain employment. He thought vaguely of wood-piles, of cutting winter fuel for people. His mind traveled in a trite strain of reasoning. Somehow wood-piles seemed the only available tasks for men of his sort.

Presently he finished his filled pipe, and arose with an air of decision. He went at a brisk pace out of the wood and was upon the road again. He progressed like a man with definite business in view until he reached a house. It was a large white farm-house with many outbuildings. It looked most promising. He approached the side door, and a dog sprang from around a corner and barked, but he spoke, and the dog's tail became eloquent. He was patting the dog, when the door opened and a man stood looking at him. Immediately the taint of the prison became evident. He had not cringed before the dog, but he did cringe before the man who lived in that fine white house, and who had never known what it was to be deprived of liberty. He hung his head, he mumbled. The house-owner, who was older than he, was slightly deaf. He looked him over curtly. The end of it was he was ordered off the premises, and went; but the dog trailed, wagging at his heels, and had to be roughly called back. The thought of the dog comforted Stebbins as he went on his way. He had always liked animals. It was something, now he was past a hand-shake, to have the friendly wag of a dog's tail.

The next house was an ornate little cottage with bay-windows, through which could be seen the flower patterns of lace draperies; the Virginia creeper which grew over the house walls was turning crimson in places. Stebbins went around to the back door and knocked, but nobody came. He waited a long time, for he had spied a great pile of uncut wood. Finally he slunk around to the front door. As he went he suddenly reflected upon his state of mind in days gone by; if he could have known that the time would come when he, Joseph Stebbins, would feel culpable at approaching any front door!

He touched the electric bell and stood close to the door, so that he might not be discovered from the windows. Presently the door opened the length of a chain, and a fair girlish head appeared. She was one of the girls who had been terrified by him in the woods, but that he did not know. Now again her eyes dilated and her pretty mouth rounded! She gave a little cry and slammed the door in his face, and he heard excited voices. Then he saw two pale, pretty faces, the faces of the two girls who had come upon him in the wood, peering at him around a corner of the lace in the bay-window, and he understood what it meant—that he was an object of terror to them. Directly he experienced such a sense of mortal insult as he had never known, not even when the law had taken hold of him. He held his head high and went away, his very soul boiling with a sort of shamed rage. "Those two girls are afraid of me," he kept saying to himself. His knees shook with the horror of it. This terror of him seemed the hardest thing to bear in a hard life. He returned to his green nook beside the brook and sat down again. He thought for the moment no more of wood-piles, of his life. He thought about those two young girls who had been afraid of him. He had never had an impulse to harm any living thing. A curious hatred toward these living things who had accused him of such an impulse came over him. He laughed sardonically. He wished that they would again come and peer at him through the bushes; he would make a threatening motion for the pleasure of seeing the silly things scuttle away.

After a while he put it all out of mind, and again returned to his problem. He lay beside the brook and pondered, and finally fell asleep in the hot air, which increased in venom, until the rattle of thunder awoke him. It was very dark—a strange, livid darkness. "A thunder-storm," he muttered, and then he thought of his new clothes—what a misfortune it would be to have them soaked. He arose and pushed through the thicket around him into a cart path, and it was then that he saw the thing which proved to be the stepping-stone toward his humble fortunes. It was only a small silk umbrella with a handle tipped with pearl. He seized upon it with joy, for it meant the salvation of his precious clothes. He opened it and held it over his head, although the rain had not yet begun. One rib of the umbrella was broken, but it was still serviceable. He hastened along the cart path; he did not know why, only the need for motion, to reach protection from the storm, was upon him; and yet what protection could be ahead of him in that woodland path? Afterward he grew to think of it as a blind instinct which led him on.

He had not gone far, not more than half a mile, when he saw something unexpected—a small untenanted house. He gave vent to a little cry of joy, which had in it something child-like and pathetic, and pushed open the door and entered. It was nothing but a tiny, unfinished shack, with one room and a small one opening from it. There was no ceiling; overhead was the tent-like slant of the roof, but it was tight. The dusty floor was quite dry. There was one rickety chair. Stebbins, after looking into the other room to make sure that the place was empty, sat down, and a wonderful wave of content and self-respect came over him. The poor human snail had found his shell; he had a habitation, a roof of shelter. The little dim place immediately assumed an aspect of home. The rain came down in torrents, the thunder crashed, the place was filled with blinding blue lights. Stebbins filled his pipe more lavishly this time, tilted his chair against the wall, smoked, and gazed about him with pitiful content. It was really so little, but to him it was so much. He nodded with satisfaction at the discovery of a fireplace and a rusty cooking-stove.

He sat and smoked until the storm passed over. The rainfall had been very heavy, there had been hail, but the poor little house had not failed of perfect shelter. A fairly cold wind from the northwest blew through the door. The hail had brought about a change of atmosphere. The burning heat was gone. The night would be cool, even chilly.

Stebbins got up and examined the stove and the pipe. They were rusty, but appeared trustworthy. He went out and presently returned with some fuel which he had found unwet in a thick growth of wood. He laid a fire handily and lit it. The little stove burned well, with no smoke. Stebbins looked at it, and was perfectly happy. He had found other treasures outside—a small vegetable-garden in which were potatoes and some corn. A man had squatted in this little shack for years, and had raised his own garden-truck. He had died only a few weeks ago, and his furniture had been pre-empted with the exception of the stove, the chair, a tilting lounge in the small room, and a few old iron pots and frying-pans. Stebbins gathered corn, dug potatoes, and put them on the stove to cook, then he hurried out to the village store and bought a few slices of bacon, half a dozen eggs, a quarter of a pound of cheap tea, and some salt. When he re-entered the house he looked as he had not for years. He was beaming. "Come, this is a palace," he said to himself, and chuckled with pure joy. He had come out of the awful empty spaces of homeless life into home. He was a man who had naturally strong domestic instincts. If he had spent the best years of his life in a home instead of a prison, the finest in him would have been developed. As it was, this was not even now too late. When he had cooked his bacon and eggs and brewed his tea, when the vegetables were done and he was seated upon the rickety chair, with his supper spread before him on an old board propped on sticks, he was supremely happy. He ate with a relish which seemed to reach his soul. He was at home, and eating, literally, at his own board. As he ate he glanced from time to time at the two windows, with broken panes of glass and curtainless. He was not afraid—that was nonsense; he had never been a cowardly man, but he felt the need of curtains or something before his windows to shut out the broad vast face of nature, or perhaps prying human eyes. Somebody might espy the light in the house and wonder. He had a candle stuck in an old bottle by way of illumination. Still, although he would have preferred to have curtains before those windows full of the blank stare of night, he *was* supremely happy.

After he had finished his supper he looked longingly at his pipe. He hesitated for a second, for he realized the necessity of saving his precious tobacco; then he became reckless: such enormous good fortune as a home must mean more to follow; it must be the first of a series of happy things. He filled his pipe and smoked. Then he went to bed on the old couch in the other room, and slept like a child until the sun shone through the trees in flickering lines. Then he rose, went out to the brook which ran near the house, splashed himself with water, returned to the house, cooked the remnant of the eggs and bacon, and ate his breakfast with the same exultant peace with which he had eaten his supper the night before. Then he sat down in the doorway upon the sunken sill and fell again to considering his main problem. He did not smoke. His tobacco was nearly exhausted and he was no longer reckless. His head was not turned now by the feeling that he was at home. He considered soberly as to the probable owner of the house and whether he would be allowed to remain its tenant. Very soon, however, his doubt concerning that was set at rest. He saw a disturbance of the shadows cast by the thick boughs over the cart path by a long outreach of darker shadow which he knew at once for that of a man. He sat upright, and his face at first assumed a defiant, then a pleading expression, like that of a child who desires to retain possession of some dear thing. His heart beat hard as he watched the advance of the shadow. It was slow, as if cast by an old man. The man was old and very stout, supporting one lopping side by a stick, who presently followed the herald of his shadow. He looked like a farmer. Stebbins rose as he approached; the two men stood staring at each other.

"Who be you, neighbor?" inquired the newcomer.

The voice essayed a roughness, but only achieved a tentative friendliness. Stebbins hesitated for a second; a suspicious look came into the farmer's misty blue eyes. Then Stebbins, mindful of his prison record and fiercely covetous of his new home, gave another name. The name of his maternal grandfather seemed suddenly to loom up in printed characters before his eyes, and he gave it glibly. "David Anderson," he said, and he did not realize a lie. Suddenly the name seemed his own. Surely old David Anderson, who had been a good man, would not grudge the gift of his unstained name to replace the stained one of his grandson. "David Anderson," he replied, and looked the other man in the face unflinchingly.

"Where do ye hail from?" inquired the farmer; and the new David Anderson gave unhesitatingly the name of the old David Anderson's birth and life and death place—that of a little village in New Hampshire.

"What do you do for your living?" was the next question, and the new David Anderson had an in-

spiration. His eyes had lit upon the umbrella which
he had found the night before.

"Umbrellas," he replied, laconically, and the
other man nodded. Men with sheaves of umbrellas,
mended or in need of mending, had always been
familiar features for him.

Then David assumed the initiative; possessed
of an honorable business as well as home, he grew
bold. "Any objection to my staying here?" he
asked.

The other man eyed him sharply. "Smoke
much?" he inquired.

"Smoke a pipe sometimes."

"Careful with your matches?"

David nodded.

"That's all I think about," said the farmer.
"These woods is apt to catch fire jest when I'm
about ready to cut. The man that squatted here
before—he died about a month ago—didn't smoke.
He was careful, he was."

"I'll be real careful," said David, humbly and
anxiously.

"I dun'no' as I have any objections to your staying, then," said the farmer. "Somebody has always
squat here. A man built this shack about twenty
year ago, and he lived here till he died. Then
t'other feller he came along. Reckon he must have
had a little money; didn't work at nothin'! Raised
some garden-truck and kept a few chickens. I took
them home after he died. You can have them now
if you want to take care of them. He rigged up
that little chicken-coop back there."

THE UMBRELLA MAN

"I'll take care of them," answered David, fervently.

"Well, you can come over by and by and get 'em. There's nine hens and a rooster. They lay pretty well. I ain't no use for 'em. I've got all the hens of my own I want to bother with."

"All right," said David. He looked blissful.

The farmer stared past him into the house. He spied the solitary umbrella. He grew facetious. "Guess the umbrellas was all mended up where you come from if you've got down to one," said he.

David nodded. It was tragically true, that guess.

"Well, our umbrella got turned last week," said the farmer. "I'll give you a job to start on. You can stay here as long as you want if you're careful about your matches." Again he looked into the house. "Guess some boys have been helpin' themselves to the furniture, most of it," he observed. "Guess my wife can spare ye another chair, and there's an old table out in the corn-house better than that one you've rigged up, and I guess she'll give ye some old bedding so you can be comfortable. Got any money?"

"A little."

"I don't want any pay for things, and my wife won't; didn't mean that; was wonderin' whether ye had anything to buy vittles with."

"Reckon I can manage till I get some work," replied David, a trifle stiffly. He was a man who had never lived at another than the state's expense.

"Don't want ye to be too short, that's all," said the other, a little apologetically.

THE COPY-CAT

"I shall be all right. There are corn and potatoes in the garden, anyway."

"So there be, and one of them hens had better be eat. She don't lay. She'll need a good deal of b'ilin'. You can have all the wood you want to pick up, but I don't want any cut. You mind that or there'll be trouble."

"I won't cut a stick."

"Mind ye don't. Folks call me an easy mark, and I guess myself I am easy up to a certain point, and cuttin' my wood is one of them points. Roof didn't leak in that shower last night, did it?"

"Not a bit."

"Didn't s'pose it would. The other feller was handy, and he kept tinkerin' all the time. Well, I'll be goin'; you can stay here and welcome if you're careful about matches and don't cut my wood. Come over for them hens any time you want to. I'll let my hired man drive you back in the wagon."

"Much obliged," said David, with an inflection that was almost tearful.

"You're welcome," said the other, and ambled away.

The new David Anderson, the good old grandfather revived in his unfortunate, perhaps graceless grandson, reseated himself on the door-step and watched the bulky, receding figure of his visitor through a pleasant blur of tears, which made the broad, rounded shoulders and the halting columns of legs dance. This David Anderson had almost forgotten that there was unpaid kindness in the whole world, and it seemed to him as if he had seen angels walking up and down. He sat for a while doing nothing except realizing happiness of the present and of the future. He gazed at the green spread of forest boughs, and saw in pleased anticipation their red and gold tints of autumn; also in pleased anticipation their snowy and icy mail of winter, and himself, the unmailed, defenseless human creature, housed and sheltered, sitting before his own fire. This last happy outlook aroused him. If all this was to be, he must be up and doing. He got up, entered the house, and examined the broken umbrella which was his sole stock in trade. David was a handy man. He at once knew that he was capable of putting it in perfect repair. Strangely enough, for his sense of right and wrong was not blunted, he had no compunction whatever in keeping this umbrella, although he was reasonably certain that it belonged to one of the two young girls who had been so terrified by him. He had a conviction that this monstrous terror of theirs, which had hurt him more than many apparently crueler things, made them quits.

After he had washed his dishes in the brook, and left them in the sun to dry, he went to the village store and purchased a few simple things necessary for umbrella-mending. Both on his way to the store and back he kept his eyes open. He realized that his capital depended largely upon chance and good luck. He considered that he had extraordinary good luck when he returned with three more umbrellas. He had discovered one propped against the counter of the store, turned inside out. He had inquired to whom it belonged, and had been answered to anybody who wanted it. David had seized upon it with secret glee. Then, unheard-of good fortune, he had found two more umbrellas on his way home; one was in an ash-can, the other blowing along like a belated bat beside the trolley track. It began to seem to David as if the earth might be strewn with abandoned umbrellas. Before he began his work he went to the farmer's and returned in triumph, driven in the farm-wagon, with his cackling hens and quite a load of household furniture, besides some bread and pies. The farmer's wife was one of those who are able to give, and make receiving greater than giving. She had looked at David, who was older than she, with the eyes of a mother, and his pride had melted away, and he had held out his hands for her benefits, like a child who has no compunctions about receiving gifts because he knows that they are his right of childhood.

Henceforth David prospered—in a humble way, it is true, still he prospered. He journeyed about the country, umbrellas over his shoulder, little bag of tools in hand, and reaped an income more than sufficient for his simple wants. His hair had grown, and also his beard. Nobody suspected his history. He met the young girls whom he had terrified on the road often, and they did not know him. He did not, during the winter, travel very far afield. Night always found him at home, warm, well fed, content, and at peace. Sometimes the old farmer on whose land he lived dropped in of an evening and they had a game of checkers. The old man was a checker expert. He played with unusual skill, but David made for himself a little code of honor. He would never beat the old man, even if he were able, oftener than once out of three evenings. He made coffee on these convivial occasions. He made very good coffee, and they sipped as they moved the men and kings, and the old man chuckled, and David beamed with peaceful happiness.

But the next spring, when he began to realize that he had mended for a while all the umbrellas in the vicinity and that his trade was flagging, he set his precious little home in order, barricaded door and windows, and set forth for farther fields. He was lucky, as he had been from the start. He found plenty of employment, and slept comfortably enough in barns, and now and then in the open. He had traveled by slow stages for several weeks before he entered a village whose familiar look gave him a shock. It was not his native village, but near it. In his younger life he had often journeyed there. It was a little shopping emporium, almost a city. He recognized building after building. Now and then he thought he saw a face which he had once known, and he was thankful that there was hardly any possibility of any one recognizing him. He had grown gaunt and thin since those far-off days; he wore a beard, grizzled, as was his hair. In those days he had not been an umbrella man. Sometimes the humor of the situation struck him. What would he have said, he the spruce, plump, head-in-the-air young man, if anybody had told him that it would come to pass that he would be an umbrella man lurking humbly in search of a job around the back doors of houses? He would laugh softly to himself as he trudged along, and the laugh would be without the slightest bitterness. His lot had been so infinitely worse, and he had such a happy nature, yielding sweetly to the inevitable, that he saw now only cause for amusement.

He had been in that vicinity about three weeks when one day he met the woman. He knew her at once, although she was greatly changed. She had grown stout, although, poor soul! it seemed as if there had been no reason for it. She was not unwieldy, but she was stout, and all the contours of earlier life had disappeared beneath layers of flesh. Her hair was not gray, but the bright brown had faded, and she wore it tightly strained back from her seamed forehead, although it was thin. One had only to look at her hair to realize that she was a woman who had given up, who no longer cared. She was humbly clad in a blue-cotton wrapper, she wore a dingy black hat, and she carried a tin pail half full of raspberries. When the man and woman met they stopped with a sort of shock, and each changed face grew like the other in its pallor. She recognized him and he her, but along with that recognition was awakened a fierce desire to keep it secret. His prison record loomed up before the man, the woman's past loomed up before her. She had possibly not been guilty of much, but her life was nothing to waken pride in her. She felt shamed before this man whom she had loved, and who felt shamed before her. However, after a second the silence was broken. The man recovered his self-possession first.

He spoke casually.

"Nice day," said he.

The woman nodded.

"Been berrying?" inquired David. The woman nodded again.

David looked scrutinizingly at her pail. "I saw better berries real thick a piece back," said he.

The woman murmured something. In spite of herself, a tear trickled over her fat, weather-beaten cheek. David saw the tear, and something warm and glorious like sunlight seemed to waken within him. He felt such tenderness and pity for this poor feminine thing who had not the strength to keep the tears back, and was so pitiably shorn of youth and grace, that he himself expanded. He had heard in the town something of her history. She had made a dreadful marriage, tragedy and suspicion had entered her life, and the direst poverty. However, he had not known that she was in the vicinity. Somebody had told him she was out West.

"Living here?" he inquired.

"Working for my board at a house back there," she muttered. She did not tell him that she had come as a female "hobo" in a freight-car from the Western town where she had been finally stranded. "Mrs. White sent me out for berries," she added. "She keeps boarders, and there were no berries in the market this morning."

"Come back with me and I will show you where I saw the berries real thick," said David.

He turned himself about, and she followed a little behind, the female failure in the dust cast by the male. Neither spoke until David stopped and pointed to some bushes where the fruit hung thick on bending, slender branches.

"Here," said David. Both fell to work. David picked handfuls of berries and cast them gaily into the pail. "What is your name?" he asked, in an undertone.

"Jane Waters," she replied, readily. Her husband's name had been Waters, or the man who had called himself her husband, and her own middle name was Jane. The first was Sara. David remembered at once. "She is taking her own middle name and the name of the man she married," he thought. Then he asked, plucking berries, with his eyes averted:

"Married?"

"No," said the woman, flushing deeply.

David's next question betrayed him. "Husband dead?"

"I haven't any husband," she replied, like the Samaritan woman.

She had married a man already provided with another wife, although she had not known it. The man was not dead, but she spoke the entire miserable truth when she replied as she did. David assumed that he was dead. He felt a throb of relief, of which he was ashamed, but he could not down it. He did not know what it was that was so alive and triumphant within him: love, or pity, or the natural instinct of the decent male to shelter and protect. Whatever it was, it was dominant.

"Do you have to work hard?" he asked.

"Pretty hard, I guess. I expect to."

"And you don't get any pay?"

"That's all right; I don't expect to get any," said she, and there was bitterness in her voice.

In spite of her stoutness she was not as strong as the man. She was not at all strong, and, moreover, the constant presence of a sense of injury at the hands of life filled her very soul with a subtle poison, to her weakening vitality. She was a child hurt and worried and bewildered, although she was to the average eye a stout, able-bodied, middle-aged woman; but David had not the average eye, and he saw her as she really was, not as she seemed. There had always been about her a little weakness and dependency which had appealed to him. Now they seemed fairly to cry out to him like the despairing voices of the children whom he had never had, and he knew he loved her as he had never loved her before, with a love which had budded and flowered and fruited and survived absence and starvation. He spoke abruptly.

"I've about got my business done in these parts," said he. "I've got quite a little money, and I've got a little house, not much, but mighty snug, back where I come from. There's a garden. It's in the woods. Not much passing nor going on."

The woman was looking at him with incredulous, pitiful eyes like a dog's. "I hate much goin' on," she whispered.

"Suppose," said David, "you take those berries home and pack up your things. Got much?"

"All I've got will go in my bag."

"Well, pack up; tell the madam where you live that you're sorry, but you're worn out—"

"God knows I am," cried the woman, with sudden force, "worn out!"

"Well, you tell her that, and say you've got another chance, and—"

"What do you mean?" cried the woman, and she hung upon his words like a drowning thing.

"Mean? Why, what I mean is this. You pack your bag and come to the parson's back there, that white house."

"I know—"

"In the mean time I'll see about getting a license, and—"

Suddenly the woman set her pail down and clutched him by both hands. "Say you are not married," she demanded; "say it, swear it!"

"Yes, I do swear it," said David. "You are the only woman I ever asked to marry me. I can support you. We sha'n't be rolling in riches, but we can be comfortable, and—I rather guess I can make you happy."

"You didn't say what your name was," said the woman.

"David Anderson."

The woman looked at him with a strange expression, the expression of one who loves and respects, even reveres, the isolation and secrecy of another soul. She understood, down to the depths of her being she understood. She had lived a hard life, she had her faults, but she was fine enough to

"WE SHA'N'T BE ROLLING IN RICHES, BUT WE CAN BE COMFORTABLE"

comprehend and hold sacred another personality. She was very pale, but she smiled. Then she turned to go.

"How long will it take you?" asked David.

"About an hour."

"All right. I will meet you in front of the parson's house in an hour. We will go back by train. I have money enough."

"I'd just as soon walk." The woman spoke with the utmost humility of love and trust. She had not even asked where the man lived. All her life she had followed him with her soul, and it would go hard if her poor feet could not keep pace with her soul.

"No, it is too far; we will take the train. One goes at half past four."

At half past four the couple, made man and wife, were on the train speeding toward the little home in the woods. The woman had frizzled her thin hair pathetically and ridiculously over her temples; on her left hand gleamed a white diamond. She had kept it hidden; she had almost starved rather than part with it. She gazed out of the window at the flying landscape, and her thin lips were curved in a charming smile. The man sat beside her, staring straight ahead as if at happy visions.

They lived together afterward in the little house in the woods, and were happy with a strange crystallized happiness at which they would have mocked in their youth, but which they now recognized as the essential of all happiness upon earth. And always the woman knew what she knew about her husband,

and the man knew about his wife, and each recognized the other as old lover and sweetheart come together at last, but always each kept the knowledge from the other with an infinite tenderness of delicacy which was as a perfumed garment veiling the innermost sacredness of love.

THE BALKING OF CHRISTOPHER

THE BALKING OF CHRISTOPHER

THE spring was early that year. It was only the last of March, but the trees were filmed with green and paling with promise of bloom; the front yards were showing new grass pricking through the old. It was high time to plow the south field and the garden, but Christopher sat in his rocking-chair beside the kitchen window and gazed out, and did absolutely nothing about it.

Myrtle Dodd, Christopher's wife, washed the breakfast dishes, and later kneaded the bread, all the time glancing furtively at her husband. She had a most old-fashioned deference with regard to Christopher. She was always a little afraid of him. Sometimes Christopher's mother, Mrs. Cyrus Dodd, and his sister Abby, who had never married, reproached her for this attitude of mind. "You are entirely too much cowed down by Christopher," Mrs. Dodd said.

"I would never be under the thumb of any man," Abby said.

"Have you ever seen Christopher in one of his spells?" Myrtle would ask.

Then Mrs. Cyrus Dodd and Abby would look

at each other. "It is all your fault, mother," Abby would say. "You really ought not to have allowed your son to have his own head so much."

"You know perfectly well, Abby, what I had to contend against," replied Mrs. Dodd, and Abby became speechless. Cyrus Dodd, now deceased some twenty years, had never during his whole life yielded to anything but birth and death. Before those two primary facts even his terrible will was powerless. He had come into the world without his consent being obtained; he had passed in like manner from it. But during his life he had ruled, a petty monarch, but a most thorough one. He had spoiled Christopher, and his wife, although a woman of high spirit, knew of no appealing.

"I could never go against your father, you know that," said Mrs. Dodd, following up her advantage.

"Then," said Abby, "you ought to have warned poor Myrtle. It was a shame to let her marry a man as spoiled as Christopher."

"I would have married him, anyway," declared Myrtle with sudden defiance; and her mother-in-law regarded her approvingly.

"There are worse men than Christopher, and Myrtle knows it," said she.

"Yes, I do, mother," agreed Myrtle. "Christopher hasn't one bad habit."

"I don't know what you call a bad habit," retorted Abby. "I call having your own way in spite of the world, the flesh, and the devil rather a bad habit. Christopher tramples on everything in his path, and he always has. He tramples on poor Myrtle."

At that Myrtle laughed. "I don't think I look trampled on," said she; and she certainly did not. Pink and white and plump was Myrtle, although she had, to a discerning eye, an expression which denoted extreme nervousness.

This morning of spring, when her husband sat doing nothing, she wore this nervous expression. Her blue eyes looked dark and keen; her forehead was wrinkled; her rosy mouth was set. Myrtle and Christopher were not young people; they were a little past middle age, still far from old in look or ability.

Myrtle had kneaded the bread to rise for the last time before it was put into the oven, and had put on the meat to boil for dinner, before she dared address that silent figure which had about it something tragic. Then she spoke in a small voice. "Christopher," said she.

Christopher made no reply.

"It is a good morning to plow, ain't it?" said Myrtle.

Christopher was silent.

"Jim Mason got over real early; I suppose he thought you'd want to get at the south field. He's been sitting there at the barn door for 'most two hours."

Then Christopher rose. Myrtle's anxious face lightened. But to her wonder her husband went into the front entry and got his best hat. "He ain't going to wear his best hat to plow," thought Myrtle. For an awful moment it occurred to her that something had suddenly gone wrong with her

271

husband's mind. Christopher brushed the hat carefully, adjusted it at the little looking-glass in the kitchen, and went out.

"Be you going to plow the south field?" Myrtle said, faintly.

"No, I ain't."

"Will you be back to dinner?"

"I don't know—you needn't worry if I'm not." Suddenly Christopher did an unusual thing for him. He and Myrtle had lived together for years, and outward manifestations of affection were rare between them. He put his arm around her and kissed her.

After he had gone, Myrtle watched him out of sight down the road; then she sat down and wept. Jim Mason came slouching around from his station at the barn door. He surveyed Myrtle uneasily.

"Mr. Dodd sick?" said he at length.

"Not that I know of," said Myrtle, in a weak quaver. She rose and, keeping her tear-stained face aloof, lifted the lid off the kettle on the stove.

"D'ye know am he going to plow to-day?"

"He said he wasn't."

Jim grunted, shifted his quid, and slouched out of the yard.

Meantime Christopher Dodd went straight down the road to the minister's, the Rev. Stephen Wheaton. When he came to the south field, which he was neglecting, he glanced at it turning emerald upon the gentle slopes. He set his face harder. Christopher Dodd's face was in any case hard-set. Now it was tragic, to be pitied, but warily, lest it turn fiercely upon the one who pitied. Christopher was a handsome man, and his face had an almost classic turn of feature. His forehead was noble; his eyes full of keen light. He was only a farmer, but in spite of his rude clothing he had the face of a man who followed one of the professions. He was in sore trouble of spirit, and he was going to consult the minister and ask him for advice. Christopher had never done this before. He had a sort of incredulity now that he was about to do it. He had always associated that sort of thing with womankind, and not with men like himself. And, moreover, Stephen Wheaton was a younger man than himself. He was unmarried, and had only been settled in the village for about a year. "He can't think I'm coming to set my cap at him, anyway," Christopher reflected, with a sort of grim humor, as he drew near the parsonage. The minister was haunted by marriageable ladies of the village.

"Guess you are glad to see a man coming, instead of a woman who has doubts about some doctrine," was the first thing Christopher said to the minister when he had been admitted to his study. The study was a small room, lined with books, and only one picture hung over the fireplace, the portrait of the minister's mother—Stephen was so like her that a question concerning it was futile.

Stephen colored a little angrily at Christopher's remark—he was a hot-tempered man, although a clergyman; then he asked him to be seated.

Christopher sat down opposite the minister. "I oughtn't to have spoken so," he apologized, "but what I am doing ain't like me."

"That's all right," said Stephen. He was a short, athletic man, with an extraordinary width of shoulders and a strong-featured and ugly face, still indicative of goodness and a strange power of sympathy. Three little mongrel dogs were sprawled about the study. One, small and alert, came and rested his head on Christopher's knee. Animals all liked him. Christopher mechanically patted him. Patting an appealing animal was as unconscious with the man as drawing his breath. But he did not even look at the little dog while he stroked it after the fashion which pleased it best. He kept his large, keen, melancholy eyes fixed upon the minister; at length he spoke. He did not speak with as much eagerness as he did with force, bringing the whole power of his soul into his words, which were the words of a man in rebellion against the greatest odds on earth and in all creation—the odds of fate itself.

"I have come to say a good deal, Mr. Wheaton," he began.

"Then say it, Mr. Dodd," replied Stephen, without a smile.

Christopher spoke. "I am going back to the very beginning of things," said he, "and maybe you will think it blasphemy, but I don't mean it for that. I mean it for the truth, and the truth which is too much for my comprehension."

"I have heard men swear when it did not seem blasphemy to me," said Stephen.

"Thank the Lord, you ain't so deep in your rut you can't see the stars!" said Christopher. "But I guess you see them in a pretty black sky sometimes.

In the beginning, why did I have to come into the world without any choice?"

"You must not ask a question of me which can only be answered by the Lord," said Stephen.

"I am asking the Lord," said Christopher, with his sad, forceful voice. "I am asking the Lord, and I ask why?"

"You have no right to expect your question to be answered in your time," said Stephen.

"But here am I," said Christopher, "and I was a question to the Lord from the first, and fifty years and more I have been on the earth."

"Fifty years and more are nothing for the answer to such a question," said Stephen.

Christopher looked at him with mournful dissent; there was no anger about him. "There was time before time," said he, "before the fifty years and more began. I don't mean to blaspheme, Mr. Wheaton, but it is the truth. I came into the world whether I would or not; I was forced, and then I was told I was a free agent. I am no free agent. For fifty years and more I have thought about it, and I have found out that, at least. I am a slave—a slave of life."

"For that matter," said Stephen, looking curiously at him, "so am I. So are we all."

"That makes it worse," agreed Christopher—"a whole world of slaves. I know I ain't talking in exactly what you might call an orthodox strain. I have got to a point when it seems to me I shall go mad if I don't talk to somebody. I know there is that awful why, and you can't answer it; and no man living can. I'm willing to admit that sometime, in another world, that why will get an answer, but meantime it's an awful thing to live in this world without it if a man has had the kind of life I have. My life has been harder for me than a harder life might be for another man who was different. That much I know. There is one thing I've got to be thankful for. I haven't been the means of sending any more slaves into this world. I am glad my wife and I haven't any children to ask 'why?'

"Now, I've begun at the beginning; I'm going on. I have never had what men call luck. My folks were poor; father and mother were good, hard-working people, but they had nothing but trouble, sickness, and death, and losses by fire and flood. We lived near the river, and one spring our house went, and every stick we owned, and much as ever we all got out alive. Then lightning struck father's new house, and the insurance company had failed, and we never got a dollar of insurance. Then my oldest brother died, just when he was getting started in business, and his widow and two little children came on father to support. Then father got rheumatism, and was all twisted, and wasn't good for much afterward; and my sister Sarah, who had been expecting to get married, had to give it up and take in sewing and stay at home and take care of the rest. There was father and George's widow—she was never good for much at work—and mother and Abby. She was my youngest sister. As for me, I had a liking for books and wanted to get an education; might just as well have wanted to get a seat on a throne. I went to work in the grist-mill of the place where we used to live when I was only a boy. Then, before I was twenty, I saw that Sarah wasn't going to hold out. She had grieved a good deal, poor thing, and worked too hard, so we sold out and came here and bought my farm, with the mortgage hitching it, and I went to work for dear life. Then Sarah died, and then father. Along about then there was a girl I wanted to marry, but, Lord, how could I even ask her? My farm started in as a failure, and it has kept it up ever since. When there wasn't a drought there was so much rain everything mildewed; there was a hail-storm that cut everything to pieces, and there was the caterpillar year. I just managed to pay the interest on the mortgage; as for paying the principal, I might as well have tried to pay the national debt.

"Well, to go back to that girl. She is married and don't live here, and you ain't like ever to see her, but she was a beauty and something more. I don't suppose she ever looked twice at me, but losing what you've never had sometimes is worse than losing everything you've got. When she got married I guess I knew a little about what the martyrs went through.

"Just after that George's widow got married again and went away to live. It took a burden off the rest of us, but I had got attached to the children. The little girl, Ellen, seemed 'most like my own. Then poor Myrtle came here to live. She did dressmaking and boarded with our folks, and I begun to see that she was one of the nervous sort of women who are pretty bad off alone in the world, and I told her about the other girl, and she said she didn't mind, and we got married. By that time mother's brother John—he had never got married—died and left her a little money, so she and my sister Abby could screw along. They bought the little house they live in and left the farm, for Abby was always hard to get along with, though she is a good woman. Mother, though she is a smart woman, is one of the sort who don't feel called upon to interfere much with men-folks. I guess she didn't interfere any too much for my good, or father's, either. Father was a set man. I guess if mother had been a little harsh with me I might not have asked that awful 'why?' I guess I might have taken my bitter pills and held my tongue, but I won't blame myself on poor mother.

"Myrtle and I get on well enough. She seems contented—she has never said a word to make me think she wasn't. She isn't one of the kind of women who want much besides decent treatment and a home. Myrtle is a good woman. I am sorry for her that she got married to me, for she deserved somebody who could make her a better husband. All the time, every waking minute, I've been growing more and more rebellious.

"You see, Mr. Wheaton, never in this world have I had what I wanted, and more than wanted—needed, and needed far more than happiness. I have never been able to think of work as anything but a way to get money, and it wasn't right, not for a man like me, with the feelings I was born with.

And everything has gone wrong even about the work for the money. I have been hampered and hindered, I don't know whether by Providence or the Evil One. I have saved just six hundred and forty dollars, and I have only paid the interest on the mortgage. I knew I ought to have a little ahead in case Myrtle or I got sick, so I haven't tried to pay the mortgage, but put a few dollars at a time in the savings-bank, which will come in handy now."

The minister regarded him uneasily. "What," he asked, "do you mean to do?"

"I mean," replied Christopher, "to stop trying to do what I am hindered in doing, and do just once in my life what I want to do. Myrtle asked me this morning if I wasn't going to plow the south field. Well, I ain't going to plow the south field. I ain't going to make a garden. I ain't going to try for hay in the ten-acre lot. I have stopped. I have worked for nothing except just enough to keep soul and body together. I have had bad luck. But that isn't the real reason why I have stopped. Look at here, Mr. Wheaton, spring is coming. I have never in my life had a chance at the spring nor the summer. This year I'm going to have the spring and the summer, and the fall, too, if I want it. My apples may fall and rot if they want to. I am going to get as much good of the season as they do."

"What are you going to do?" asked Stephen.

"Well, I will tell you. I ain't a man to make mystery if I am doing right, and I think I am. You know, I've got a little shack up on Silver Mountain in the little sugar-orchard I own there; never got enough sugar to say so, but I put up the shack one year when I was fool enough to think I might get something. Well, I'm going up there, and I'm going to live there awhile, and I'm going to sense the things I have had to hustle by for the sake of a few dollars and cents."

"But what will your wife do?"

"She can have the money I've saved, all except enough to buy me a few provisions. I sha'n't need much. I want a little corn meal, and I will have a few chickens, and there is a barrel of winter apples left over that she can't use, and a few potatoes. There is a spring right near the shack, and there are trout-pools, and by and by there will be berries, and there's plenty of fire-wood, and there's an old bed and a stove and a few things in the shack. Now, I'm going to the store and buy what I want, and I'm going to fix it so Myrtle can draw the money when she wants it, and then I am going to the shack, and"—Christopher's voice took on a solemn tone—"I will tell you in just a few words the gist of what I am going for. I have never in my life had enough of the bread of life to keep my soul nourished. I have tried to do my duties, but I believe sometimes duties act on the soul like weeds on a flower. They crowd it out. I am going up on Silver Mountain to get once, on this earth, my fill of the bread of life."

Stephen Wheaton gasped. "But your wife, she will be alone, she will worry."

"I want you to go and tell her," said Christopher, "and I've got my bank-book here; I'm going to write some checks that she can get cashed when she needs money. I want you to tell her. Myrtle won't make a fuss. She ain't the kind. Maybe she will be a little lonely, but if she is, she can go and visit somewhere." Christopher rose. "Can you let me have a pen and ink?" said he, "and I will write those checks. You can tell Myrtle how to use them. She won't know how."

Stephen Wheaton, an hour later, sat in his study, the checks in his hand, striving to rally his courage. Christopher had gone; he had seen him from his window, laden with parcels, starting upon the ascent of Silver Mountain. Christopher had made out many checks for small amounts, and Stephen held the sheaf in his hand, and gradually his courage to arise and go and tell Christopher's wife gained strength. At last he went.

Myrtle was looking out of the window, and she came quickly to the door. She looked at him, her round, pretty face gone pale, her plump hands twitching at her apron.

"What is it?" said she.

"Nothing to be alarmed about," replied Stephen.

Then the two entered the house. Stephen found his task unexpectedly easy. Myrtle Dodd was an unusual woman in a usual place.

"It is all right for my husband to do as he pleases," she said with an odd dignity, as if she were defending him.

"Mr. Dodd is a strange man. He ought to have been educated and led a different life," Stephen said, lamely, for he reflected that the words might be hard for the woman to hear, since she seemed obviously quite fitted to her life, and her life to her.

But Myrtle did not take it hardly, seemingly rather with pride. "Yes," said she, "Christopher ought to have gone to college. He had the head for it. Instead of that he has just stayed round here and dogged round the farm, and everything has gone wrong lately. He hasn't had any luck even with that." Then poor Myrtle Dodd said an unexpectedly wise thing. "But maybe," said Myrtle, "his bad luck may turn out the best thing for him in the end."

Stephen was silent. Then he began explaining about the checks.

"I sha'n't use any more of his savings than I can help," said Myrtle, and for the first time her voice quavered. "He must have some clothes up there," said she. "There ain't bed-coverings, and it is cold nights, late as it is in the spring. I wonder how I can get the bedclothes and other things to him. I can't drive, myself, and I don't like to hire anybody; aside from its being an expense, it would make talk. Mother Dodd and Abby won't make talk outside the family, but I suppose it will have to be known."

"Mr. Dodd didn't want any mystery made over it," Stephen Wheaton said.

"There ain't going to be any mystery. Christopher has got a right to live awhile on Silver Mountain if he wants to," returned Myrtle with her odd, defiant air.

"But I will take the things up there to him, if you will let me have a horse and wagon," said Stephen.

"I will, and be glad. When will you go?"

"To-morrow."

"I'll have them ready," said Myrtle.

After the minister had gone she went into her own bedroom and cried a little and made the moan of a loving woman sadly bewildered by the ways of man, but loyal as a soldier. Then she dried her tears and began to pack a load for the wagon.

The next morning early, before the dew was off the young grass, Stephen Wheaton started with the wagon-load, driving the great gray farm-horse up the side of Silver Mountain. The road was fairly good, making many winds in order to avoid steep ascents, and Stephen drove slowly. The gray farm-horse was sagacious. He knew that an unaccustomed hand held the lines; he knew that of a right he should be treading the plowshares instead of climbing a mountain on a beautiful spring morning.

But as for the man driving, his face was radiant, his eyes of young manhood lit with the light of the morning. He had not owned it, but he himself had sometimes chafed under the dull necessity of his life, but here was excitement, here was exhilaration. He drew the sweet air into his lungs, and the deeper meaning of the spring morning into his soul. Christopher Dodd interested him to the point of enthusiasm. Not even the uneasy consideration of the lonely, mystified woman in Dodd's deserted home could deprive him of admiration for the man's flight into the spiritual open. He felt that these rights of the man were of the highest, and that other rights, even human and pitiful ones, should give them the right of way.

It was not a long drive. When he reached the shack—merely a one-roomed hut, with a stove-pipe chimney, two windows, and a door—Christopher stood at the entrance and seemed to illuminate it. Stephen for a minute doubted his identity. Christopher had lost middle age in a day's time. He had the look of a triumphant youth. Blue smoke was curling from the chimney. Stephen smelled bacon frying, and coffee.

Christopher greeted him with the joyousness of a child. "Lord!" said he, "did Myrtle send you up with all those things? Well, she is a good woman. Guess I would have been cold last night if I hadn't been so happy. How is Myrtle?"

"She seemed to take it very sensibly when I told her."

Christopher nodded happily and lovingly. "She would. She can understand not understanding, and that is more than most women can. It was mighty good of you to bring the things. You are in time for breakfast. Lord! Mr. Wheaton, smell the trees, and there are blooms hidden somewhere that smell sweet. Think of having the common food of man sweetened this way! First time I fully sensed I was something more than just a man. Lord, I am paid already. It won't be so very long before I get my fill, at this rate, and then I can go back. To think I needn't plow to-day! To think all I have to do is to have the spring! See the light under those trees!"

"FIRST TIME I FULLY SENSED I WAS SOMETHING MORE THAN JUST
A MAN"

Christopher spoke like a man in ecstasy. He tied the gray horse to a tree and brought a pail of water for him from the spring near by.

Then he said to Stephen: "Come right in. The bacon's done, and the coffee and the corn-cake and the eggs won't take a minute."

The two men entered the shack. There was nothing there except the little cooking-stove, a few kitchen utensils hung on pegs on the walls, an old table with a few dishes, two chairs, and a lounge over which was spread an ancient buffalo-skin.

Stephen sat down, and Christopher fried the eggs. Then he bade the minister draw up, and the two men breakfasted.

"Ain't it great, Mr. Wheaton?" said Christopher.

"You are a famous cook, Mr. Dodd," laughed Stephen. He was thoroughly enjoying himself, and the breakfast was excellent.

"It ain't that," declared Christopher in his exalted voice. "It ain't that, young man. It's because the food is blessed."

Stephen stayed all day on Silver Mountain. He and Christopher went fishing, and had fried trout for dinner. He took some of the trout home to Myrtle.

Myrtle received them with a sort of state which defied the imputation of sadness. "Did he seem comfortable?" she asked.

· "Comfortable, Mrs. Dodd? I believe it will mean a new lease of life to your husband. He is an uncommon man."

"Yes, Christopher is uncommon; he always was," assented Myrtle.

"You have everything you want? You were not timid last night alone?" asked the minister.

"Yes, I was timid. I heard queer noises," said Myrtle, "but I sha'n't be alone any more. Christopher's niece wrote me she was coming to make a visit. She has been teaching school, and she lost her school. I rather guess Ellen is as uncommon for a girl as Christopher is for a man. Anyway, she's lost her school, and her brother's married, and she don't want to go there. Besides, they live in Boston, and Ellen, she says she can't bear the city in spring and summer. She wrote she'd saved a little, and she'd pay her board, but I sha'n't touch a dollar of her little savings, and neither would Christopher want me to. He's always thought a sight of Ellen, though he's never seen much of her. As for me, I was so glad when her letter came I didn't know what to do. Christopher will be glad. I suppose you'll be going up there to see him off and on." Myrtle spoke a bit wistfully, and Stephen did not tell her he had been urged to come often.

"Yes, off and on," he replied.

"If you will just let me know when you are going, I will see that you have something to take to him —some bread and pies."

"He has some chickens there," said Stephen.

"Has he got a coop for them?"

"Yes, he had one rigged up. He will have plenty of eggs, and he carried up bacon and corn meal and tea and coffee."

"I am glad of that," said Myrtle. She spoke with

a quiet dignity, but her face never lost its expression of bewilderment and resignation.

The next week Stephen Wheaton carried Myrtle's bread and pies to Christopher on his mountainside. He drove Christopher's gray horse harnessed in his old buggy, and realized that he himself was getting much pleasure out of the other man's idiosyncrasy. The morning was beautiful, and Stephen carried in his mind a peculiar new beauty, besides. Ellen, Christopher's niece, had arrived the night before, and, early as it was, she had been astir when he reached the Dodd house. She had opened the door for him, and she was a goodly sight: a tall girl, shaped like a boy, with a fearless face of great beauty crowned with compact gold braids and lit by unswerving blue eyes. Ellen had a square, determined chin and a brow of high resolve.

"Good morning," said she, and as she spoke she evidently rated Stephen and approved, for she smiled genially. "I am Mr. Dodd's niece," said she. "You are the minister?"

"Yes."

"And you have come for the things aunt is to send him?"

"Yes."

"Aunt said you were to drive uncle's horse and take the buggy," said Ellen. "It is very kind of you. While you are harnessing, aunt and I will pack the basket."

Stephen, harnessing the gray horse, had a sense of shock; whether pleasant or otherwise, he could not determine. He had never seen a girl in the least like Ellen. Girls had never impressed him. She did.

When he drove around to the kitchen door she and Myrtle were both there, and he drank a cup of coffee before starting, and Myrtle introduced him. "Only think, Mr. Wheaton," said she, "Ellen says she knows a great deal about farming, and we are going to hire Jim Mason and go right ahead." Myrtle looked adoringly at Ellen.

Stephen spoke eagerly. "Don't hire anybody," he said. "I used to work on a farm to pay my way through college. I need the exercise. Let me help."

"You may do that," said Ellen, "on shares. Neither aunt nor I can think of letting you work without any recompense."

"Well, we will settle that," Stephen replied. When he drove away, his usually calm mind was in a tumult.

"Your niece has come," he told Christopher, when the two men were breakfasting together on Silver Mountain.

"I am glad of that," said Christopher. "All that troubled me about being here was that Myrtle might wake up in the night and hear noises."

Christopher had grown even more radiant. He was effulgent with pure happiness.

"You aren't going to tap your sugar-maples?" said Stephen, looking up at the great symmetrical efflorescence of rose and green which towered about them.

Christopher laughed. "No, bless 'em," said he, "the trees shall keep their sugar this season. This week is the first time I've had a chance to get acquainted with them and sort of enter into their feelings. Good Lord! I've seen how I can love those trees, Mr. Wheaton! See the pink on their young leaves! They know more than you and I. They know how to grow young every spring."

Stephen did not tell Christopher how Ellen and Myrtle were to work the farm with his aid. The two women had bade him not. Christopher seemed to have no care whatever about it. He was simply happy. When Stephen left, he looked at him and said, with the smile of a child, "Do you think I am crazy?"

"Crazy? No," replied Stephen.

"Well, I ain't. I'm just getting fed. I was starving to death. Glad you don't think I'm crazy, because I couldn't help matters by saying I wasn't. Myrtle don't think I am, I know. As for Ellen, I haven't seen her since she was a little girl. I don't believe she can be much like Myrtle; but I guess if she is what she promised to turn out she wouldn't think anybody ought to go just her way to have it the right way."

"I rather think she is like that, although I saw her for the first time this morning," said Stephen.

"I begin to feel that I may not need to stay here much longer," Christopher called after him. "I begin to feel that I am getting what I came for so fast that I can go back pretty soon."

But it was the last day of July before he came. He chose the cool of the evening after a burning day, and descended the mountain in the full light of the

289

moon. He had gone up the mountain like an old man; he came down like a young one.

When he came at last in sight of his own home, he paused and stared. Across the grass-land a heavily laden wagon was moving toward his barn. Upon this wagon heaped with hay, full of silver lights from the moon, sat a tall figure all in white, which seemed to shine above all things. Christopher did not see the man on the other side of the wagon leading the horses; he saw only this wonderful white figure. He hurried forward and Myrtle came down the road to meet him. She had been watching for him, as she had watched every night.

"Who is it on the load of hay?" asked Christopher.

"Ellen," replied Myrtle.

"Oh!" said Christopher. "She looked like an angel of the Lord, come to take up the burden I had dropped while I went to learn of Him."

"Be you feeling pretty well, Christopher?" asked Myrtle. She thought that what her husband had said was odd, but he looked well, and he might have said it simply because he was a man.

Christopher put his arm around Myrtle. "I am better than I ever was in my whole life, Myrtle, and I've got more courage to work now than I had when I was young. I had to go away and get rested, but I've got rested for all my life. We shall get along all right as long as we live."

"Ellen and the minister are going to get married come Christmas," said Myrtle.

"She is lucky. He is a man that can see with the eyes of other people," said Christopher.

THE BALKING OF CHRISTOPHER

It was after the hay had been unloaded and Christopher had been shown the garden full of lusty vegetables, and told of the great crop with no drawback, that he and the minister had a few minutes alone together at the gate.

"I want to tell you, Mr. Wheaton, that I am settled in my mind now. I shall never complain again, no matter what happens. I have found that all the good things and all the bad things that come to a man who tries to do right are just to prove to him that he is on the right path. They are just the flowers and sunbeams, and the rocks and snakes, too, that mark the way. And—I have found out more than that. I have found out the answer to my 'why?'"

"What is it?" asked Stephen, gazing at him curiously from the wonder-height of his own special happiness.

"I have found out that the only way to heaven for the children of men is through the earth," said Christopher.

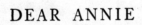

DEAR ANNIE

DEAR ANNIE

ANNIE HEMPSTEAD lived on a large family canvas, being the eldest of six children. There was only one boy. The mother was long since dead. If one can imagine the Hempstead family, the head of which was the Reverend Silas, pastor of the Orthodox Church in Lynn Corners, as being the subject of a mild study in village history, the high light would probably fall upon Imogen, the youngest daughter. As for Annie, she would apparently supply only a part of the background.

This afternoon in late July, Annie was out in the front yard of the parsonage, assisting her brother Benny to rake hay. Benny had not cut it. Annie had hired a man, although the Hempsteads could not afford to hire a man, but she had said to Benny, "Benny, you can rake the hay and get it into the barn if Jim Mullins cuts it, can't you?" And Benny had smiled and nodded acquiescence. Benny Hempstead always smiled and nodded acquiescence, but there was in him the strange persistency of a willow bough, the persistency of pliability, which is the most unconquerable of all. Benny swayed gracefully in response to all the wishes of others, but always he remained in his own inadequate attitude toward life.

Now he was raking to as little purpose as he could and rake at all. The clover-tops, the timothy grass, and the buttercups moved before his rake in a faint foam of gold and green and rose, but his sister Annie raised whirlwinds with hers. The Hempstead yard was large and deep, and had two great squares given over to wild growths on either side of the gravel walk, which was bordered with shrubs, flowering in their turn, like a class of children at school saying their lessons. The spring shrubs had all spelled out their floral recitations, of course, but great clumps of peonies were spreading wide skirts of gigantic bloom, like dancers courtesying low on the stage of summer, and shafts of green-white Yucca lilies and Japan lilies and clove-pinks still remained in their school of bloom.

Benny often stood still, wiped his forehead, leaned on his rake, and inhaled the bouquet of sweet scents, but Annie raked with never-ceasing energy. Annie was small and slender and wiry, and moved with angular grace, her thin, peaked elbows showing beneath the sleeves of her pink gingham dress, her thin knees outlining beneath the scanty folds of the skirt. Her neck was long, her shoulder-blades troubled the back of her blouse at every movement. She was a creature full of ostentatious joints, but the joints were delicate and rhythmical and charming. Annie had a charming face, too. It was thin and sun-burnt, but still charming, with a sweet, eager, intent-to-please outlook upon life. This last was the real attitude of Annie's mind; it was, in fact, Annie. She was intent to please from her toes to the crown of her brown head. She radiated good will and loving-kindness as fervently as a lily in the border radiated perfume.

It was very warm, and the northwest sky had a threatening mountain of clouds. Occasionally An-nie glanced at it and raked the faster, and thought complacently of the water-proof covers in the little barn. This hay was valuable for the Reverend Silas's horse.

Two of the front windows of the house were filled with girls' heads, and the regular swaying movement of white-clad arms sewing. The girls sat in the house because it was so sunny on the piazza in the afternoon. There were four girls in the sitting-room, all making finery for themselves. On the other side of the front door one of the two windows was blank; in the other was visible a nodding gray head, that of Annie's father taking his afternoon nap.

Everything was still except the girls' tongues, an occasional burst of laughter, and the crackling shrill of locusts. Nothing had passed on the dusty road since Benny and Annie had begun their work. Lynn Corners was nothing more than a hamlet. It was even seldom that an automobile got astray there, being diverted from the little city of Anderson, six miles away, by turning to the left instead of the right.

Benny stopped again and wiped his forehead, all pink and beaded with sweat. He was a pretty young man—as pretty as a girl, although large. He glanced furtively at Annie, then he went with a soft, padding glide, like a big cat, to the piazza and settled down. He leaned his head against a post, closed his eyes, and inhaled the sweetness of flowers alive and dying, of new-mown hay. Annie glanced at him and an angelic look came over her face. At that moment the sweetness of her nature seemed actually visible.

"He is tired, poor boy!" she thought. She also thought that probably Benny felt the heat more because he was stout. Then she raked faster and faster. She fairly flew over the yard, raking the severed grass and flowers into heaps. The air grew more sultry. The sun was not yet clouded, but the northwest was darker and rumbled ominously.

The girls in the sitting-room continued to chatter and sew. One of them might have come out to help this little sister toiling alone, but Annie did not think of that. She raked with the uncomplaining sweetness of an angel until the storm burst. The rain came down in solid drops, and the sky was a sheet of clamoring flame. Annie made one motion toward the barn, but there was no use. The hay was not half cocked. There was no sense in running for covers. Benny was up and lumbering into the house, and her sisters were shutting windows and crying out to her. Annie deserted her post and fled before the wind, her pink skirts lashing her heels, her hair dripping.

When she entered the sitting-room her sisters, Imogen, Eliza, Jane, and Susan, were all there; also her father, Silas, tall and gaunt and gray. To the Hempsteads a thunder-storm partook of the nature of a religious ceremony. The family gathered together, and it was understood that they were all offering prayer and recognizing God as present on the wings of the tempest. In reality they were all very nervous in thunder-storms, with the exception of Annie. She always sent up a little silent petition that her sisters and brother and father, and the horse and dog and cat, might escape danger, although she had never been quite sure that she was not wicked in including the dog and cat. She was surer about the horse because he was the means by which her father made pastoral calls upon his distant sheep. Then afterward she just sat with the others and waited until the storm was over and it was time to open windows and see if the roof had leaked. To-day, however, she was intent upon the hay. In a lull of the tempest she spoke.

"It is a pity," she said, "that I was not able to get the hay cocked and the covers on."

Then Imogen turned large, sarcastic blue eyes upon her. Imogen was considered a beauty, pink and white, golden-haired, and dimpled, with a curious calculating hardness of character and a sharp tongue, so at variance with her appearance that people doubted the evidence of their senses.

"If," said Imogen, "you had only made Benny work instead of encouraging him to dawdle and finally to stop altogether, and if you had gone out directly after dinner, the hay would have been all raked up and covered."

Nothing could have exceeded the calm and instructive superiority of Imogen's tone. A mass of soft white fabric lay upon her lap, although she had removed scissors and needle and thimble to a safe

299

distance. She tilted her chin with a royal air. When the storm lulled she had stopped praying.

Imogen's sisters echoed her and joined in the attack upon Annie.

"Yes," said Jane, "if you had only started earlier, Annie. I told Eliza when you went out in the yard that it looked like a shower."

Eliza nodded energetically.

"It was foolish to start so late," said Susan, with a calm air of wisdom only a shade less exasperating than Imogen's.

"And you always encourage Benny so in being lazy," said Eliza.

Then the Reverend Silas joined in. "You should have more sense of responsibility toward your brother, your only brother, Annie," he said, in his deep pulpit voice.

"It was after two o'clock when you went out," said Imogen.

"And all you had to do was the dinner-dishes, and there were very few to-day," said Jane.

Then Annie turned with a quick, cat-like motion. Her eyes blazed under her brown toss of hair. She gesticulated with her little, nervous hands. Her voice was as sweet and intense as a reed, and withal piercing with anger.

"It was not half past one when I went out," said she, "and there was a whole sinkful of dishes."

"It was after two. I looked at the clock," said Imogen.

"It was not."

"And there were very few dishes," said Jane.

"A whole sinkful," said Annie, tense with wrath.

"You always are rather late about starting," said Susan.

"I am not! I was not! I washed the dishes, and swept the kitchen, and blacked the stove, and cleaned the silver."

"I swept the kitchen," said Imogen, severely. "Annie, I am surprised at you."

"And you know I cleaned the silver yesterday," said Jane.

Annie gave a gasp and looked from one to the other.

"You know you did not sweep the kitchen," said Imogen.

Annie's father gazed at her severely. "My dear," he said, "how long must I try to correct you of this habit of making false statements?"

"Dear Annie does not realize that they are false statements, father," said Jane. Jane was not pretty. but she gave the effect of a long, sweet stanza of some fine poetess. She was very tall and slender and large-eyed, and wore always a serious smile. She was attired in a purple muslin gown, cut V-shaped at the throat, and, as always, a black velvet ribbon with a little gold locket attached. The locket contained a coil of hair. Jane had been engaged to a young minister, now dead three years, and he had given her the locket.

Jane no doubt had mourned for her lover, but she had a covert pleasure in the romance of her situation. She was a year younger than Annie, and she had loved and lost, and so had achieved a sentimental distinction. Imogen always had admirers. Eliza had been courted at intervals half-heartedly by a widower, and Susan had had a few fleeting chances. But Jane was the only one who had been really definite in her heart affairs. As for Annie, nobody ever thought of her in such a connection. It was supposed that Annie had no thought of marriage, that she was foreordained to remain unwed and keep house for her father and Benny.

When Jane said that dear Annie did not realize that she made false statements, she voiced an opinion of the family before which Annie was always absolutely helpless. Defense meant counter-accusation. Annie could not accuse her family. She glanced from one to the other. In her blue eyes were still sparks of wrath, but she said nothing. She felt, as always, speechless, when affairs reached such a juncture. She began, in spite of her good sense, to feel guiltily responsible for everything—for the spoiling of the hay, even for the thunder-storm. What was more, she even wished to feel guiltily responsible. Anything was better than to be sure her sisters were not speaking the truth, that her father was blaming her unjustly.

Benny, who sat hunched upon himself with the effect of one set of bones and muscles leaning upon others for support, was the only one who spoke for her, and even he spoke to little purpose.

"One of you other girls," said he, in a thick, sweet voice, "might have come out and helped Annie; then she could have got the hay in."

They all turned on him.

"It is all very well for you to talk," said Imogen. "I saw you myself quit raking hay and sit down on the piazza."

"Yes," assented Jane, nodding violently, "I saw you, too."

"You have no sense of your responsibility, Benjamin, and your sister Annie abets you in evading it," said Silas Hempstead with dignity.

"Benny feels the heat," said Annie.

"Father is entirely right," said Eliza. "Benjamin has no sense of responsibility, and it is mainly owing to Annie."

"But dear Annie does not realize it," said Jane.

Benny got up lumberingly and left the room. He loved his sister Annie, but he hated the mild simmer of feminine rancor to which even his father's presence failed to add a masculine flavor. Benny was always leaving the room and allowing his sisters "to fight it out."

Just after he left there was a tremendous peal of thunder and a blue flash, and they all prayed again, except Annie, who was occupied with her own perplexities of life, and not at all afraid. She wondered, as she had wondered many times before, if she could possibly be in the wrong, if she were spoiling Benny, if she said and did things without knowing that she did so, or the contrary. Then suddenly she tightened her mouth. She knew. This sweet-tempered, anxious-to-please Annie was entirely sane, she had unusual self-poise. She *knew* that she knew what she did and said, and what she did not do or say, and a strange comprehension of her family over-whelmed her. Her sisters were truthful; she would not admit anything else, even to herself; but they confused desires and impulses with accomplishment. They had done so all their lives, some of them from intense egotism, some possibly from slight twists in their mental organisms. As for her father, he had simply rather a weak character, and was swayed by the majority. Annie, as she sat there among the praying group, made the same excuse for her sisters that they made for her. "They don't realize it," she said to herself.

When the storm finally ceased she hurried up-stairs and opened the windows, letting in the rain-fresh air. Then she got supper, while her sisters resumed their needlework. A curious conviction seized her, as she was hurrying about the kitchen, that in all probability some, if not all, of her sisters considered that they were getting the supper. Pos-sibly Jane had reflected that she ought to get supper, then she had taken another stitch in her work and had not known fairly that her impulse of duty had not been carried out. Imogen, presumably, was sew-ing with the serene consciousness that, since she was herself, it followed as a matter of course that she was performing all the tasks of the house.

While Annie was making an omelet Benny came out into the kitchen and stood regarding her, hands in pockets, making, as usual, one set of muscles rest upon another. His face was full of the utmost good nature, but it also convicted him of too much sloth to obey its commands.

"Say, Annie, what on earth makes them all pick on you so?" he observed.

"Hush, Benny! They don't mean to. They don't know it."

"But say, Annie, you must know that they tell whoppers. You *did* sweep the kitchen."

"Hush, Benny! Imogen really thinks she swept it."

"Imogen always thinks she has done everything she ought to do, whether she has done it or not," said Benny, with unusual astuteness. "Why don't you up and tell her she lies, Annie?"

"She doesn't really lie," said Annie.

"She does lie, even if she doesn't know it," said Benny; "and what is more, she ought to be made to know it. Say, Annie, it strikes me that you are doing the same by the girls that they accuse you of doing by me. Aren't you encouraging them in evil ways?"

Annie started, and turned and stared at him.

Benny nodded. "I can't see any difference," he said. "There isn't a day but one of the girls thinks she has done something you have done, or hasn't done something you ought to have done, and they blame you all the time, when you don't deserve it, and you let them, and they don't know it, and I don't think myself that they know they tell whoppers; but they ought to know. Strikes me you are just spoiling the whole lot, father thrown in, Annie. You are a dear, just as they say, but you are too much of a dear to be good for them."

Annie stared.

305

"You are letting that omelet burn," said Benny. "Say, Annie, I will go out and turn that hay in the morning. I know I don't amount to much, but I ain't a girl, anyhow, and I haven't got a cross-eyed soul. That's what ails a lot of girls. They mean all right, but their souls have been cross-eyed ever since they came into the world, and it's just such girls as you who ought to get them straightened out. You know what has happened to-day. Well, here's what happened yesterday. I don't tell tales, but you ought to know this, for I believe Tom Reed has his eye on you, in spite of Imogen's being such a beauty, and Susan's having manners like silk, and Eliza's giving everybody the impression that she is too good for this earth, and Jane's trying to make everybody think she is a sweet martyr, without a thought for mortal man, when that is only her way of trying to catch one. You know Tom Reed was here last evening?"

Annie nodded. Her face turned scarlet, then pathetically pale. She bent over her omelet, carefully lifting it around the edges.

"Well," Benny went on, "I know he came to see you, and Imogen went to the door and ushered him into the parlor, and I was out on the piazza, and she didn't know it, but I heard her tell him that she thought you had gone out. She hinted, too, that George Wells had taken you to the concert in the town hall. He did ask you, didn't he?"

"Yes."

"Well, Imogen spoke in this way." Benny lowered his voice and imitated Imogen to the life.

"'Yes, we are all well, thank you. Father is busy, of course; Jane has run over to Mrs. Jacobs's for a pattern; Eliza is writing letters; and Susan is somewhere about the house. Annie—well, Annie— George Wells asked her to go to the concert— I rather—' Then," said Benny, in his natural voice, "Imogen stopped, and she could say truthfully that she didn't lie, but anybody would have thought from what she said that you had gone to the concert with George Wells."

"Did Tom inquire for me?" asked Annie, in a low voice.

"Didn't have a chance. Imogen got ahead of him."

"Oh, well, then it doesn't matter. I dare say he did come to see Imogen."

"He didn't," said Benny, stoutly. "And that isn't all. Say, Annie—"

"What?"

"Are you going to marry George Wells? It is none of my business, but are you?"

Annie laughed a little, although her face was still pale. She had folded the omelet and was carefully watching it.

"You need not worry about that, Benny dear," she said.

"Then what right have the girls to tell so many people the nice things they hear you say about him?"

Annie removed the omelet skilfully from the pan to a hot plate, which she set on the range shelf, and turned to her brother.

"What nice things do they hear me say?"

"That he is so handsome; that he has such a good position; that he is the very best young man in the place; that you should think every girl would be head over heels in love with him; that every word he speaks is so bright and clever."

Annie looked at her brother.

"I don't believe you ever said one of those things," remarked Benny.

Annie continued to look at him.

"Did you?"

"Benny dear, I am not going to tell you."

"You won't say you never did, because that would be putting your sisters in the wrong and admitting that they tell lies. Annie, you are a dear, but I do think you are doing wrong and spoiling them as much as they say you are spoiling me."

"Perhaps I am," said Annie. There was a strange, tragic expression on her keen, pretty little face. She looked as if her mind was contemplating strenuous action which was changing her very features. She had covered the finished omelet and was now cooking another.

"I wish you would see if everybody is in the house and ready, Benny," said she. "When this omelet is done they must come right away, or nothing will be fit to eat. And, Benny dear, if you don't mind, please get the butter and the cream-pitcher out of the ice-chest. I have everything else on the table."

"There is another thing," said Benny. "I don't go about telling tales, but I do think it is time you knew. The girls tell everybody that you like to do

the housework so much that they don't dare interfere. And it isn't so. They may have taught themselves to think it is so, but it isn't. You would like
a little time for fancy-work and reading as well as
they do."

"Please get the cream and butter, and see if
they are all in the house," said Annie. She spoke
as usual, but the strange expression remained in her
face. It was still there when the family were all
gathered at the table and she was serving the puffy
omelet. Jane noticed it first.

"What makes you look so odd, Annie?" said she.

"I don't know how I look odd," replied Annie.
They all gazed at her then, her father with some
anxiety. "You don't look yourself," he said. "You
are feeling well, aren't you, Annie?"

"Quite well, thank you, father."

But after the omelet was served and the tea
poured Annie rose.

"Where are you going, Annie?" asked Imogen,
in her sarcastic voice.

"To my room, or perhaps out in the orchard."

"It will be sopping wet out there after the shower,"
said Eliza. "Are you crazy, Annie?"

"I have on my black skirt, and I will wear rub-
bers," said Annie, quietly. "I want some fresh air."

"I should think you had enough fresh air. You
were outdoors all the afternoon, while we were
cooped up in the house," said Jane.

"Don't you feel well, Annie?" her father asked
again, a golden bit of omelet poised on his fork, as
she was leaving the room.

"Quite well, father dear."

"But you are eating no supper."

"I have always heard that people who cook don't need so much to eat," said Imogen. "They say the essence of the food soaks in through the pores."

"I am quite well," Annie repeated, and the door closed behind her.

"Dear Annie! She is always doing odd things like this," remarked Jane.

"Yes, she is, things that one cannot account for, but Annie is a dear," said Susan.

"I hope she is well," said Annie's father.

"Oh, she is well enough. Don't worry, father," said Imogen. "Dear Annie is always doing the unexpected. She looks very well."

"Yes, dear Annie is quite stout, for her," said Jane.

"I think she is thinner than I have ever seen her, and the rest of you look like stuffed geese," said Benny, rudely.

Imogen turned upon him in dignified wrath. "Benny, you insult your sisters," said she. "Father, you should really tell Benny that he should bridle his tongue a little."

"You ought to bridle yours, every one of you," retorted Benny. "You girls nag poor Annie every single minute. You let her do all the work, then you pick at her for it."

There was a chorus of treble voices. "We nag dear Annie! We pick at dear Annie! We make her do everything! Father, you should remonstrate with Benjamin. You know how we all love dear Annie!"

DEAR ANNIE

"Benjamin," began Silas Hempstead, but Benny, with a smothered exclamation, was up and out of the room.

Benny quite frankly disliked his sisters, with the exception of Annie. For his father he had a sort of respectful tolerance. He could not see why he should have anything else. His father had never done anything for him except to admonish him. His scanty revenue for his support and college expenses came from his maternal grandmother, who had been a woman of parts and who had openly scorned her son-in-law.

Grandmother Loomis had left a will which occasioned much comment. By its terms she had provided sparsely but adequately for Benjamin's education and living until he should graduate; and her house, with all her personal property, and the bulk of the sum from which she had derived her own income, fell to her granddaughter Annie. Annie had always been her grandmother's favorite. There had been covert dismay when the contents of the will were made known, then one and all had congratulated the beneficiary, and said abroad that they were glad dear Annie was so well provided for. It was intimated by Imogen and Eliza that probably dear Annie would not marry, and in that case Grandmother Loomis's bequest was so fortunate. She had probably taken that into consideration. Grandmother Loomis had now been dead four years, and her deserted home had been for rent, furnished, but it had remained vacant.

Annie soon came back from the orchard, and after

she had cleared away the supper-table and washed the dishes she went up to her room, carefully re-arranged her hair, and changed her dress. Then she sat down beside a window and waited and watched, her pointed chin in a cup of one little thin hand, her soft muslin skirts circling around her, and the scent of queer old sachet emanating from a flowered ribbon of her grandmother's which she had tied around her waist. The ancient scent always clung to the rib-bon, suggesting faintly as a dream the musk and roses and violets of some old summer-time.

Annie sat there and gazed out on the front yard, which was silvered over with moonlight. Annie's four sisters all sat out there. They had spread a rug over the damp grass and brought out chairs. There were five chairs, although there were only four girls. Annie gazed over the yard and down the street. She heard the chatter of the girls, which was inconsequent and absent, as if their minds were on other things than their conversation. Then sud-denly she saw a small red gleam far down the street, evidently that of a cigar, and also a dark, moving figure. Then there ensued a subdued wrangle in the yard. Imogen insisted that her sisters should go into the house. They all resisted, Eliza the most vehemently. Imogen was arrogant and compelling. Finally she drove them all into the house except Eliza, who wavered upon the threshold of yielding. Imogen was obliged to speak very softly lest the ap-proaching man hear, but Annie, in the window above her, heard every word.

"You know he is coming to see me," said Imogen,

passionately. "You know—you know, Eliza, and yet every single time he comes, here are you girls, spying and listening."

"He comes to see Annie, I believe," said Eliza, in her stubborn voice, which yet had indecision in it.

"He never asks for her."

"He never has a chance. We all tell him, the minute he comes in, that she is out. But now I am going to stay, anyway."

"Stay if you want to. You are all a jealous lot. If you girls can't have a beau yourselves, you begrudge one to me. I never saw such a house as this for a man to come courting in."

"I will stay," said Eliza, and this time her voice was wholly firm. "There is no use in my going, anyway, for the others are coming back."

It was true. Back flitted Jane and Susan, and by that time Tom Reed had reached the gate, and his cigar was going out in a shower of sparks on the gravel walk, and all four sisters were greeting him and urging upon his acceptance the fifth chair. Annie, watching, saw that the young man seemed to hesitate. Then her heart leaped and she heard him speak quite plainly, with a note of defiance and irritation, albeit with embarrassment.

"Is Miss Annie in?" asked Tom Reed.

Imogen answered first, and her harsh voice was honey-sweet.

"I fear dear Annie is out," she said. "She will be so sorry to miss you."

Annie, at her window, made a sudden passionate motion, then she sat still and listened. She argued fiercely that she was right in so doing. She felt that the time had come when she must know, for the sake of her own individuality, just what she had to deal with in the natures of her own kith and kin. Dear Annie had turned in her groove of sweetness and gentle yielding, as all must turn who have any strength of character underneath the sweetness and gentleness. Therefore Annie, at her window above, listened.

At first she heard little that bore upon herself, for the conversation was desultory, about the weather and general village topics. Then Annie heard her own name. She was "dear Annie," as usual. She listened, fairly faint with amazement. What she heard from that quartette of treble voices down there in the moonlight seemed almost like a fairy-tale. The sisters did not violently incriminate her. They were too astute for that. They told half-truths. They told truths which were as shadows of the real facts, and yet not to be contradicted. They built up between them a story marvelously consistent, unless prearranged, and that Annie did not think possible. George Wells figured in the tale, and there were various hints and pauses concerning herself and her own character in daily life, and not one item could be flatly denied, even if the girl could have gone down there and, standing in the midst of that moonlit group, given her sisters the lie.

Everything which they told, the whole structure of falsehood, had beams and rafters of truth. Annie felt helpless before it all. To her fancy, her sisters and Tom Reed seemed actually sitting in a fairy building whose substance was utter falsehood, and yet which could not be utterly denied. An awful sense of isolation possessed her. So these were her own sisters, the sisters whom she had loved as a matter of the simplest nature, whom she had admired, whom she had served.

She made no allowance, since she herself was perfectly normal, for the motive which underlay it all. She could not comprehend the strife of the women over the one man. Tom Reed was in reality the one desirable match in the village. Annie knew, or thought she knew, that Tom Reed had it in mind to love her, and she innocently had it in mind to love him. She thought of a home of her own and his with delight. She thought of it as she thought of the roses coming into bloom in June, and she thought of it as she thought of the every-day happenings of life—cooking, setting rooms in order, washing dishes. However, there was something else to reckon with, and that Annie instinctively knew. She had been long-suffering, and her long-suffering was now regarded as endless. She had cast her pearls, and they had been trampled. She had turned her other cheek, and it had been promptly slapped. It was entirely true that Annie's sisters were not quite worthy of her, that they had taken advantage of her kindness and gentleness, and had mistaken them for weakness, to be despised. She did not understand them, nor they her. They were, on the whole, better than she thought, but with her there was a stern limit of endurance. Something whiter and hotter than mere wrath was in the girl's soul as she sat there and listened to the building of that structure of essential falsehood about herself.

She waited until Tom Reed had gone. He did not stay long. Then she went down-stairs with flying feet, and stood among them in the moonlight. Her father had come out of the study, and Benny had just been entering the gate as Tom Reed left. Then dear Annie spoke. She really spoke for the first time in her life, and there was something dreadful about it all. A sweet nature is always rather dreadful when it turns and strikes, and Annie struck with the whole force of a nature with a foundation of steel. She left nothing unsaid. She defended herself and she accused her sisters as if before a judge. Then came her ultimatum.

"To-morrow morning I am going over to Grandmother Loomis's house, and I am going to live there a whole year," she declared, in a slow, steady voice. "As you know, I have enough to live on, and—in order that no word of mine can be garbled and twisted as it has been to-night, I speak not at all. Everything which I have to communicate shall be written in black and white, and signed with my own name, and black and white cannot lie."

It was Jane who spoke first. "What will people say?" she whimpered, feebly.

"From what I have heard you all say to-night, whatever you make them," retorted Annie—the Annie who had turned.

Jane gasped. Silas Hempstead stood staring, quite dumb before the sudden problem. Imogen

316

DEAR ANNIE

alone seemed to have any command whatever of the situation.

"May I inquire what the butcher and grocer are going to think, no matter what your own sisters think and say, when you give your orders in writing?" she inquired, achieving a jolt from tragedy to the commonplace.

"That is my concern," replied Annie, yet she recognized the difficulty of that phase of the situation. It is just such trifling matters which detract from the dignity of extreme attitudes toward existence. Annie had taken an extreme attitude, yet here were the butcher and the grocer to reckon with. How could she communicate with them in writing without appearing absurd to the verge of insanity? Yet even that difficulty had a solution.

Annie thought it out after she had gone to bed that night. She had been imperturbable with her sisters, who had finally come in a body to make entreaties, although not apologies or retractions. There was a stiff-necked strain in the Hempstead family, and apologies and retractions were bitterer cuds for them to chew than for most. She had been imperturbable with her father, who had quoted Scripture and prayed at her during family worship. She had been imperturbable even with Benny, who had whispered to her: "Say, Annie, I don't blame you, but it will be a hell of a time without you. Can't you stick it out?"

But she had had a struggle before her own vision of the butcher and the grocer, and their amazement when she ceased to speak to them. Then she settled that with a sudden leap of inspiration. It sounded too apropos to be life, but there was a little deaf-and-dumb girl, a far-away relative of the Hempsteads, who lived with her aunt Felicia in Anderson. She was a great trial to her aunt Felicia, who was a widow and well-to-do, and liked the elegancies and normalities of life. This unfortunate little Effie Hempstead could not be placed in a charitable institution on account of the name she bore. Aunt Felicia considered it her worldly duty to care for her, but it was a trial.

Annie would take Effie off Aunt Felicia's hands, and no comment would be excited by a deaf-and-dumb girl carrying written messages to the tradesmen, since she obviously could not give them orally. The only comment would be on Annie's conduct in holding herself aloof from her family and the village people generally.

The next morning, when Annie went away, there was an excited conclave among the sisters.

"She means to do it," said Susan, and she wept.

Imogen's handsome face looked hard and set. "Let her, if she wants to," said she.

"Only think what people will say!" wailed Jane.

Imogen tossed her head. "I shall have something to say myself," she returned. "I shall say how much we all regret that dear Annie has such a difficult disposition that she felt she could not live with her own family and must be alone."

"But," said Jane, blunt in her distress, "will they believe it?"

"Why will they not believe it, pray?"

DEAR ANNIE

"Why, I am afraid people have the impression that dear Annie has—" Jane hesitated.

"What?" asked Imogen, coldly. She looked very handsome that morning. Not a waved golden hair was out of place on her carefully brushed head. She wore the neatest of blue linen skirts and blouses, with a linen collar and white tie. There was something hard but compelling about her blond beauty.

"I am afraid," said Jane, "that people have a sort of general impression that dear Annie has perhaps as sweet a disposition as any of us, perhaps sweeter."

"Nobody says that dear Annie has not a sweet disposition," said Imogen, taking a careful stitch in her embroidery. "But a sweet disposition is very often extremely difficult for other people. It constantly puts them in the wrong. I am well aware of the fact that dear Annie does a great deal for all of us, but it is sometimes irritating. Of course it is quite certain that she must have a feeling of superiority because of it, and she should not have it."

Sometimes Eliza made illuminating speeches. "I suppose it follows, then," said she, with slight irony, "that only an angel can have a very sweet disposition without offending others."

But Imogen was not in the least nonplussed. She finished her line of thought. "And with all her sweet disposition," said she, "nobody can deny that dear Annie is peculiar, and peculiarity always makes people difficult for other people. Of course it is horribly peculiar what she is proposing to do

319

now. That in itself will be enough to convince people that dear Annie must be difficult. Only a difficult person could do such a strange thing."

"Who is going to get up and get breakfast in the morning, and wash the dishes?" inquired Jane, irrelevantly.

"All I ever want for breakfast is a bit of fruit, a roll, and an egg, besides my coffee," said Imogen, with her imperious air.

"Somebody has to prepare it."

"That is a mere nothing," said Imogen, and she took another stitch.

After a little, Jane and Eliza went by themselves and discussed the problem.

"It is quite evident that Imogen means to do nothing," said Jane.

"And also that she will justify herself by the theory that there is nothing to be done," said Eliza.

"Oh, well," said Jane, "I will get up and get breakfast, of course. I once contemplated the prospect of doing it the rest of my life."

Eliza assented. "I can understand that it will not be so hard for you," she said, "and although I myself always aspired to higher things than preparing breakfasts, still, you did not, and it is true that you would probably have had it to do if poor Henry had lived, for he was not one to ever have a very large salary."

"There are better things than large salaries," said Jane, and her face looked sadly reminiscent. After all, the distinction of being the only one who had been on the brink of preparing matrimonial breakfasts was much. She felt that it would make early rising and early work endurable to her, although she was not an active young woman.

"I will get a dish-mop and wash the dishes," said Eliza. "I can manage to have an instructive book propped open on the kitchen table, and keep my mind upon higher things as I do such menial tasks."

Then Susan stood in the doorway, a tall figure gracefully swaying sidewise, long-throated and prominent-eyed. She was the least attractive-looking of any of the sisters, but her manners were so charming, and she was so perfectly the lady, that it made up for any lack of beauty.

"I will dust," said Susan, in a lovely voice, and as she spoke she involuntarily bent and swirled her limp muslins in such a way that she fairly suggested a moral duster. There was the making of an actress in Susan. Nobody had ever been able to decide what her true individual self was. Quite unconsciously, like a chameleon, she took upon herself the characteristics of even inanimate things. Just now she was a duster, and a wonderfully creditable duster.

"Who," said Jane, "is going to sweep? Dear Annie has always done that."

"I am not strong enough to sweep. I am very sorry," said Susan, who remained a duster, and did not become a broom.

"If we have system," said Eliza, vaguely, "the work ought not to be so very hard."

"Of course not," said Imogen. She had come in and seated herself. Her three sisters eyed her, but she embroidered imperturbably. The same thought

21 321

was in the minds of all. Obviously Imogen was the very one to take the task of sweeping upon herself. That hard, compact, young body of hers suggested strenuous household work. Embroidery did not seem to be her rôle at all.

But Imogen had no intention of sweeping. Indeed, the very imagining of such tasks in connection with herself was beyond her. She did not even dream that her sisters expected it of her.

"I suppose," said Jane, "that we might be able to engage Mrs. Moss to come in once a week and do the sweeping."

"It would cost considerable," said Susan.

"But it has to be done."

"I should think it might be managed, with system, if you did not hire anybody," said Imogen, calmly.

"You talk of system as if it were a suction cleaner," said Eliza, with a dash of asperity. Sometimes she reflected how she would have hated Imogen had she not been her sister.

"System is invaluable," said Imogen. She looked away from her embroidery to the white stretch of country road, arched over with elms, and her beautiful eyes had an expression as if they sighted system, the justified settler of all problems.

Meantime, Annie Hempstead was traveling to Anderson in the jolting trolley-car, and trying to settle her emotions and her outlook upon life, which jolted worse than the car upon a strange new track. She had not the slightest intention of giving up her plan, but she realized within herself the sensations of a revolutionist. Who in her family, for generations and generations, had ever taken the course which she was taking? She was not exactly frightened —Annie had splendid courage when once her blood was up—but she was conscious of a tumult and grind of adjustment to a new level which made her nervous.

She reached the end of the car line, then walked about half a mile to her Aunt Felicia Hempstead's house. It was a handsome house, after the standard of nearly half a century ago. It had an opulent air, with its swelling breasts of bay windows, through which showed fine lace curtains; its dormer-windows, each with its carefully draped curtains; its black-walnut front door, whose side-lights were screened with medallioned lace. The house sat high on three terraces of velvet-like grass, and was surmounted by stone steps in three instalments, each of which was flanked by stone lions.

Annie mounted the three tiers of steps between the stone lions and rang the front-door bell, which was polished so brightly that it winked at her like a brazen eye. Almost directly the door was opened by an immaculate, white-capped and white-aproned maid, and Annie was ushered into the parlor. When Annie had been a little thing she had been enamoured of and impressed by the splendor of this parlor. Now she had doubts of it, in spite of the long, magnificent sweep of lace curtains, the sheen of carefully kept upholstery, the gleam of alabaster statuettes, and the even piles of gilt-edged books upon the polished tables.

Soon Mrs. Felicia Hempstead entered, a tall, well-set-up woman, with a handsome face and keen eyes. She wore her usual morning costume—a breakfast sacque of black silk profusely trimmed with lace, and a black silk skirt. She kissed Annie, with a slight peck of closely set lips, for she liked her. Then she sat down opposite her and regarded her with as much of a smile as her sternly set mouth could manage, and inquired politely regarding her health and that of the family. When Annie broached the subject of her call, the set calm of her face relaxed, and she nodded.

"I know what your sisters are. You need not explain to me," she said.

"But," returned Annie, "I do not think they realize. It is only because I—"

"Of course," said Felicia Hempstead. "It is because they need a dose of bitter medicine, and you hope they will be the better for it. I understand you, my dear. You have spirit enough, but you don't get it up often. That is where they make their mistake. Often the meek are meek from choice, and they are the ones to beware of. I don't blame you for trying it. And you can have Effie and welcome. I warn you that she is a little wearing. Of course she can't help her affliction, poor child, but it is dreadful. I have had her taught. She can read and write very well now, poor child, and she is not lacking, and I have kept her well dressed. I take her out to drive with me every day, and am not ashamed to have her seen with me. If she had all her faculties she would not be a bad-looking little girl. Now, of course, she has something of a vacant expression. That comes, I suppose, from her not being able to hear. She has learned to speak a few words, but I don't encourage her doing that before people. It is too evident that there is something wrong. She never gets off one tone. But I will let her speak to you. She will be glad to go with you. She likes you, and I dare say you can put up with her. A woman when she is alone will make a companion of a brazen image. You can manage all right for everything except her clothes and lessons. I will pay for them."

"Can't I give her lessons?"

"Well, you can try, but I am afraid you will need to have Mr. Freer come over once a week. It seems to me to be quite a knack to teach the deaf and dumb. You can see. I will have Effie come in and tell her about the plan. I wanted to go to Europe this summer, and did not know how to manage about Effie. It will be a godsend to me, this arrangement, and of course after the year is up she can come back."

With that Felicia touched a bell, the maid appeared with automatic readiness, and presently a tall little girl entered. She was very well dressed. Her linen frock was hand-embroidered, and her shoes were ultra. Her pretty shock of fair hair was tied with French ribbon in a fetching bow, and she made a courtesy which would have befitted a little princess. Poor Effie's courtesy was the one feature in which Felicia Hempstead took pride. After making it the child always glanced at her for approval, and her face lighted up with pleasure at the faint smile which her little performance evoked. Effie would have been a pretty little girl had it not been for that vacant, bewildered expression of which Felicia had spoken. It was the expression of one shut up with the darkest silence of life, that of her own self, and beauty was incompatible with it.

Felicia placed her stiff forefinger upon her own lips and nodded, and the child's face became transfigured. She spoke in a level, awful voice, utterly devoid of inflection, and full of fright. Her voice was as the first attempt of a skater upon ice. However, it was intelligible.

"Good morning," said she. "I hope you are well." Then she courtesied again. That little speech and one other, "Thank you, I am very well," were all she had mastered. Effie's instruction had begun rather late, and her teacher was not remarkably skilful.

When Annie's lips moved in response, Effie's face fairly glowed with delight and affection. The little girl loved Annie. Then her questioning eyes sought Felicia, who beckoned, and drew from the pocket of her rustling silk skirt a tiny pad and pencil. Effie crossed the room and stood at attention while Felicia wrote. When she had read the words on the pad she gave one look at Annie, then another at Felicia, who nodded.

Effie courtesied before Annie like a fairy dancer. "Good morning. I hope you are well," she said. Then she courtesied again and said, "Thank you, I am very well." Her pretty little face was quite eager with love and pleasure, and yet there was an effect as of a veil before the happy emotion in it. The contrast between the awful, level voice and the grace of motion and evident delight at once shocked and compelled pity. Annie put her arms around Effie and kissed her.

"You dear little thing," she said, quite forgetting that Effie could not hear.

Felicia Hempstead got speedily to work, and soon Effie's effects were packed and ready for transportation upon the first express to Lynn Corners, and Annie and the little girl had boarded the trolley thither.

Annie Hempstead had the sensation of one who takes a cold plunge—half pain and fright, half exhilaration and triumph—when she had fairly taken possession of her grandmother's house. There was genuine girlish pleasure in looking over the stock of old china and linen and ancient mahoganies, in starting a fire in the kitchen stove, and preparing a meal, the written order for which Effie had taken to the grocer and butcher. There was genuine delight in sitting down with Effie at her very own table, spread with her grandmother's old damask and pretty dishes, and eating, without hearing a word of unfavorable comment upon the cookery. But there was a certain pain and terror in trampling upon that which it was difficult to define, either her conscience or sense of the divine right of the conventional.

But that night after Effie had gone to bed, and the house was set to rights, and she in her cool muslin was sitting on the front-door step, under the hooded trellis covered with wistaria, she was conscious of entire emancipation. She fairly gloated over her new estate.

"To-night one of the others will really have to get the supper, and wash the dishes, and not be able to say she did it and I didn't, when I did," Annie thought with unholy joy. She knew perfectly well that her viewpoint was not sanctified, but she felt that she must allow her soul to have its little witch-caper or she could not answer for the consequences. There might result spiritual atrophy, which would be much more disastrous than sin and repentance. It was either the continuance of her old life in her father's house, which was the ignominious and harmful one of the scapegoat, or this. She at last reveled in this. Here she was mistress. Here what she did, she did, and what she did not do remained undone. Here her silence was her invincible weapon. Here she was free.

The soft summer night enveloped her. The air was sweet with flowers and the grass which lay still unraked in her father's yard. A momentary feeling of impatience seized her; then she dismissed it, and peace came. What had she to do with that hay? Her father would be obliged to buy hay if it were not raked over and dried, but what of that? She had nothing to do with it.

She heard voices and soft laughter. A dark shadow passed along the street. Her heart quickened its beat. The shadow turned in at her father's gate. There was a babel of welcoming voices, of which Annie could not distinguish one articulate word. She sat leaning forward, her eyes intent upon the road. Then she heard the click of her father's gate and the dark, shadowy figure reappeared in the road. Annie knew who it was; she knew that Tom Reed was coming to see her. For a second, rapture seized her, then dismay. How well she knew her sisters—how very well! Not one of them would have given him the slightest inkling of the true situation. They would have told him, by the sweetest of insinuations, rather than by straight statements, that she had left her father's roof and come over here, but not one word would have been told him concerning her vow of silence. They would leave that for him to discover, to his amazement and anger.

Annie rose and fled. She closed the door, turned the key softly, and ran up-stairs in the dark. Kneeling before a window on the farther side from her old home, she watched with eager eyes the young man open the gate and come up the path between the old-fashioned shrubs. The clove-like fragrance of the pinks in the border came in her face. Annie watched Tom Reed disappear beneath the trellised hood of the door; then the bell tinkled through the house. It seemed to Annie that she heard it as she had never heard anything before. Every nerve in her body seemed urging her to rise and go down-stairs and admit this young man whom she loved. But her will, turned upon itself, kept her back. She could not rise and go down; something stronger than her own wish restrained her. She suffered horribly, but she remained. The bell tinkled again. There was a pause, then it sounded for the third time.

Annie leaned against the window, faint and trembling. It was rather horrible to continue such a fight between will and inclination, but she held out. She would not have been herself had she not done so. Then she saw Tom Reed's figure emerge from under the shadow of the door, pass down the path between the sweet-flowering shrubs, seeming to stir up the odor of the pinks as he did so. He started to go down the road; then Annie heard a loud, silvery call, with a harsh inflection, from her father's house. "Imogen is calling him back," she thought.

Annie was out of the room, and, slipping softly down-stairs and out into the yard, crouched close to the fence overgrown with sweetbrier, its foundation hidden in the mallow, and there she listened. She wanted to know what Imogen and her other sisters were about to say to Tom Reed, and she meant to know. She heard every word. The distance was not great, and her sisters' voices carried far, in spite of their honeyed tones and efforts toward secrecy. By the time Tom had reached the gate of the parsonage they had all crowded down there, a fluttering assembly in their snowy summer muslins, like white doves. Annie heard Imogen first. Imogen was always the ringleader.

"Couldn't you find her?" asked Imogen.

"No. Rang three times," replied Tom. He had a boyish voice, and his chagrin showed plainly in it. Annie knew just how he looked, how dear and big and foolish, with his handsome, bewildered face, blurting out to her sisters his disappointment, with innocent faith in their sympathy.

Then Annie heard Eliza speak in a small, sweet voice, which yet, to one who understood her, carried in it a sting of malice. "How very strange!" said Eliza.

Jane spoke next. She echoed Eliza, but her voice was more emphatic and seemed multiple, as echoes do. "Yes, very strange indeed," said Jane.

"Dear Annie is really very singular lately. It has distressed us all, especially father," said Susan, but deprecatingly.

Then Imogen spoke, and to the point. "Annie must be in that house," said she. "She went in there, and she could not have gone out without our seeing her."

Annie could fairly see the toss of Imogen's head as she spoke.

"What in thunder do you all mean?" asked Tom Reed, and there was a bluntness, almost a brutality, in his voice which was refreshing.

"I do not think such forcible language is becoming, especially at the parsonage," said Jane.

Annie distinctly heard Tom Reed snort. "Hang it if I care whether it is becoming or not," said he.

"You seem to forget that you are addressing ladies, sir," said Jane.

"Don't forget it for a blessed minute," returned Tom Reed. "Wish I could. You make it too evident that you are—ladies, with every word you speak, and all your beating about the bush. A man would blurt it out, and then I would know where I am at. Hang it if I know now. You all say that your sister is singular and that she distresses your father, and you"—addressing Imogen—"say that she must be in that house. You are the only one who does make a dab at speaking out; I will say that much for you. Now, if she is in that house, what in thunder is the matter?"

"I really cannot stay here and listen to such profane language," said Jane, and she flitted up the path to the house like an enraged white moth. She had a fleecy white shawl over her head, and her pale outline was triangular.

"If she calls that profane, I pity her," said Tom Reed. He had known the girls since they were children, and had never liked Jane. He continued, still addressing Imogen. "For Heaven's sake, if she is in that house, what is the matter?" said he. "Doesn't the bell ring? Yes, it does ring, though it is as cracked as the devil. I heard it. Has Annie gone deaf? Is she sick? Is she asleep? It is only eight o'clock. I don't believe she is asleep. Doesn't she want to see me? Is that the trouble? What have I done? Is she angry with me?"

Eliza spoke, smoothly and sweetly. "Dear Annie is singular," said she.

"What the dickens do you mean by singular? I have known Annie ever since she was that high. It never struck me that she was any more singular than other girls, except she stood an awful lot of nagging without making a kick. Here you all say she is singular, as if you meant she was"—Tom hesitated a second—"crazy," said he. "Now, I know that Annie is saner than any girl around here, and that simply does not go down. What do you all mean by singular?"

DEAR ANNIE

"Dear Annie may not be singular, but her actions are sometimes singular," said Susan. "We all feel badly about this."

"You mean her going over to her grandmother's house to live? I don't know whether I think that is anything but horse-sense. I have eyes in my head, and I have used them. Annie has worked like a dog here; I suppose she needed a rest."

"We all do our share of the work," said Eliza, calmly, "but we do it in a different way from dear Annie. She makes very hard work of work. She has not as much system as we could wish. She tires herself unnecessarily."

"Yes, that is quite true," assented Imogen. "Dear Annie gets very tired over the slightest tasks, whereas if she went a little more slowly and used more system the work would be accomplished well and with no fatigue. There are five of us to do the work here, and the house is very convenient."

There was a silence. Tom Reed was bewildered. "But—doesn't she want to see me?" he asked, finally.

"Dear Annie takes very singular notions sometimes," said Eliza, softly.

"If she took a notion not to go to the door when she heard the bell ring, she simply wouldn't," said Imogen, whose bluntness of speech was, after all, a relief.

"Then you mean that you think she took a notion not to go to the door?" asked Tom, in a desperate tone.

"Dear Annie is very singular," said Eliza, with

such softness and deliberation that it was like a minor chord of music.

"Do you know of anything she has against me?" asked Tom of Imogen; but Eliza answered for her.

"Dear Annie is not in the habit of making confidantes of her sisters," said she, "but we do know that she sometimes takes unwarranted dislikes."

"Which time generally cures," said Susan.

"Oh yes," assented Eliza, "which time generally cures. She can have no reason whatever for avoiding you. You have always treated her well."

"I have always meant to," said Tom, so miserably and helplessly that Annie, listening, felt her heart go out to this young man, badgered by females, and she formed a sudden resolution.

"You have not seen very much of her, anyway," said Imogen.

"I have always asked for her, but I understood she was busy," said Tom, "and that was the reason why I saw her so seldom."

"Oh," said Eliza, "busy!" She said it with an indescribable tone.

"If," supplemented Imogen, "there was system, there would be no need of any one of us being too busy to see our friends."

"Then she has not been busy? She has not wanted to see me?" said Tom. "I think I understand at last. I have been a fool not to before. You girls have broken it to me as well as you could. Much obliged, I am sure. Good night."

"Won't you come in?" asked Imogen.

"We might have some music," said Eliza.

DEAR ANNIE

"And there is an orange cake, and I will make coffee," said Susan.

Annie reflected rapidly how she herself had made that orange cake, and what queer coffee Susan would be apt to concoct.

"No, thank you," said Tom Reed, briskly. "I will drop in another evening. Think I must go home now. I have some important letters. Good night, all."

Annie made a soft rush to the gate, crouching low that her sisters might not see her. They flocked into the house with irascible murmurings, like scolding birds, while Annie stole across the grass, which had begun to glisten with silver wheels of dew. She held her skirts closely wrapped around her, and stepped through a gap in the shrubs beside the walk, then sped swiftly to the gate. She reached it just as Tom Reed was passing with a quick stride.

"Tom," said Annie, and the young man stopped short.

He looked in her direction, but she stood close to a great snowball-bush, and her dress was green muslin, and he did not see her. Thinking that he had been mistaken, he started on, when she called again, and this time she stepped apart from the bush and her voice sounded clear as a flute.

"Tom," she said. "Stop a minute, please."

Tom stopped and came close to her. In the dim light she could see that his face was all aglow, like a child's, with delight and surprise.

"Is that you, Annie?" he said.

"Yes, I want to speak to you, please."

"I have been here before, and I rang the bell three times. Then you were out, although your sisters thought not."

"No, I was in the house."

"You did not hear the bell?"

"Yes, I heard it every time."

"Then why—?"

"Come into the house with me and I will tell you; at least I will tell you all I can."

Annie led the way and the young man followed. He stood in the dark entry while Annie lit the parlor lamp. The room was on the farther side of the house from the parsonage.

"Come in and sit down," said Annie. Then the young man stepped into a room which was pretty in spite of itself. There was an old Brussels carpet with an enormous rose pattern. The haircloth furniture gave out gleams like black diamonds under the light of the lamp. In a corner stood a what-not piled with branches of white coral and shells. Annie's grandfather had been a sea-captain, and many of his spoils were in the house. Possibly Annie's own occupation of it was due to an adventurous strain inherited from him. Perhaps the same impulse which led him to voyage to foreign shores had led her to voyage across a green yard to the next house.

Tom Reed sat down on the sofa. Annie sat in a rocking-chair near by. At her side was a Chinese teapoy, a nest of lacquer tables, and on it stood a small, squat idol. Annie's grandmother had been taken to task by her son-in-law, the Reverend Silas, for harboring a heathen idol, but she had only laughed.

DEAR ANNIE

"Guess as long as I don't keep heathen to bow down before him, he can't do much harm," she had said.

Now the grotesque face of the thing seemed to stare at the two Occidental lovers with the strange, calm sarcasm of the Orient, but they had no eyes or thought for it.

"Why didn't you come to the door if you heard the bell ring?" asked Tom Reed, gazing at Annie, slender as a blade of grass in her clinging green gown.

"Because I was not able to break my will then. I had to break it to go out in the yard and ask you to come in, but when the bell rang I hadn't got to the point where I could break it."

"What on earth do you mean, Annie?"

Annie laughed. "I don't wonder you ask," she said, "and the worst of it is I can't half answer you. I wonder how much, or rather how little explanation will content you?"

Tom Reed gazed at her with the eyes of a man who might love a woman and have infinite patience with her, relegating his lack of understanding of her woman's nature to the background, as a thing of no consequence.

"Mighty little will do for me," he said, "mighty little, Annie dear, if you will only tell a fellow you love him."

Annie looked at him, and her thin, sweet face seemed to have a luminous quality, like a crescent moon. Her look was enough.

"Then you do?" said Tom Reed.

"You have never needed to ask," said Annie. "You knew."

"I haven't been so sure as you think," said Tom. "Suppose you come over here and sit beside me. You look miles away."

Annie laughed and blushed, but she obeyed. She sat beside Tom and let him put his arm around her. She sat up straight, by force of her instinctive maidenliness, but she kissed him back when he kissed her.

"I haven't been so sure," repeated Tom. "Annie darling, why have I been unable to see more of you? I have fairly haunted your house, and seen the whole lot of your sisters, especially Imogen, but somehow or other you have been as slippery as an eel. I have always asked for you, but you were always out or busy."

"I have been very busy," said Annie, evasively. She loved this young man with all her heart, but she had an enduring loyalty to her own flesh and blood.

Tom was very literal. "Say, Annie," he blurted out, "I begin to think you have had to do most of the work over there. Now, haven't you? Own up."

Annie laughed sweetly. She was so happy that no sense of injury could possibly rankle within her. "Oh, well," she said, lightly. "Perhaps. I don't know. I guess housekeeping comes rather easier to me than to the others. I like it, you know, and work is always easier when one likes it. The other girls don't take to it so naturally, and they get very tired, and it has seemed often that I was the one who could hurry the work through and not mind."

338

DEAR ANNIE

"I wonder if you will stick up for me the way you do for your sisters when you are my wife?" said Tom, with a burst of love and admiration. Then he added: "Of course you are going to be my wife, Annie? You know what this means?"

"If you think I will make you as good a wife as you can find," said Annie.

"As good a wife! Annie, do you really know what you are?"

"Just an ordinary girl, with no special talent for anything."

"You are the most wonderful girl that ever walked the earth," exclaimed Tom. "And as for talent, you have the best talent in the whole world; you can love people who are not worthy to tie your shoe-strings, and think you are looking up when in reality you are looking down. That is what I call the best talent in the whole world for a woman." Tom Reed was becoming almost subtle.

Annie only laughed happily again. "Well, you will have to wait and find out," said she.

"I suppose," said Tom, "that you came over here because you were tired out, this hot weather. I think you were sensible, but I don't think you ought to be here alone."

"I am not alone," replied Annie. "I have poor little Effie Hempstead with me."

"That deaf-and-dumb child? I should think this heathen god would be about as much company."

"Why, Tom, she is human, if she is deaf and dumb."

Tom eyed her shrewdly. "What did you mean
339

when you said you had broken your will?" he inquired.

"My will not to speak for a while," said Annie, faintly.

"Not to speak—to any one?"

Annie nodded.

"Then you have broken your resolution by speaking to me?"

Annie nodded again.

"But why shouldn't you speak? I don't understand."

"I wondered how little I could say, and have you satisfied," Annie replied, sadly.

Tom tightened his arm around her. "You precious little soul," he said. "I am satisfied. I know you have some good reason for not wanting to speak, but I am plaguey glad you spoke to me, for I should have been pretty well cast down if you hadn't, and to-morrow I have to go away."

Annie leaned toward him. "Go away!"

"Yes; I have to go to California about that confounded Ames will case. And I don't know exactly where, on the Pacific coast, the parties I have to interview may be, and I may have to be away weeks, possibly months. Annie darling, it did seem to me a cruel state of things to have to go so far, and leave you here, living in such a queer fashion, and not know how you felt. Lord! but I'm glad you had sense enough to call me, Annie."

"I couldn't let you go by, when it came to it, and Tom—"

"What, dear?"

"I did an awful mean thing: something I never was guilty of before. I—listened."

"Well, I don't see what harm it did. You didn't hear much to your or your sisters' disadvantage, that I can remember. They kept calling you 'dear.'"

"Yes," said Annie, quickly. Again, such was her love and thankfulness that a great wave of love and forgiveness for her sisters swept over her. Annie had a nature compounded of depths of sweetness; nobody could be mistaken with regard to that. What they did mistake was the possibility of even sweetness being at bay at times, and remaining there.

"You don't mean to speak to anybody else?" asked Tom.

"Not for a year, if I can avoid it without making comment which might hurt father."

"Why, dear?"

"That is what I cannot tell you," replied Annie, looking into his face with a troubled smile.

Tom looked at her in a puzzled way, then he kissed her.

"Oh, well, dear," he said, "it is all right. I know perfectly well you would do nothing in which you were not justified, and you have spoken to me, anyway, and that is the main thing. I think if I had been obliged to start to-morrow without a word from you I shouldn't have cared a hang whether I ever came back or not. You are the only soul to hold me here; you know that, darling."

"Yes," replied Annie.

"You are the only one," repeated Tom, "but it seems to me this minute as if you were a whole host, you dear little soul. But I don't quite like to leave you here living alone, except for Effie."

"Oh, I am within a stone's-throw of father's," said Annie, lightly.

"I admit that. Still, you are alone. Annie, when are you going to marry me?"

Annie regarded him with a clear, innocent look. She had lived such a busy life that her mind was unfilmed by dreams. "Whenever you like, after you come home," said she.

"It can't be too soon for me. I want my wife and I want my home. What will you do while I am gone, dear?"

Annie laughed. "Oh, I shall do what I have seen other girls do—get ready to be married."

"That means sewing, lots of hemming and tucking and stitching, doesn't it?"

"Of course."

"Girls are so funny," said Tom. "Now imagine a man sitting right down and sewing like mad on his collars and neckties and shirts the minute a girl said she'd marry him!"

"Girls like it."

"Well, I suppose they do," said Tom, and he looked down at Annie from a tender height of masculinity, and at the same time seemed to look up from the valley of one who cannot understand the subtle and poetical details in a woman's soul.

He did not stay long after that, for it was late. As he passed through the gate, after a tender farewell, Annie watched him with shining eyes. She was now to be all alone, but two things she had, her freedom and her love, and they would suffice.

The next morning Silas Hempstead, urged by his daughters, walked solemnly over to the next house, but he derived little satisfaction. Annie did not absolutely refuse to speak. She had begun to realize that carrying out her resolution to the extreme letter was impossible. But she said as little as she could.

"I have come over here to live for the present. I am of age, and have a right to consult my own wishes. My decision is unalterable." Having said this much, Annie closed her mouth and said no more. Silas argued and pleaded. Annie sat placidly sewing beside one front window of the sunny sitting-room. Effie, with a bit of fancy-work, sat at another. Finally Silas went home defeated, with a last word, half condemnatory, half placative. Silas was not the sort to stand firm against such feminine strength as his daughter Annie's. However, he secretly held her dearer than all his other children.

After her father had gone, Annie sat taking even stitch after even stitch, but a few tears ran over her cheeks and fell upon the soft mass of muslin. Effie watched with shrewd, speculative silence, like a pet cat. Then suddenly she rose and went close to Annie, with her little arms around her neck, and the poor dumb mouth repeating her little speeches: "Thank you, I am very well, thank you, I am very well," over and over.

Annie kissed her fondly, and was aware of a sense of comfort and of love for this poor little Effie. Still, after being nearly two months with the child, she was relieved when Felicia Hempstead came, the first of September, and wished to take Effie home with her. She had not gone to Europe, after all, but to the mountains, and upon her return had missed the little girl.

Effie went willingly enough, but Annie discovered that she too missed her. Now loneliness had her fairly in its grip. She had a telephone installed, and gave her orders over that. Sometimes the sound of a human voice made her emotional to tears. Besides the voices over the telephone, Annie had nobody, for Benny returned to college soon after Effie left. Benny had been in the habit of coming in to see Annie, and she had not had the heart to check him. She talked to him very little, and knew that he was no telltale as far as she was concerned, although he waxed most communicative with regard to the others. A few days before he left he came over and begged her to return.

"I know the girls have nagged you till you are fairly worn out," he said. "I know they don't tell things straight, but I don't believe they know it, and I don't see why you can't come home, and insist upon your rights, and not work so hard."

"If I come home now it will be as it was before," said Annie.

"Can't you stand up for yourself and not have it the same?"

Annie shook her head.

"Seems as if you could," said Benny. "I always thought a girl knew how to manage other girls. It is rather awful the way things go now over there.

344

Father must be uncomfortable enough trying to eat the stuff they set before him and living in such a dirty house."

Annie winced. "Is it so very dirty?"

Benny whistled.

"Is the food so bad?"

Benny whistled again.

"You advised me—or it amounted to the same thing—to take this stand," said Annie.

"I know I did, but I didn't know how bad it would be. Guess I didn't half appreciate you myself, Annie. Well, you must do as you think best, but if you could look in over there your heart would ache."

"My heart aches as it is," said Annie, sadly.

Benny put an arm around her. "Poor girl!" he said. "It is a shame, but you are going to marry Tom. You ought not to have the heartache."

"Marriage isn't everything," said Annie, "and my heart does ache, but—I can't go back there, unless—I can't make it clear to you, Benny, but it seems to me as if I couldn't go back there until the year is up, or I shouldn't be myself, and it seems, too, as if I should not be doing right by the girls. There are things more important even than doing work for others. I have got it through my head that I can be dreadfully selfish being unselfish."

"Well, I suppose you are right," admitted Benny with a sigh.

Then he kissed Annie and went away, and the blackness of loneliness settled down upon her. She had wondered at first that none of the village people

came to see her, although she did not wish to talk to
them; then she no longer wondered. She heard, without hearing, just what her sisters had said about her.

That was a long winter for Annie Hempstead.
Letters did not come very regularly from Tom Reed,
for it was a season of heavy snowfalls and the mails
were often delayed. The letters were all that she
had for comfort and company. She had bought a
canary-bird, adopted a stray kitten, and filled her
sunny windows with plants. She sat beside them
and sewed, and tried to be happy and content, but
all the time there was a frightful uncertainty deep
down within her heart as to whether or not she was
doing right. She knew that her sisters were unworthy, and yet her love and longing for them
waxed greater and greater. As for her father, she
loved him as she had never loved him before. The
struggle grew terrible. Many a time she dressed
herself in outdoor array and started to go home,
but something always held her back. It was a
strange conflict that endured through the winter
months, the conflict of a loving, self-effacing heart
with its own instincts.

Toward the last of February her father came over
at dusk. Annie ran to the door, and he entered.
He looked unkempt and dejected. He did not say
much, but sat down and looked about him with a
half-angry, half-discouraged air. Annie went out
into the kitchen and broiled some beefsteak, and
creamed some potatoes, and made tea and toast.
Then she called him into the sitting-room, and he
ate like one famished.

DEAR ANNIE

"Your sister Susan does the best she can," he said, when he had finished, "and lately Jane has been trying, but they don't seem to have the knack. I don't want to urge you, Annie, but—"

"You know when I am married you will have to get on without me," Annie said, in a low voice.

"Yes, but in the mean time you might, if you were home, show Susan and Jane."

"Father," said Annie, "you know if I came home now it would be just the same as it was before. You know if I give in and break my word with myself to stay away a year what they will think and do."

"I suppose they might take advantage," admitted Silas, heavily. "I fear you have always given in to them too much for their own good."

"Then I shall not give in now," said Annie, and she shut her mouth tightly.

There came a peal of the cracked door-bell, and Silas started with a curious, guilty look. Annie regarded him sharply. "Who is it, father?"

"Well, I heard Imogen say to Eliza that she thought it was very foolish for them all to stay over there and have the extra care and expense, when you were here."

"You mean that the girls—?"

"I think they did have a little idea that they might come here and make you a little visit—"

Annie was at the front door with a bound. The key turned in the lock and a bolt shot into place. Then she returned to her father, and her face was very white.

347

"You did not lock your door against your own sisters?" he gasped.

"God forgive me, I did."

The bell pealed again. Annie stood still, her mouth quivering in a strange, rigid fashion. The curtains in the dining-room windows were not drawn. Suddenly one window showed full of her sisters' faces. It was Susan who spoke.

"Annie, you can't mean to lock us out?" Susan's face looked strange and wild, peering in out of the dark. Imogen's handsome face towered over her shoulder.

"We think it advisable to close our house and make you a visit," she said, quite distinctly through the glass.

Then Jane said, with an inaudible sob, "Dear Annie, you can't mean to keep us out!"

Annie looked at them and said not a word. Their half-commanding, half-imploring voices continued a while. Then the faces disappeared.

Annie turned to her father. "God knows if I have done right," she said, "but I am doing what you have taken me to account for not doing."

"Yes, I know," said Silas. He sat for a while silent. Then he rose, kissed Annie—something he had seldom done—and went home. After he had gone Annie sat down and cried. She did not go to bed that night. The cat jumped up in her lap, and she was glad of that soft, purring comfort. It seemed to her as if she had committed a great crime, and as if she had suffered martyrdom. She loved her father and her sisters with such intensity that

348

her heart groaned with the weight of pure love. For the time it seemed to her that she loved them more than the man whom she was to marry. She sat there and held herself, as with chains of agony, from rushing out into the night, home to them all, and breaking her vow.

It was never quite so bad after that night, for Annie compromised. She baked bread and cake and pies, and carried them over after nightfall and left them at her father's door. She even, later on, made a pot of coffee, and hurried over with it in the dawn-light, always watching behind a corner of a curtain until she saw an arm reached out for it. All this comforted Annie, and, moreover, the time was drawing near when she could go home.

Tom Reed had been delayed much longer than he expected. He would not be home before early fall. They would not be married until November, and she would have several months at home first.

At last the day came. Out in Silas Hempstead's front yard the grass waved tall, dotted with disks of clover. Benny was home, and he had been over to see Annie every day since his return. That morning when Annie looked out of her window the first thing she saw was Benny waving a scythe in awkward sweep among the grass and clover. An immense pity seized her at the sight. She realized that he was doing this for her, conquering his indolence. She almost sobbed.

"Dear, dear boy, he will cut himself," she thought. Then she conquered her own love and pity, even as her brother was conquering his sloth. She understood clearly that it was better for Benny to go on with his task even if he did cut himself.

The grass was laid low when she went home, and Benny stood, a conqueror in a battle-field of summer, leaning on his scythe.

"Only look, Annie," he cried out, like a child. "I have cut all the grass."

Annie wanted to hug him. Instead she laughed. "It was time to cut it," she said. Her tone was cool, but her eyes were adoring.

Benny laid down his scythe, took her by the arm, and led her into the house. Silas and his other daughters were in the sitting-room, and the room was so orderly it was painful. The ornaments on the mantel-shelf stood as regularly as soldiers on parade, and it was the same with the chairs. Even the cushions on the sofa were arranged with one corner overlapping another. The curtains were drawn at exactly the same height from the sill. The carpet looked as if swept threadbare.

Annie's first feeling was of worried astonishment; then her eye caught a glimpse of Susan's kitchen apron tucked under a sofa pillow, and of layers of dust on the table, and she felt relieved. After all, what she had done had not completely changed the sisters, whom she loved, faults and all. Annie realized how horrible it would have been to find her loved ones completely changed, even for the better. They would have seemed like strange, aloof angels to her.

They all welcomed her with a slight stiffness, yet with cordiality. Then Silas made a little speech.

DEAR ANNIE

"Your father and your sisters are glad to welcome you home, dear Annie," he said, "and your sisters wish me to say for them that they realize that possibly they may have underestimated your tasks and overestimated their own. In short, they may not have been—"

Silas hesitated, and Benny finished. "What the girls want you to know, Annie, is that they have found out they have been a parcel of pigs."

"We fear we have been selfish without realizing it," said Jane, and she kissed Annie, as did Susan and Eliza. Imogen, looking very handsome in her blue linen, with her embroidery in her hands, did not kiss her sister. She was not given to demonstrations, but she smiled complacently at her.

"We are all very glad to have dear Annie back, I am sure," said she, "and now that it is all over, we all feel that it has been for the best, although it has seemed very singular, and made, I fear, considerable talk. But, of course, when one person in a family insists upon taking everything upon herself, it must result in making the others selfish."

Annie did not hear one word that Imogen said. She was crying on Susan's shoulder.

"Oh, I am so glad to be home," she sobbed.

And they all stood gathered about her, rejoicing and fond of her, but she was the one lover among them all who had been capable of hurting them and hurting herself for love's sake.

THE END